Dark Sister

ALSO BY GRAHAM JOYCE

Dreamside
House of Lost Dreams
Requiem
The Tooth Fairy
The Stormwatcher

GRAHAM JOYCE
Dark Sister

TOR®

A Tom Doherty Associates Book
New York

DARK SISTER

Copyright © 1999 by Graham Joyce

This book is printed on acid-free paper.

A Tor Book
Published by Tom Doherty Associates, LLC
175 Fifth Avenue
New York, NY 10010

www.tor.com

Library of Congress Cataloging-in-Publication

Joyce, Graham.
    Dark sister / Graham Joyce.—1st ed.
        p.   cm.
    "A Tom Doherty Associates book."
    ISBN 0-312-86632-1
    I. Title.
  PR6060.093D37   1999
  823'.914—dc21
                                       99-22202
                                        CIP

First Edition: August 1999

Printed in the United States of America

0 9 8 7 6 5 4 3 2 1

TO: MY MOTHER AND FATHER, WHO NEVER PUT
ME THROUGH ANY OF THIS

Dark Sister

ONE

When Alex had ripped out the boards, in a cracking and splintering of wood, he called Maggie. The kids came too, along with Dot, their Labrador-cross, who had a sniff at the results.

"I knew it!" Maggie said. "It's beautiful!"

Alex was more doubtful. "It might be when it's cleaned up."

It was a standard Victorian fireplace, with a wrought-iron and tiled surround. Maggie was already rubbing at the tiles, exposing bright, floral patterns. The grate was intact, though choked with soot and debris.

"It's got to be swept. Kids, take all this wood out the back."

Alex liked to have his gofors around when he was doing a job. Maggie was already making inroads into the debris with a dustpan and brush when she leapt back.

"Ugh!"

The children crowded closer. "What is it?"

Maggie looked as though she wanted to be sick. "Come away from it."

"What is it, Mummy?"

Alex poked at the debris in the grate. Mixed in with the soot were what seemed like sticks and straw. "I see it," he said. "It's nothing. Only a dead bird." He lifted it out on the dustpan. It was a large, black-feathered bird with wings spread. Obviously it had been there for some time. Dessicated, though not decayed, its feathers were choked with dust and soot, and its eye had whitened over. Its beak hung open. Alex waved it at the kids.

"Ugh!" said Amy.

"Ugh!" said Sam, with fascinated eyes.

Even Dot seemed to wince.

"Take it away, Alex."

"It must have nested in the chimney at some time. Then got trapped. Happens all the time."

"What will you do with it, Daddy?"

"We'll have it for Sunday dinner. Blackbird in parsley sauce."

"Take no notice, Amy, he's being silly. Get it out of the house, Alex."

"Will we give it a proper burial, like Ulysses?" Amy wanted to know.

When Amy's goldfish Ulysses had died, they'd given it a state funeral in the back garden, so Alex took the bird outside, dug a hole for it, and covered it over.

Amy patted the soil with the spade. "Will it go to heaven now?"

"Yep," said Alex. "If you look up at the sky, you'll see its white soul flying towards heaven."

It was an afternoon in late October, and the sky was as blue as a bird's egg. Amy looked up at the sky for a long time. Then she looked back at her father. He could see that at five years old she was already beginning to distrust some of the things he said. It made him sad.

"Let's go back inside."

It had all started the night they'd gone over to the Suzmans for dinner. First the car wouldn't start.

"What are you getting mad about?" Maggie said.

It was the kind of remark guaranteed to infuriate Alex. He wasn't mad until Maggie had told him not to *get* mad. Now he was mad. He took a deep breath and tried to think why he was getting angry. It had started to rain, the kids were playing slap in the back of the car and Maggie was looking at him. She wore too much blusher and eye-shadow. Whenever they went to the Suzmans, Maggie felt insecure; and whenever Maggie felt insecure she put on too much makeup.

He got out of the car, flung open the bonnet, and was impotently fiddling with the plug leads when the engine coughed into life, fan blades narrowly missing lopping off the tops of his fingers. Now he really had something to be mad about, and this made him feel a lot better.

Maggie still had her hand on the ignition keys. "Magic touch," she said, smiling at him as he climbed back inside.

"Trying to amputate my fingers, were you?" Her smile disappeared. He looked at the heavy red lipstick at war with her flaming chestnut hair. Who could stay angry with someone so nervous about meeting old friends that she had to plaster her face like that? Alex couldn't. "Forget it."

He turned to the kids in the back. "If you two don't stop slapping each other, I'm going to bang your heads together." He'd never banged heads, and probably never would, but Maggie turned and nodded to them as if to say *he means it*.

"This is supposed to be enjoyable," she said.

"So why isn't it enjoyable?" said Amy.

"That kid's five," Alex shouted. "*Five!*" And Maggie knew everything was fine.

And the visit to the Suzmans had turned out to be enjoyable after all. Amy and three-year-old Sam were whisked off by the Suzman kids, giving their parents the chance to show Alex and Maggie around their monster of a new house. Bill Suzman, a commercial lawyer, had managed to get in before the house prices went crazy. Alex had missed the boat, as usual.

After Alex and Maggie were conducted on a grand tour

(where they were expected to admire the way the towels were folded in the bathroom, and to comment on the parquet floor) Bill cracked open the wine. Anita drew attention to their new integrated sound system and located the right music before they settled down in front of a rip-roaring log fire.

Maggie looked into the flames, firelight reflecting in her hair and in the wine glass at her lips, and Alex knew exactly what she was thinking. Marriage, proximity to another person, he supposed, cultivated a knowingness, a rough telepathy. It was something you acquired in exchange, when ardor faded. But he loved to do things to make her happy, and if she, too, wanted an open fire, she could have one.

"Nice fireplace," Alex observed.

"Original to the house," Bill said, getting up to stroke the marble mantelpiece. He always stroked anything he wanted others to admire: his CD player, his mantelpiece, his wife.

"Look at those tiles. Perfect condition. Been boarded up for years. We had to rip out an old gas fire to get to it."

"That old fire had protected it," said Anita.

"You wouldn't believe," Bill continued, "the state of the thing we took out. You're an archaeologist, Alex; you'd appreciate it. One of those sixties plastic log-effect things. You plug 'em in and a rotating fan casts shadows on a very unconvincing orange light."

"Ghastly," Maggie agreed, and they laughed more at the word than at Bill's description.

"We've still got one," said Alex.

There was a pause. "I'd forgotten about that," said Anita.

"What the hell," said Bill. "Is dinner ready?"

Dinner was indeed ready, because Anita had hired some help for the evening, a gesture beyond Maggie's comprehension and budget. Silverware gleamed, crystal glimmered, and no one seemed unduly worried when Sam seemed deliberately to tip a glass of claret on to the snow-white tablecloth.

"Why did you do that?" said Alex, exasperated.

Sam giggled and showed everyone a mouthful of half-chewed dinner.

Otherwise the meal went well. Alex and Bill cackled a lot and guzzled wine. Anita said sophisticated things about antiques, in which she had a "hobby" business, and Bill stroked her arm a great deal. Maggie paid attention to keeping the children in order. Then she won the others' interest by telling them about a psychic evening she'd attended.

"It was a birthday present from Alex," she said.

Alex coloured slightly. "It was what she asked me for. It was a joke."

Maggie began to relay the events of the evening, but she caught herself in the middle of the story. The two men were gazing at her, entranced by her enthusiasm, but Anita was looking at her strangely, so she allowed the story to tail off.

But it had been a pleasant evening, the conversation had stayed light, friendly. With the kids asleep in the back of the car, Maggie drove them home.

Alex, mellowed by the wine, said, "Why did you stop halfway through your story about the psychic?"

"I don't think Anita liked me grabbing the limelight."

"Why d'you say that?"

"Just a feeling."

"It's your imagination. Anyway, to hell with Anita. That was your story, and your chance to tell it. She wouldn't stop for you."

"No. You're right. I think Anita doesn't like me because I've got red hair."

"Nonsense. You're drunk."

"No I'm not. Anyway it's not my hair. Not just that anyway. It was a . . . feeling. Sometimes I look at people and I. . . ."

"And you what?"

"Never mind."

"Go on! Say it!"

"No. You'd just laugh at me. You always do."

"Yes, I probably would."

"Did you see that lovely open fireplace, Alex? Do you think . . ."

"Don't ask. The answer is yes."

Which is how Alex had come to be tearing out the old gas fire from their lounge the following day, a Saturday. The moment he'd seen Maggie staring into the fire at the Suzmans, he'd remembered what had irritated him.

Every time they visited Bill and Anita's immaculate house, Maggie returned discontented. Consequently his precious weekends (designated for watching *Sports Report* from the comfort of the sofa while lubricated by tins of beer) were spent trailing around home improvement stores the size of aircraft hangars. Death by DIY. Previous visits to the Suzmans had spurred the conversion of the cellar into a playroom for Amy and Sam, and the erection of a lopsided conservatory at the rear of the house. However long-suffering he was about it, Alex just wanted to make Maggie happy. He would look at her moist eyes and her long, curling chestnut hair, like a Preraphaelite painting, and generally he would give in to whatever she wanted.

With the gas disconnected, the fire had lifted out easily enough. Alex had had more difficulty with the nailed-up boarding. A strong timber frame had at some time been constructed out of thick lengths, leaving only a small vent for the passage of the gas fumes up the chimney. But now that part of the job was done. Meanwhile someone had to stop Sam juggling with the loose soot, and Alex decided that was women's work. He put his coat on and adjourned to the Merry Fiddler.

Theirs was a large Victorian villa with a huge, over-hanging gable. It was described by estate agents, when they'd first bought it, as a character property, and character properties were Maggie's enthusiasm but not Alex's. Character properties were like character people. Their qualities, entertainments, and rewards came in equal measure with their usually hidden but considerable faults. Alex had doggedly devoted much of his leisure time in the past five years to beating back elements permanently poised to invade the sanctuary he was trying to build for his family.

There was the ongoing damp problem that made him sometimes wonder if the house were built over a river. There was a woodworm blight he'd poisoned into submission. There was a silverfish infestation astonishing even the experts from Rentokil. The high-ceilinged rooms had demanded the installation of powerful central heating just to secure the beautiful plaster moldings round the light fittings. And he was still embattled over a roof leak which thwarted him by shifting nine inches every time it was "fixed."

Embattled yes, and if occasionally he broke ranks and deserted the front line in favour of the Merry Fiddler, Maggie let him go. She said nothing as he went out, and checked the Yellow Pages for a chimney sweep.

She primed the children for the arrival of the sweep. They'd seen *Mary Poppins* on video, and she told them stories from her own childhood. When she was a kid, the chimneys had been serviced by a local man who played ventriloquist to keep curious children amused. He pretended to have a midget assistant who spoke from the chimney, and would send Maggie outside to check if his brush had cleared the chimney pot. Amy and Sam were fascinated. They sat by the window, waiting eagerly for the man to arrive. Maggie told them they should "touch" the sweep for luck.

When he arrived that afternoon, Maggie was enormously disappointed that he wasn't black from head to foot, and that he brought with him a suction machine instead of a set of brushes. The modern version was a bespectacled young man arriving for his first job of the day in a clean set of blue overalls. He had no sweep's humor for her children. When Amy and Sam ran forward to touch him almost before he got through the door, the young man looked at the spot on his overalls where the children had put their fingers. Then he looked (sourly, Maggie thought) at the children. Maggie quickly showed him where to set up his gear.

Sam rapidly lost interest in this unpicturesque sweep and waddled away to play with Dot, but Amy remained, watching his every move. She was utterly spellbound. She inched forward, gazing over the shoulder of the man as he knelt before the fireplace, until she was almost breathing on his neck. Maggie was about to shift her out of his way, but she was checked by a second thought, almost like another voice in her head. *Why not? Why not let her look?*

The first thing the sweep did (though it didn't seem right to call him a sweep when he was only a man with a machine which sucked) was to put his arm up the flue, bringing down more debris, straw, and sticks into the grate.

"Hello," he said, withdrawing his arm. "Something else here." He was holding some dirty object in his hand. It was a book. He scraped away the soot and the dust. "People hide things up chimneys, then forget all about them."

He flicked the pages open, as if looking for something pressed between the leaves. Maggie was mesmerised. She felt a thrill of possessiveness, almost childish in its intensity. *My book,* she wanted to say. *My house, my chimney, my book.* She objected to his large, sooty thumbs imprinting on the cover. She wanted to snatch it from him, but instead she said, "Do you find many things?"

"I once found five hundred quid—"

"Sweeps are lucky," she blurted, unable to take her eyes from the object in his blackened hands.

"You didn't let me finish. It was in forged notes." Finding nothing between the pages, he lost interest in the book.

"Here." He passed it to her and proceeded with the task of sweeping, or rather sucking, the chimney.

That evening they had a crackling log fire going in the lounge. They all sat round it staring into the flames as if it was some new form of light entertainment, except for Dot, who commanded the place in front of the fire and immediately went to sleep, as if the entire thing had been introduced for her benefit alone. The newly exposed fireplace showed off to great effect. An ornate, black, cast-iron surround was inset with beautiful ceramic tiles in rich autumnal colours. The design had an oriental feel, depicting peacocks and other exotic birds entwined in mysterious looking shrubs and trees. Maggie had polished them until they gleamed. The glaze on the tiles was perfectly preserved, not a single chip or scratch anywhere.

It was, they both agreed happily, even better than the Suzman specimen.

Alex was initially fascinated by what had been found hidden inside the chimney, and every now and then broke the hypnotic spell of the fire by reading aloud from the book.

It was a leatherbound diary. It was soiled and slightly charred, but still legible. Alex struggled to decipher the handwriting, and insisted on reading out what seemed to be mostly shopping lists. His first flush of excitement soon dulled though, as Maggie knew it would. Maggie's had not; but for some reason she felt compelled to disguise her interest in the thing.

"It belonged to someone who lived here," said Alex. "Actually lived here over a hundred years ago!"

Maggie pretended to stifle a yawn. "Will you give it to your museum?"

"No, I bloody won't. It'll end up in a box on a shelf in a cupboard in a back room on a forgotten inventory."

"Some archaeologist you are."

"I know too much about the bloody business."

"Did Daddy swear?" said Sam.

"He said it's time for your bed," said Maggie.

"No, he didn't," said Amy.

Amy had a pageboy head of silky blond hair, and a habit of looking suddenly from under her fringe. Her eyes were the impenetrable blue-gray of the mist from a lake. They disarmed. They challenged. Sometimes it was mightily disconcerting to be wrong-footed by a five-year-old.

"You never miss a trick, do you?" said her father.

"No," said Amy, looking into the fire.

TWO

Amy had been home from school about an hour. She and Sam had been playing spitting games in the garden. It was three days after the discovery of the diary in the fireplace. Maggie was busy at the kitchen sink—busy in that abstract way of gazing into the soap suds as if they revealed fleeting, irridescent patterns of the future—when a bespattered Amy and Sam hurtled into the kitchen.

"Dot dug it up! Dot dug it up!"

"And it wasn't dead and it's gone on the roof!"

"If you've been spitting . . ." Maggie started, noticing the suspicious dribble on Sam's chin, but something about the children's urgency arrested her.

"She did! Dot dug it up, so it isn't dead!"

"What isn't dead?"

"The bird we buried on Saturday. It isn't dead yet."

"Nonsense."

But Amy insisted Maggie should come and look for herself.

Out in the garden, Dot was snuffling in the corner by the wall, looking vaguely guilty as Maggie approached. The dog was hacking, as if trying to clear its throat of something unpleasant. Amy pointed to the spot where Alex and the children had made a shallow grave for the bird they'd removed from the fireplace. The earth had been disturbed.

"Dot dug it up and got it in her mouth and then the bird flew away. I saw it."

"Yes it did," said Sam.

Maggie looked hard into the cloudless blue of Sam's three-year-old eyes. He was going through a phase of lying habitually about almost anything. But Amy was usually a more reliable witness.

"It can't fly away when it's dead, Amy. Dot must have eaten it."

"Dot ate it," said Sam.

"No, she didn't!" Amy protested. "I saw it fly!"

Maggie took a stick and poked at the disturbed soil. It was true, nothing remained there now.

"There it is!" Amy shouted, pointing above her mother's head.

Maggie turned. Perched on the rusting pole of her washing line, not six feet away, was a sleek blackbird, feathers a lustrous blue-black, its eye fixed on her. She motioned her arm, expecting it to fly off, but it didn't move. It squatted there, immobile, watching her. Maggie took a step backwards.

"That's not the same one. There are hundreds of blackbirds around here."

"It is the same one," said Amy, "it is."

"Kill it," said Sam.

Maggie felt the prickly contagion of their childish fear. It transmitted to her, like static. It paralysed her. It left her shocked, unable to step out of the moment. She had a brief vision in which she saw herself, all of them, her children and the bird, all caught twitching at the fine strands of some miraculous web.

Then she became conscious that Sam and Amy were waiting for her to do something. Ridiculous! It was ridiculous that this small, unremarkable bird should make her afraid like this! At last she picked up a rotting wicket of wood from the garden. Advancing slowly, she waved the stick before her. The bird, in its own time, hopped from the pole to the wall before flying away.

Maggie collected up the children and ushered them indoors.

THREE

Alex came home late that evening complaining bitterly about the dig at the castle. A policy change had been enacted over his head. Since the episode with the bird, Maggie had had a particularly tiresome day with the kids. Amy had stood on watch in the garden and had flatly refused to come in even when it had begun to rain; and when Maggie took her eye off Sam for three seconds while fetching Amy, he'd promptly emptied a box of breakfast cereal into the dog's dish. What's more, her period was about to start, and she frankly didn't give a shit about Alex's grubbing about in the castle ruins.

Meanwhile Alex directed at Maggie the speeches he would like to have made at work. "Living archaeology they call it! So now we have to build a walkway round our work just so Joe Public can come and watch us in action. Maybe I should scatter a few dog bones around the site."

"Haven't you ever stopped to watch three men digging a hole in the road?"

Alex ignored her, tearing off his work clothes and throwing them in a corner of the kitchen. "I told them, just so long as you don't want to dress me up like Indiana Jones. Didn't know what I was talking about. Pretended not to. How would they like it?

How many people have to tolerate having their work closely observed by the public?"

"Footballers. Actors. Policemen. Dentists—"

"Exactly. Run me a bath, would you?"

"Any particular temperature?"

Alex switched to a wheedling voice. "Sorry; but you know how I like to be pampered when I get steamed up about the job. And it's not as if you have anything to do all day."

Alex flinched as he heard his own words crash. He reached out to her, but she pushed past him and went hammering up the stairs. In the bathroom she slapped the plug in the hole and throttled the taps open to release ferocious jets of hot and cold water; she then thumped heavily back down the stairs, shoved him aside, and snatched up his discarded work clothes. Alex made to say something conciliatory, thought better of it, and quietly made his way up to his bath.

While Alex soaked, groaning and cooing loudly in the tub, Maggie shepherded the kids to bed, nursing a poisonous indignation. She came downstairs and put a match to their new living-room fire. It was crackling nicely when Alex appeared wearing a threadbare dressing gown she hated. He collapsed into an armchair and snatched up a magazine.

She waved a glossy leaflet at him. "This came today. Want to look at it with me?"

Alex glanced up, and winced. His sciatic nerve always rebelled when this subject came up. It was a prospectus for the local university. Maggie had a yearning to study for a degree in Psychology.

"Do we have to go through this again? We've discussed it enough times."

They had. Alex had expressed the view that psychology was a pseudoscience. Maggie said she didn't give a pseudo-damn about that. Alex complained that psychology promoted simplistic views of human nature. Good, Maggie had replied, I'm a simplistic person. Alex had had a dream about climbing through an open window one night, and made the mistake of telling it to Maggie. Now he pointedly referred to windows as "vagina-adultery-suicide-apparatus."

"Alex. I really want to do this course. It's important to me."

"But it's such lousy timing. You've got a young family to think about. Responsibilities."

Yes, they had discussed it before; many times, and without resolution. The language they used had been repeated so often it had become symbolic. Maggie employed words like "important" as a stinging missile. Alex in turn sent up big barrage-balloon words like "family" and "responsibilities." The words were made available, but they'd stopped talking to each other.

Underneath it all, Alex was secretly afraid he might lose her. It was an unspecified anxiety he chose not to analyze. He never took Maggie for granted; he counted her value above rubies and emeralds, and feared that one day someone might plot to take her away from him. And the more Maggie sensed this secret fear, the more trapped she felt.

"I'll go mad if I don't do something. I mean really mad. I'm already going mad hanging around here. Weird things have started to happen."

"What weird things?" He put down his magazine.

"Today. There was a bird. In the garden. It *looked* at me."

"It looked at you?"

"Yes. It *looked* at me."

Alex laughed. "Well. I daresay it did."

Maggie stared at him. He pretended to duck back behind his magazine.

"You," Maggie said at length.

"Uh?"

"You."

The magazine dipped again. "Are you premenstrual?" he said. "Do you want a cuddle?"

She outstared him. The grin vanished from his face. She

had to take deep breaths between her words. "You don't—
know—what—I'm talking about! You just—sit—there and you—
DON'T KNOW WHAT I'M TALKING ABOUT!"

"All right ! Stop shouting and tell me what you *are* talking
about!"

She waited until she felt more composed. "There was a bird,
in the garden, and it looked at me! Not in any ordinary way. And
it frightened me. The children saw it too."

"What kind of a bird?"

"A blackbird."

"An ordinary blackbird?"

"It wasn't ordinary at all. It looked *into* me. Through me. I
can't explain it. It was as near to me as you are now, and it wasn't
at all afraid. I tried to make it go away and it wouldn't."

"Perhaps someone had tamed it. Looked after it."

"Not this one."

"How do you know?"

"You weren't there." She chewed her lip, wondering whether
to tell him the rest. "The children said it was the bird you buried
in the garden."

"What?"

"Amy said that Dot dug it up and it flapped its wings and
jumped onto the roof."

"Ridiculous."

"I know it sounds ridiculous, but the bird was gone from
where you put it and I told Amy that Dot must have eaten it or
something but I didn't believe it myself."

"Look, you're just—"

"I know! I know! I'm just neurotic! A completely neurotic
housewife with two children and a dog and a dog's dish and a
husband in a dirty old dressing gown! You don't seem to see the
point!"

"So what is the point?"

"The point is . . ." Maggie had to draw a deep breath so that she could remember the point. "The point is that every day I'm stuck here I feel like a bird in a wire cage and I want to get out!"

They simultaneously became aware of Sam standing in the doorway in his pyjamas. The shouting had woken him, and he was blinking at them with moist, frightened eyes. Alex leapt to his feet, gathered the boy to him, and brought him over by the fire. He kissed Sam's neck, a big, bruising, wet, noisy kiss. He told him it was all right, they were only playing a shouting game.

That night in bed, she did something which she didn't do very often. When Alex put his hand on her belly, she turned away from him. He said nothing. They lay awake in the dark, and it was some time before either of them drifted off to sleep.

FOUR

Amy was at school and Sam was asleep on the sofa. Maggie
had a precious moment to herself. She'd been woken in the middle
of the night by a thump from downstairs, where she'd found Sam
sleepwalking. She'd tried to pick him up to carry him back to bed,
but he'd woken to complain about nightmares, so she let him
climb in with them. Alex had snored on and Maggie had sighed
with guilt. She knew the shouting had disturbed Sam.

Sam had developed a touch of conjunctivitis, and after a bad
night his eye looked sore. Maggie had a large, very old *Family
Medical Dictionary* passed on to her by her grandmother. Her family doctor told her the healthiest thing she could do with it was
toss it on a bonfire; he told her books like that only scared people.
But she kept it, consulting the brittle, yellowing pages every time
her children suffered some complaint or other.

She read that conjunctivitis was an inflammation of the
membrane that linked the eyelids and covered the white of the
eye; she read that any but the slightest cases required immediate
attention as blindness might result; and she read that a serious
form was caused by gonorrhoea. She felt rather alarmed by all of
this information. The book was returned to its shelf under the
stairs, out of the doctor's sight.

Sam turned in his sleep. Maggie thought about phoning the

clinic for advice; it might even produce another visit from the doctor. She liked him. He was a young, handsome Asian GP with a wonderful sense of humor, who always seemed prepared to stay longer than was strictly necessary. She picked up the telephone, looked up the number, and then something made her replace the handset.

She noticed the diary resting on the mantelpiece above the fire. The diary the sweep had found up the chimney. Alex must have left it there.

She made herself a coffee and sat down to leaf through the pages. As well as what appeared to be shopping lists, the diary contained lists of herbs, what Alex had called "folk remedies." Her idea was to see if she might find some gentle salve to apply to Sam's eye.

Opening a page at random, she found a list written in beautiful copperplate handwriting. In places the blue ink had mellowed to purple and black with age, but the author was meticulous and neat:

Acacia	*Anise*	*Broom*
Comfrey	*Elder*	*Eucalyptus*
Eyebright	*Hazel*	*Lavender*
Marjoram	*Mastic*	*Mistletoe*
Mugwort	*Nutmeg*	*Peppermint*
Pimpernel	*Sandalwood*	*Spearmint*
Thyme	*Wormwood*	

That was all. There was no other entry on the page. Whether it had any relation to the date at the head of the page, 7th February 1891, Maggie had no idea. Neither did she know enough about herbs to deduce why this selection had been grouped together. The previous page contained a similar list:

Balm of Gilead	*Cedar*	*Cinquefoil*
Cypress	*Fern*	*Honeysuckle*

On the following page, another list of herbs, rather longer. Maggie turned the pages more quickly. Some entries seemed to be no more than shopping lists, with no reference to herbs; occasionally there was a more intriguing entry. On one page was written simply:

Sell your coat and buy betony.

There were also practical remedies.

All headaches. Make herbal sachet of light-blue cloth, sew into equal parts bruised leaves lavender peppermint mugwort clove marjoram tie on blue thread and wear round neck. Sniffing is efficacious.

But beneath that entry was written:

A. hates me because of my red hair.

So, the diarist too was a redhead. Maggie instantly felt an affinity with the writer, for reasons unclear. This detail of physical appearance, trivial in itself, excited a disproportionate wave of sympathy and identification. Sure, it was irrational: redheads weren't denied the fruits of the earth any more than anyone else and, in her experience, never laid claim to any sisterhood which might exclude a blonde or a brunette. Yet there it was, and Maggie decided that whoever the diarist was, she liked her for it.

She leafed through the diary rapidly, alighting on whatever looked interesting. There were several "remedies," listing the preparation of poultices, salves, ointments, oils, and some which seemed simply intended to make smells. Many, however, were useless, since they didn't say what complaint they claimed to remedy. The diarist might have known, but Maggie couldn't guess. Then she found something for Sam.

Soreness of eyes all eye complaints. wax.m. juice of fern camo-
mile eyebright. Salve the sachet w clove garlic 1 eucalyptus 2
sage 2 saffron. Blue cloth. Can also bring f. to light.

It all sounded a bit messy. But, she reasoned, it couldn't be
any worse than having chemicals dropped into your eye, which
was all the family doctor—however kindly he was—would prescribe. These were earth remedies, Maggie argued to herself, natural healing agents that had been handed down over hundreds
and hundreds of years only to be ridiculed and dismissed by a
medical industry hell-bent on profit and too clever for its own
good.

She put down the diary and moved to where Sam was sleeping
on the sofa. She stood over him for a moment. When she put her
hand on his forehead, he opened his eyes. There was still some
inflammation in the corner of one eye.

"Want to come shopping with me?" she asked.

"No," said Sam.

"No?"

"Yes."

FIVE

Three days later Sam was still running around with a sore eye. He also had a dirty brown stain near the bridge of his nose where Maggie applied her homemade herbal remedy. Alex had quizzed her about it.

"Ointment," she'd said. He'd sniffed and let the matter drop.

Alex didn't seem to notice that Sam wore a sachet of herbs on a string round his neck. The herbs were sewn into a light blue cloth, and Sam carried it cheerfully, calling it his treasure.

Unfortunately it just wasn't working.

Maggie had been conscientious. She'd dragged Sam around the shops to pick up every herb mentioned in the list. There'd been no difficulty in collecting them from general health food stores, except for the one called eyebright. The assistants all looked blank at that one, and when pressed on where she might try, they shook their heads pathetically. Then another customer, over-hearing, suggested she might try a shop in the Gilded Arcade.

The Gilded Arcade was an original four-story Victorian shopping precinct. It was unfashionable and off the main drag; consequently the many tiny stores operating from it were special interest or frankly eccentric. Rents were low and businesses had a habit of changing hands rapidly. The hollow echo of the arcade, its fitful little flights of business, and the peeling gold-leaf railings of its catwalks gave it the impression of a giant aviary. Colorfully dressed young people with startling hair and ironmongery in their ears and noses looked over the railings for hours, like exotic birds perched at different levels. Maggie approved of the unorthodoxy of the place, and of its dilapidated grandeur.

The shop she was looking for was called Omega. She passed kiosk-sized shops peddling memorabilia and second-hand period clothes; tattooists and body-piercing studios; comic-marts and specialist bookshops; eventually finding Omega on the uppermost level. Pulling Sam by the hand, she opened the door and a tiny bell tinkled. A man sat behind the counter, engrossed in a book. He glanced up from the book, but didn't speak.

The shop seemed chiefly devoted to herbs and spices and to books about alternative medicine; that is to say, its shelves contained rows and rows of jars with handwritten labels, and where there were no jars there were books and pamphlets.

Maggie turned her back on the man at the counter, pretending to study a selection of pestles and mortars, but she felt his eyes tracking her. She picked up one set made of stone but quickly replaced it on the shelf. When she turned back to him, he raised his eyebrows in a jocular fashion. Sam just stared at the man.

"Eyebright. I want a herb called eyebright. Do you know what it is?"

"Of course." It was said in a lethargic manner. The man was in his mid-forties, with thinning shoulder-length hair and a wispy beard. His weathered face and heavy build seemed at odds with his thin, reedy voice. "Euphrasia officinalis if you want to get technical. Euphrosyne by any other name. Red eyebright to me and thee. What d'you want it for?"

She resented the question. "I only need a small amount."

"Please yourself," he said, getting up and crossing to a shelf on the far side of the shop. He reached for a jar. "Only trying to be helpful."

He weighed some of the herb on a beautiful set of brass scales. "Gender, Male. Planet, Sun. Element, Air. Ask for Euphrosyne another time, because that's what most people call it."

"Do you know a lot about herbs?"

The man opened his eyes wide and looked at her as if the question was as stupid as it gets.

"Anything else?"

She shook her head and paid for the herb. Her fingers trembled in her purse. As she was bustling Sam out of the door, the man said, "Next time come to me for the other things as well. I do it half the price you paid in those health shops." She turned to look at him, but he already had his head back in his book.

After that she drove out of town to Osier's Wood. It wasn't necessary to drive so far to collect a few stalks of fern, but the place had pleasant associations. She and Alex used to walk there. They'd even made love there one hot summer afternoon; but only once. Alex was put off after claiming to have seen an adder weaving through the fern stalks. She had an idea Sam had been conceived that time in the woods.

"Know what, Sam? You were made in these woods."

"No," said Sam.

"No? I'll give you no!" She waved a freshly cut fern at him.

"Yes!" said Sam, running away. They played hide-and-seek in among the trees before going back to the car.

The following day Maggie had to return to the Gilded Arcade. When she went into the shop, the man was seated in exactly the same position, reading the same book, as if he hadn't shifted a millimeter since she'd left the premises the previous day. Almost without looking up, he pointed to the selection of pestles and mortars. "They're all over there."

She had indeed returned to buy a pestle-and-mortar set, having decided the previous evening that, if she was going to make an ointment out of her ingredients, they'd need to be pounded first.

"Are you a mind-reader as well as a herbalist?"

The man looked up, pleased with himself. "Where's the little boy?"

"With his childminder. I get two hours' relief a week. I'm glad to see there's something you don't know."

"I can always spot a first-timer. They come here to ask for the more obscure stuff. Then they get it home and realize they need some way of preparing it. Then they remember seeing all these."

"How did you know I'd been to the health food store first?"

"That was more difficult. You had a carrier bag spelling out their name in big letters."

Maggie smiled to herself and turned to finger the implements lined up in the window. She liked the man now that she realized his offhand manner was nothing other than gamesome. She picked up a brass pestle. "What do you recommend?"

"The ceramic ones chip if you're not careful; the wooden ones splinter and don't take to anything hot; and I don't like to think of the metal ones leaving some of themselves in your mix."

"Stone, then?"

"Every time."

"Not cheap, are they?"

"Please yourself. Take the brass."

"No, I'll take the stone."

"And I wasn't being nosy yesterday. I was genuinely trying to be helpful."

"Then you must know the eyebright is for eye infections."

"The little chap. I noticed his eye was sore."

"Isn't that how it got its name?"

"Eyebright? No. Applied to the eyelids it aids clairvoyance."

"Are you serious?"

He looked at her hard, but his eyes were swimming with suppressed mirth. "I never joke. Tell me what you're making."

She told him. He nodded thoughtfully. "Not my first choice. But it's an interesting one, and it won't do him any harm. Where did you get it from?"

So she told him, too, about the diary and the lists of remedies. "And there were the words 'wax.m.' Does that mean anything to you?"

He regarded her steadily. "As for the sachet, that's a bit of indirect herbalism, if you follow me."

"Should I ignore that part?"

"Oh no. And it'll give you something to do with your time." There wasn't a flicker from him to indicate irony. Then he gave her some useful advice for preparing Sam's eye ointment. As she turned to leave the shop, he said, "This diary. I'd really like to have a look at it some time."

"I might show it you," she said, "and then again I might not."

And the tiny bell tinkled as she went out.

Three days later, all Sam had to show for his mother's incursion into the world of herbalism was a dirty face; that and the gay little sachet round his neck. Maggie inspected the remains of the sticky paste she'd concocted and judged it time to revert to orthodox pharmacy.

For some reason she'd hidden from Alex her new collection of herbs and her stone pestle and mortar. She wasn't sure why exactly she'd made a secret of the thing. Perhaps she was placing it beyond his ridicule, because nothing was more certain than his skepticism for anything unscientific.

Unscientific.

No, it was more than that. Much more. Alex's was like many people's skepticism: it was almost rabid, it was desperate. He used skepticism to seal himself off from whatever he was afraid lay out there. Like the yards of draughtproofing he bought for the house, or his dampproofing, or his endless leak treatments. Worse, she knew that in his darkest heart he nursed some kind of suspicion about her. Something they'd never discussed, and never would, but which lay between them, like a sword hidden beneath the sheets.

She knew what Alex feared was her power. Powers he didn't

possess. The power to be surprised, to be delighted, to exult, to be mystified by events. The power to be afraid without fear of showing it. The power to resist the stolid pull of the ground. There was something in her he recognized as a deep flirtatiousness, not necessarily with other men, but with the world itself, with the unknown, and he was afraid that one day it would carry her away from him.

Beyond all that, she wanted this to be something exclusively her own. That's why she'd hidden the herbs. She wanted the opportunity to experiment freely. Somehow that gave her a feeling of another kind of power; power not just over Alex, but over the preparations she made with her herbs.

So she hid everything in a lockable trunk in the spare room. It was full of old photographs and memorabilia neither she nor Alex could bear to dispose of but at which they never looked from one year to another. She bundled everything in a black scarf and buried it at the bottom of the trunk.

Sam came out of the garden and into the kitchen waving a stick. Maggie held his face to the light and looked doubtfully into the corner of his eye. "It was worth a try, Sam. But we'll have to stop using that stuff, it's not doing any good."

"No!" said Sam.

"For God's sake stop saying no every time I speak to you."

"The lady said."

"What?"

"The lady in the garden."

"What lady?" Maggie felt a shiver run through her.

"In the garden. She said use it tonight. She did. She told me."

Maggie looked out of the window at the walled garden with the dwarf birch in the comer. There was no one there. She knelt on the floor beside Sam. "Tell me about this lady."

"You can't see her. She's gone. And she's only this big." He stretched out his thumb and first finger. Then he changed his mind and made her a bit smaller. "No, this big. She rides on a rat."

"What did she say about the ointment?"

"She said you have to put it on me tonight. Yes she did."

"That boy," said Alex angrily. Maggie was startled. He was towering in the kitchen doorway, gazing down at them. He must have been watching them for some time. He looked huge and frightening, his eyebrows knitted, his brow full of thunder. "We're going to have to do something about this constant lie telling. He needs a good shaking."

Alex stormed past them and clumped heavily upstairs. He'd had another bad day at work. Maggie collected Sam to her and hugged him.

SIX

Maggie applied her herbal ointment to Sam's eye that night, and the next morning there was a distinct improvement. By the following morning, his conjunctivitis had cleared up completely. Now all they had to worry about, said Alex, was Sam's deep-rooted habit of telling lies.

"He's just a child. He makes up stories. So what? That's what children are supposed to do. He'll grow out of it."

Alex wasn't having any of it. "It's not stories. It's lies. Lies. Every single word that comes out of his mouth is a lie. Ask him what his name is and he says anything other than Sam. Ask him where he lives and he talks rubbish. He tells people his mother is the lady at the sweet shop. If he says yes, we all have to pretend he means no."

"He's only three years old, for Christ's sake!"

"He's nearly four and there's something wrong!"

"It's just a phase he's going through, Alex. Your mother told me you were still wetting the bed when you were nine."

Alex didn't like to he reminded of such things. Maggie could tell that the remark had angered him, because unlike most people, Alex spoke more quietly when he was angry, pausing occasionally for big breaths. "It is not a phase. It is a steady condition."

"I mean all children do it. Have pretend playmates and the like. That's what I meant to say."

"Amy certainly never did it. Not on this scale. And neither did any of our friends' children. He needs to see a child psychiatrist."

"At three years of age! You're the one who's crazy, Alex!"

"You think it'll help him if we wait until he's thirty? Now's the time to do it, so he can be straightened out."

"Straightened out? I don't want him straightened out. I'm not putting Sam at the mercy of a shrink."

"What's a shrink?" Amy wanted to know.

"It's a special doctor," said Alex, "who looks after little children."

"No it's not," said Sam.

It seemed easier to communicate through pointless argument than by any other means; at least that's all Maggie and Alex seemed to be doing. The matter went unresolved, they turned their backs on each other.

Meanwhile Maggie returned to the diary, flushed with the success of her first efforts. She found the page listing the remedy she had used and underneath it made an entry herself. She wrote the dates, the quantity she had used, and the words *Sam's conjunctivitis cleared up*. If only the diary had a herbal for banishing fibs and tall stories.

While flicking through the pages, settling here and there on remedies, she made a discovery. Some of the pages with ink entries contained further notes, but in pencil and so faintly written that a cursory glance could easily miss them. These entries, too, were mainly lists, written in the same perfectly penned copperplate hand, but they occasionally included additional commentaries. Maggie was astonished she'd failed to notice them before; but then the pencil marks were so weak, they were a strain to read.

Rue is a mighty powerful one, a mother of herbs. I heard her called Ruta, Bashoush and Herb of Grace and more. This is of Diana, though it is hot and indeed it is of the element of Fire.

Now rue they used for that Great Plague, but it was denied. It grows best if stolen, which I have. Gather in the fresh morning because a poison to pick later. Some say the sight. I know that to eat leaves will not talk in sleep, which is the tongue of angels and demons. The crushed leaf when breathed back full, will clear the brain of envious thought. And rue water kills the flea.

Now I will use rue on A. she bothers me so. I know this one for she taught it me: Nine drops of the rue oil added to a bath with salt for the nine nights as follows the moon in her waning will break the spell she has on me, for she wearies me. And I know others:

> *Rue, vervain, St John's wort, dill*
> *Hinder witches of their will.*

Maggie felt a strange thrill. She set the diary down and turned to check on Sam. He was playing happily behind her chair, swinging an old biscuit tin loaded with toy soldiers. She picked the book up again and reread the page. What she'd taken to be simple herbalism was obviously something more. *Rue, vervain, St John's wort, dill* . . .

She leafed through the pages, searching for more pencil entries.

Listening. This I dearly love above all things. And I can with or without I make a simple. On a windy day, with the sun just up, or fast on the dusk which is my favourite to lie down in a tall leafy bower or such and listen and wait on the wind. And I wait and I wait and there he comes with such messages as are written on the wind in the leaves some time I fear my heart will break. And should I infuse a simple it is the mugwort and I make a tea and sweeten with honey. Or that I make a pot then into the boil the bay laurel mugwort and cinquefoil and I breathe them. But for listening I say I can without a simple or a pot.

Maggie read on:

Some words of the mugwort, also called witch herb and old uncle harry and artemesia and felon herb. Why "uncle" I cannot tell, for mugwort is a she-plant and another of Diana whose other name is Artemis. Her planet is Venus and her element the Air.

    Now she is very good for the sight; in a simple or pot or the fresh leaves rubbed on mirror or the crystal. She also wards off fatigue and I have walked long distances: and wild beasts stay away from it. Now pluck before sunrise during the wax moon: A. says, and is insistent, that it should be from a plant as leans northward. Also her powers are strongest when picked at the Full.

A few pages on, Maggie stumbled across the name of the diarist.

P. B. come to me and was full of woe, I never seen so much woe, she being barren. Bella, she says to me, three years and no child! I counselled her and I had a bit of Patience Dock so I stitched her a sachet as we talked. I didn't want to give her any of my Man, he being so rare these days so I put bryony, which is good and she wasn't to know. I told her eat poppy and sunflower seed in a cake, and sent her off to find some mistletoe. Well I hope for her but I'm afraid I can't see it.

    Now A. chid me for all this, for her saying is "be silent as the sacred oak." She says folk turn. But I say we must help, and there's the end of it.

So now she had the diarist's name. It was Bella. Red-haired Bella. And Bella was some kind of witch.

Maggie read on as if the diary contained hard news. Some of the pencilled entries she didn't entirely understand; others were merely the elaboration of uses of herbs. So absorbed in the diary was she that she jumped when Sam gave a yelp from behind the chair.

"It bit me!" he bawled. He held his hand up to her and she saw a thin stream of blood running between his finger and thumb.

Maggie saw the culprit. The corner of the biscuit tin had become twisted and a sliver of metal extruded from the edge. It was razor-sharp. "Naughty tin!" she said. "We'll throw you away for doing that!"

"It wasn't the tin," said Sam. "The tin didn't bite me."

Maggie took Sam's little white hand and put it to her mouth, sucking the crimson beads of blood. "Who did, then?" she said soothingly.

SEVEN

Alex came back from work to find Maggie, Amy, and Sam playing a game in the yard. A large blue candle was set in a brass holder in the middle of the flagstones, its flame flickering in the light breeze. It was Amy's turn to jump.

> *Jack be nimble,*
> *Jack be quick,*
> *Jack jump over the Candlestick.*

And Amy jumped. She cleared the candle easily and shouted, "Mummy's turn!" Maggie stepped a few paces backwards, repeated the rhyme, and took a healthy run. She cleared the candle by several feet. "Cheating!" shrieked Amy. "Cheating! You have to stand still and then jump."

"What's going on?" said Alex.

"Shut up!" Amy shouted. "Sam's turn!"

But Sam was afraid to try. "Scaredy-pants!" Amy bawled. "It's easy."

"Don't want to."

"Can I have a go?" said Alex.

Alex stood before the candle and cleared it easily from a standing position. "No!" Amy bellowed. "You have to say Jack! You have to say it."

"Okay." So Alex did it again, reciting the rhyme.

"Now Sam has to do it."

"Not if he doesn't want to."

"He's boring."

"No I'm not."

"I know," said Alex, lifting up Sam. "I'll do it holding Sam, then we'll have done it together. All right, Sam?"

Sam nodded. Amy complained that it didn't count, but they did it anyway, reciting the rhyme together. Maggie hadn't done it properly, so she was put to the task again. "Did you know that Jack's another name for the Devil?" said Alex. "This game was supposed to he an old pagan cure for something or other."

"Eczema," said Maggie. "And Jack isn't the devil in this case; it's a herb."

"Really? That's handy, because Amy's got a touch of..." He looked at his wife strangely.

"What does pagan mean?" Amy wanted to know.

"Sort of... wild," said Alex.

"No it doesn't, Amy. It means the people before Christianity. They had lots of different gods."

Alex considered for a moment. Then, still holding Sam, he said, "Bet you can't do it backwards!"

"Backwards?" said Amy.

Alex stood with his back to the flaming candle and said:

> *Candlestick the over jump Jack*
> *Quick be Jack nimble be Jack*

He jumped backwards. He landed awkwardly, his leg buckling under him. Sam landed on his chest.

"Careful!" Maggie shouted.

Sam thought it was a giggle, but Alex had sprained his ankle. He picked himself up.

Amy noticed the candle had gone out. "You said that's bad luck, Mummy. You said it's bad luck if the candle goes out."

"It's always bad luck," said Alex, hobbling back up the path, "to twist your ankle."

"Bad luck stupid shit!" cackled Sam. He picked up the candle and threw it at his father. "Stupid shit backwards!"

Alex unfolded himself and looked at Maggie in astonishment.

"I don't know!" she protested. "He must have picked it up from the kids at the childminder's."

That evening, with the children in bed, they sat by the fire. Alex, his foot up on a stool and a bag of ice cubes draped over his ankle, was watching a game show on the television. Maggie had her head in a magazine.

"You know that journal we found?"

"Ummm?" Maggie murmured. She didn't look up.

"I was looking for it earlier. I couldn't find it."

"It's around somewhere."

"I was telling a colleague at work about it. He's interested. I said I'd let him have a look at it."

She turned a page.

"So where is it?"

"Where's what?"

"The journal. The diary."

She glanced up. "Where have you looked?"

"I've looked all over."

"Last time I saw it it was on the mantelpiece."

"The mantelpiece?" said Alex.

"Yes. The mantelpiece."

"Well it's not there now. So where is it?"

"I don't think it's a good idea to lend it out."

"Oh, you don't?" Alex was getting annoyed. "Can I ask why not?"

"We won't get it back."

"Don't be ridiculous. It's only Geoff at the museum; he wants to see it."

"It's fragile and it's valuable," she flashed angrily, "and it belongs to this family."

Alex was rather taken aback by this show of defiance. "All right. All right. It's no big deal." He pretended to become re-engrossed in the TV game show. After a while he snapped the television off and stood up.

"What are you up to?"

"What?"

"You're up to something, Maggie. What is it?"

"What the hell are you talking about?"

"All right. Have it your own way. Meanwhile let me say this: something's got to be done about Sam."

"Something?"

"He's out of control. Completely out of control."

Maggie took the remark as it was intended: a criticism of her capacity as a mother. She pursed her mouth. Though she was boiling, she said nothing.

Alex went to bed, hobbling up the stairs with his twisted ankle. Maggie followed an hour later. It was a cold bed. Two backs turned make a deep, dark valley of ill will, down the middle, where sleep is hard to find.

EIGHT

Alex had Sam booked in to see a child psychiatrist within the week. He made private arrangements, an expensive move calculated to infuriate Maggie. Mr. De Sang—he didn't like to be called doctor, although he possessed all the credentials—insisted on an initial meeting with the parents together, followed by individual meetings, followed at last by meeting with Sam.

Maggie had put up massive resistance, but Alex was determined. It had been their single biggest dispute in seven years of marriage. Maggie said it would only happen over her dead body, Alex declared that could be arranged. Alex said he'd drag her there kicking and screaming if necessary, and Maggie claimed that would be the only way. Alex alluded to a history of mental illness in Maggie's family (a minor nervous complaint), and Maggie reminded him of disorders in his own (a single case of epilepsy).

"If you *really* want to screw him up," bawled Maggie, "why not just throw him into a pit of snakes?"

"Seems like you've already accomplished that much."

"What do you mean by that?"

"Work it out for yourself."

The truth was Alex didn't know what he meant. It was just something to be said in the momentum of fierce argument. It was a wild shot, but it silenced Maggie for a minute.

She recovered to say, "So Sam's got to be dragged off to a qualified child abuser just because you're for some reason furious with me?"

To Alex's credit, he'd considered that possibility. He'd analyzed his own motives for wanting Sam examined. He was genuinely uneasy about Sam's relentlessly disruptive behavior. Amy was growing up as straight as a pine tree, while Sam, psychologically speaking, was like something from a hall of mirrors. He'd enjoyed none of the closeness with the boy he'd adored in bringing up his daughter. Maggie had found a way of handling him, sure enough, but all he ever got from the child was a gaudy procession of lies, tantrums, breakages, blue fits, and foul language. He loved Sam, but found the boy a minute-by-minute horror show.

To Alex's debit, he failed to understand his proposal for dealing with Sam masked a deeper unease. His self-analysis wasn't thorough enough to make him realize he was trying to get a grip on a family he sensed was nudging away from his sphere of protection. It frightened him at too plunging a level to admit this might be happening. He sensed malign things incubating in the umbrageous waters of the family relationships, but the knowledge of it only ever spoke to him in his dreams. He was a rational man. He grabbed at rational, surface solutions. He thought all that was needed was a strong hand on the tiller.

De Sang wore suede boots, a feature Maggie had always held to be a floggable offense. He also wore a drab suit, his jacket supplementing a large cardigan buttoned underneath. He was a tall, thin man with a fleecy white head of hair. Though he had a chair behind his desk, he didn't seem to like to sit on it: throughout his interviews with Maggie and Alex he sat variously on the arm of his chair, on the edge of his desk, on his windowsill, and indeed anywhere but his chair. In a day's work he covered miles of ground without leaving his office.

When agreeing to take on Sam he managed to convey the

impression he was doing all concerned a favor. "Meanwhile what Sam needs above all else," he said, parking his butt on the warm radiator and folding his arms, "is stability."

"He's got stability," said Maggie.

De Sang looked at her a long time before answering. "Children Sam's age are moving through a precise stage of development. They have a habit of responding acutely to the emotional environment in which they're located. If Mother is pleased, they know it without anything being said by Mother. If Father is angry, they know it even before Father has outwardly shown his anger."

Alex nodded sagely, interested. Maggie looked away, guessing where all this was leading.

"This empathy of early childhood begins to thin out as kids become more verbal—as they learn to talk better. It's a survival faculty we mostly lose. But Sam here, he's still in that empathy mode, reflecting some of the emotions generated around him."

Alex agreed. "Makes sense. I mean—"

"You can tell all that from one meeting?" Maggie interrupted rudely.

"I can recognize a pattern when I see one," said De Sang. "We all like to think of ourselves and our relationships as unique—and in some ways they are. But underneath . . . If there is tension in the house, Sam will find a way to reflect it back. If there's a mood of opposition, or contradiction—"

"But what's been said about tension or opposition?" She looked at Alex.

"Mrs. Sanders. You're paying me to be blunt."

"It's all right," said Alex, getting up to leave. "I appreciate the directness. It's already making sense."

He shook De Sang by the hand.

Maggie was livid.

"What the hell did you tell him about us?"

"I didn't tell him anything."

"Bullshit. You practically did his job for him. Now he doesn't even have to earn his fee. Stability! Stability? Couldn't you even let him look at Sam first, before blaming everything on our disagreements?"

"The idea is to help the man sort it out, not to mystify him!"

"Rubbish! You had your tongue so far up his arse I couldn't even see your head waggling."

Alex stared at her. She'd never previously directed language like this at him.

"All I said was that there are certain tensions in the household. That's all I said."

"Did he ask you if we're fucking?"

"Sam is listening to every sweet word you have to say."

"Did he ask you? Did he?"

"What's that got to do with it?"

"That means he did! Yes! I'm right! And you told him. Jesus Christ!"

Sam looked up wide-eyed at his mother. "Baby Jesus."

"All right! What do you suggest we do with the child? I'm sure you've got some terrific ideas. What does your book say? Rub him down with mustard and garlic? Or thrash it out of him with a hazel switch? When are you going to be a *proper mother to our children*?"

Now it was Maggie's turn to stare at him for raising his voice. Alex stormed off to work, leaving her to take Sam home.

But before she did, she stopped by the Gilded Arcade, to look in on the man she thought of as Mr. Omega. She peered through the window and thought he must have finished reading his book; at any rate he had his back turned and was weighing out measures of herbs in small plastic bags. He didn't look up when the bell tinkled. Sam pointed up at the tiny bell, waiting for it to ring again as the door closed.

"Rue, vervain," said Maggie, "St. John's wort, dill . . ."

"Hindreth witches of their will." He didn't look up from his task, but she could tell he was smiling. "You've learned something."

"Only we say hinder. We don't go in for 'Hindreth'."

"Brought that book in for me to see?"

"No."

"Right. Sell her old stock, won't we, Sam?" He winked at the child. Sam buried himself in Maggie's long skirt.

"How did you know his name?"

"You let it slip. Last time you were in." She suddenly remembered telling him, and she felt stupid.

"If you're going to ask me all these questions," he said a few minutes later, "you'd better sit down. I'll make you some coffee. Or herb tea if you prefer, but personally I can't stand the stuff." He dragged a chair beside the counter and she sat. He gave Sam a doll on strings to play with.

"Coffee will be fine. What does it mean when certain herbs are referred to as 'hot' or 'cold'?"

"It refers to the energy of the plant. If its effects are stimulating and aggressive, or electric, then they're said to be hot. If they're relaxing, passive, and magnetic, then cold. I prefer it as a gender classification, male and female, but then I suppose I'm an old chauvinist." He sat down and swept a hand through his thinning hair.

"I suppose you are." She looked across her coffee cup at him and their eyes settled on each other a moment too long. Maggie looked away. "What if a plant was said to be of Diana?"

"Oh, you're getting a bit fey there. All these herbs are supposed to have associated deities. The old gods. I can't be bothered with all that stuff."

"Does it matter when a plant is picked?"

"Does it matter how long you cook a lasagne? Or a panful of carrots? Of course it matters!"

"I still don't see why."

"She doesn't see why, Sam. Look, if you want to be scientific about it, did you know the weight of a plant increases during the waxing of a moon? Fact. Photosynthesis. So some new matter must be created. Then the weight returns to normal as the moon wanes. Fact."

There was something invitingly humorous and ironic about the way he levitated his eyebrows each time on the word *fact*. As though he was seducing her into a conspiracy to which he only jokingly subscribed. Certainly he wasn't the most physically attractive man in the world, but he exuded a deep sense of calm and self-possession; it tempted one to want to stay and bathe in it for a while.

Maggie had a deeply intuitive nature, and great powers of empathy when they were allowed exercise. It depended on context or on precise individuals, on the combination of active agents, like sugar and yeast. Here was such an interaction. The bond was immediate. She saw through to him. She saw a level of sadness beneath all of his ironies. It excited her instincts. Questions fizzed.

"What's manzanilla?"

"Camomile."

"What's devil's milk?"

"Celandine."

"And old gal?"

"Old gal is elder."

"And old man's mustard?"

"Yarrow. Where are you getting all these names from?"

"You seem to know them all. Can you sell me some laurel, mugwort, and cinquefoil?"

"Going listening, are we? I really wouldn't mind getting a look at that book of yours."

Maggie giggled. "Got any suggestions for a love potion? Or at least I'll settle for a peace potion. Something to restore a bit of harmony to a fractious household."

"Not getting along with the old man, eh?" He jumped out of

his chair and started to reach down jars from the shelf behind him. "Let's see what we can do."

Maggie too got to her feet, bombarding him with questions as he shook herbs into the brass pan of his weighing scales. She leaned comfortably against the counter. Both were too preoccupied to notice the door open. Sam, playing with his doll on the shop floor, did notice. His eyes shot up to the bell as he waited for it to tinkle; but this time it failed to ring. An old woman stood in the open doorway.

Sam looked at his mother and the shopkeeper, but they had their backs turned. He looked again at the silent bell, and then at the woman standing over him. She wore a long gray coat, black woollen stockings, and heavy black shoes. A dark hat was pulled over her head, shadowing her face. Wisps of hair the color of smoke poked out from under the brim. She stared hard at the two people engrossed at the counter, her face set in an expression of impatience. Then she noticed Sam.

The old woman bent down toward him. Her movement was slow, snakelike. She put her face close enough to his that he recoiled from her pungent breath. Sam looked over to his mother. He wanted to call her, but the space across the floor of the shop seemed to expand outwards until she was a great distance away, too far to hear him. The woman took the doll from him and put it inside her coat. She straightened her back, turned and walked out of the shop, closing the door behind her. Sam raised his eyes to the bell again. It was silent.

Maggie suddenly looked up from the counter, where they were still measuring out herbs.

"What is it?" the shopkeeper wanted to know.

"I don't know." She looked at Sam and snatched him up from the floor.

"Something wrong?"

"Nothing. Only ... just a strange feeling. Forget it."

He dispensed the herbs in little plastic sachets. "As for your old man, blend the oil I told you about. Then rent a porn film from the video shop."

"Should I drop the oil in his food?"

"Not unless you want to poison him. You're meant to wear it. It smells good." Maggie paid for what she'd bought. "Can I have my dolly back?" the shopkeeper asked Sam.

Sam buried his head in his mother's clothes. "Come on, Sam. Where's the dolly? Give it back to Mr. Omega."

"The lady took it."

Maggie apologized. "He makes up porky pies, I'm afraid."

"The lady took it!" Sam almost screamed.

"Don't worry about it. It must be around here somewhere. My name's not Mr. Omega, by the way. It's Ash. Let me know how you get on." He opened the door for her, and this time Sam heard the bell tinkle over their heads, and then again as Ash closed it after them.

NINE

Alex came home in buoyant mood. He picked up the kids and swung them round and chattered about his work. He made lip-fart noises with Sam until Maggie told him he ought to know better. His nostrils twitched once or twice, but whether in savor of the spicy goulash simmering on the stove, or of Maggie's newly acquired and liberally applied oil, it was impossible to tell since he made no comment.

"Things are going haywire at the castle; all our ideas have been scrambled by things turning up which shouldn't really be there."

"What sort of things?" Maggie stirred the goulash.

He stood behind her, pressing his knees into the hollows at the back of her knees. "The layer we've worked for the last three months is supposed to be fifteenth century; today we suddenly find our way into the twelfth century with all this stuff."

"Stuff? Get off."

"Yes, stuff. Stuff. Nothing important. Shards of pottery. A coin and a tin plate. Just all from the wrong period. We'll have to go back to the drawing board and retrace the foundations."

"Were there any bones?" Amy, appearing behind them, put a stop to Alex's knee-trembling activities. Amy always wanted to know if there were any bones.

Alex had once brought a skull home to show them, but Maggie had refused to keep it in the house. If her own unease wasn't enough, Amy had demonstrated far too great a fascination for the object. She'd treated it as some kind of pet, and the line had to be drawn when Maggie had discovered her cleaning its grinning teeth with a pink toothbrush. Out went the skull. "No Bones. No skeletons. Not even a dog bone." His nostrils twitched again and he sniffed. He looked at Maggie. "What's for tea?"

Maggie had prepared her perfume using an eyedropper she had originally purchased to treat Sam's conjunctivitis. Ash had sold her oils of gardenia, musk, jasmine, and rose geranium, and she blended them a drop at a time until the scent seemed satisfactory. Ash had told her to use her instincts in judging the strength of the smell.

It wasn't that she was prepared to compromise over the issues which divided them; she was still angry about the question of Sam and his visits to De Sang's private practice. But she was exhausted by the arguments, and genuinely concerned that the tension in the household might be harming her children. Despite her antipathies towards De Sang, his words hadn't completely missed their mark.

So she made her scent, her oil perfume, and hoped for the best. She applied it behind her ears, and on her wrists; and for good measure she also anointed the pillows in the bedroom and the cushions on the sofa in the lounge.

Alex complimented her on the goulash, which was a good sign, and the first kind words in over a week. Then after dinner he switched on the TV, plumped up the cushions, and stretched out on the sofa to watch a game show. "Pollution," he said. "Everything on TV is intellectual pollution."

"So why are you watching it?"

He didn't answer, and by the time she had put the children to bed and washed the dishes, he was almost asleep dozing in front of the set. She sat in her chair, looking at him, asking herself if she still loved him. She thought she did, thought she might. Once he'd been the one with all the ideas, the motivator, the initiator of adventures. Now he dozed in front of game shows and cartoons. The routines of work and the responsibilities of parenthood had strapped him in. She felt a wave of compassion for him; he was doing all he could to protect her and the children from the storm, while she longed for nothing more than to be allowed an occasional walk in the wind and the rain.

Alex roused himself. He got to his feet, blinked at her and smiled weakly. Then he went up to bed. After a while she followed him, but he was asleep before she got there. Undressed, she held her scented wrist to her face, inhaling the perfume as she looked at him. The scent produced a deep, sensuous ripple in her and she had to smile. It wasn't love and it wasn't passion and it wasn't enchantment either; but it was better than arguing.

Tomorrow she would go listening. .

In the afternoon she deposited Sam with Mary the childminder and returned home to consult the diary. It sanctioned dawn and dusk as the best moments for the exercise, but these were times not usually available to her: the afternoon would have to do.

She boiled spring water—from the supermarket—on the kitchen stove. Then she shredded the bay laurel, the mugwort, and the cinquefoil and tipped it all into the pan. She covered the pan with a lid and left the mixture to simmer.

Returning to it half an hour later, she lifted the lid and sniffed the fumes. It didn't smell particularly strong, so she inhaled more deeply, twice, before replacing the lid. She felt nothing in particular. She was disappointed. There seemed nothing stimulating about the concoction; if anything it made her feel slightly drowsy.

But she was committed. She took a thermos flask and filled it with the hot brew, screwing the cap on tight. She put on her coat, picked up the flask and her car keys, went out and drove to Osier's Wood.

All was quiet but for the breeze stirring in the trees. Maggie left the car and crossed the brook into the willow-fringed woods, finding a spot near the place where she believed she and Alex had created Sam. Here she sat under an oak. She unscrewed the cap of the thermos flask and inhaled the hot fumes rising from the brew. She practiced breathing in from her diaphragm, pushing out below the rib cage as she inhaled. She did this until the brew went cold; then she sat back to wait.

When Alex got back from work that evening, the telephone was ringing and no one was answering. He unlocked the front door and burst in to answer the phone before the caller hung up. It was Mary the childminder. She didn't mind that Maggie hadn't been to collect Sam, but she wanted Alex to know she expected to he paid for the extra hours. Alex mumbled an apology and promised to collect Sam himself.

He replaced the receiver and looked uselessly around the living room. The car was missing from the driveway, and he hadn't a clue why. His only thought was that something might have happened with Amy, and that Maggie must be with her. He was ready to trudge round to the childminder's to collect Sam when the telephone rang again. This time it was Anita Suzman on the line.

Anita had gone to school to collect her own children, who finished half an hour later than Amy's younger class, only to find Amy hanging around in the playground with a teacher. She'd waited a while longer and had then decided to take Amy home with her. That had been over two hours ago, and she'd been telephoning intermittently ever since. Was anything wrong?

"Wrong?" said Alex. "I don't know. I've just this minute got in. And there's nobody here."

"Well, you're there now."

Alex, his mind still on other things, was astonished at the logic of this remark. "Yes."

"So. Would you like to come and collect Amy?"

"Amy?"

"Yes. She's your daughter, remember?"

"I'm sorry, Anita, I'm not with it. Thanks for picking up Amy; it's good of you. I'd come at once, but Maggie seems to have taken the car somewhere."

"Would it help if I brought Amy to you?"

Anita even offered to pick up Sam on the way after Alex had explained his predicament.

The children looked none the worse when she arrived with them. She took off her coat and sat down without being invited. It wasn't even six o'clock, but Anita looked as though she was dressed for a big night out. "Going somewhere this evening?" Alex gave her a glass of wine.

"No. Why do you ask?"

"I can't think why," said Alex. He hadn't seen Anita since they'd all dined together at her house and he was reminded how lusciously attractive she was. She relaxed easily into his sofa and crossed her long legs. The sheer nylon of her tights hissed as they meshed.

"I see you got your open fire," she said.

"Oh, that. Yes."

"Cosy and romantic. An open fire."

"Is it? Yes, I suppose it is."

She put down her wineglass. "What's going on?"

Alex took a deep breath. "Maggie wants to go and study a course at university. I don't want her to, so she's finding all sorts of ways to punish me."

Anita was about to answer, but suddenly Maggie was standing in the doorway.

"Maggie! We were just talking about you."

"I heard. How are you, Anita?" She unbuttoned her coat, sat down and picked up a magazine.

"We were worried about you. Everything okay?"

"Why shouldn't it be?"

"Anita collected Amy from school," said Alex calmly. "She

also collected Sam. Mary has been phoning all afternoon to ask what's going on."

"Are the kids all right?"

"The kids are fine," said Anita.

"That's all right then." Maggie looked at Alex. "Isn't it."

TEN

"This garden needs digging. And it needs a pond."

"What?" Alex had followed Maggie outside after Anita left.

"I'm going to plant a herb garden. I want my own herbs. Lots of them."

"Why the hell are you talking about herb gardens? Where have you been all afternoon?"

"And I want the money for some good garden tools."

"Did you have to be so bloody rude to Anita?"

"I don't like her."

"You made that pretty obvious."

"Didn't you see why she was waiting? So she could enjoy the spectacle of us having a row."

"Anita is our friend!"

"Correction: she's your friend. Correction: she's the wife of your friend."

"She was looking after Amy and Sam while you were falling down on the job of being a mother."

"It won't happen again."

"Are you going to tell me where you were?"

She turned to look him in the eye. "I was having a conversation. With myself. I found out some things. I found out you don't love me, for example."

"Here we go again. Here we go."

"You only want to own me. You can't stand the idea of me having any life of my own. I'm not allowed my own life. I'm just a clip-on accessory to your own world."

"That old song."

"I also found out that this garden badly needs a fucking pond."

Alex looked up in exasperation. He saw Amy and Sam watching them from a bedroom window. "Look at that! Look at those kids! No wonder they're so twisted and fucked-up and miserable and unhappy when they've got you for a mother, disappearing and reappearing without a word! Just look at them!" Alex dived back indoors.

Maggie glanced up at the children, saw them move away from the window. Twisted and fucked-up and miserable and unhappy. She knew it wasn't the children Alex was describing at all; it was themselves.

She turned and saw the bird perched on the washing-line pole. It was a blackbird, stock-still, head cocked to one side as if listening. Its eye was focused on her. She stared at it for a long time, until it flapped away.

That evening hit a new low. They failed to exchange a single word and Alex made himself a bed on the sofa.

Maggie lay awake in the feverish dark. She felt anxious, troubled by thoughts too abstract to pin down. Still light-headed from the episode in the woods, she was unable to keep her mind from what had transpired there. In one sense there was little to be said. Listening, that's all that had occurred. No more, no less than that. Yet it was as if she had listened for the first time in her life, and discovered that beneath the ordinary sounds of the world was something else.

The first change was a miraculous softening. Her brittle edginess dissolved in the peace of the woods, and so too did her visual impression of the trees, branches, ferns, grasses, and the silky feel of the leaf mold beneath her. Everything softened. The silence of the place distilled out, and even when a wood pigeon broke cover, the whirr of wings and flicking of branches was muted and distant.

At one point she thought she might have fallen asleep, but knew she hadn't. Time had simply broken out of its tram lines. She had overstayed her allotted period by two hours. And she had indeed heard a voice, whether in the leaves or in her own head. It was soothing and, in turns, excitable. It was reassuring. It knew things she had thought forgotten. It was a voice she hadn't heard for many years, a neglected, private voice.

It was her own, inner voice, demanding an audience. It spoke to her in a language half-formed, in fragments of words, sometimes archaic in sound; it whispered in strange accents. Strange, but familiar enough to be none other than her own mind, yet shredded and reformulated, and at last fractured into a small crowd of ghostly women at her back.

No, she hadn't fallen asleep, because as she opened her eyes and looked around her she felt intensely awake, her perception had sharpened. Squinting up through the branches, she saw that the leaves formed patterns. They structured the light between the leaves, stringing it together like beads on a necklace, or suspending the light in parabolas, like spiders' cobwebs.

The woods took on a moist-canvas effect. She too felt she helped to generate this moistness, and was happy to be a part of the rich mulch of woodland decay and fertility. She found herself blowing gently on the back of her hand, to remind herself to stay conscious; and the act chased a sensuous ripple through her body. She felt moist, inside and out.

And then as she closed her eyes again, the effortless whispering returned. Sometimes it was no more than a beat under the surface of life, a rhythm, an existential hum. Then it was the versifying rustle again, which she knew must be the leaves in the trees, but which was urgent in its desire to speak, to tell, to reveal. She had opened a faucet on something shut down for a very long time, and now it would not be closed off. It waited for the twilight between dozing and sleeping, and then it began again, elusive, at the periphery of consciousness, but relentless as a river.

The following day, with Alex at work and Amy at school, Maggie set about cleaning up in the kitchen. The pan of dirty herb water sat on the stove. She tossed the reeking remains into the sink where they instantly formed a pattern on the stainless steel. A face suggested itself in the mash of leaves; but Maggie'd had enough of clairvoyance for a while, and she rinsed the leaves away.

She did some washing, and when she came to peg it out she found something dangling from the line. It was the wooden doll on puppet strings which Ash had given Sam to play with in his shop. Maggie couldn't think how Sam had managed to bring it home with him unnoticed, but there it was. She took it down. It was an expensive toy, hand-carved and brightly painted. She decided to return it, or even to offer to pay for it, that afternoon. She also decided to show Ash the diary.

Fetching the thing from its hiding place, she began leafing through the pages. It was a curious feature of the diary that she continued to discover, here and there, pages of faintly pencilled entries she'd previously dismissed as blank. As if the volume of contributions increased every time she closed the book. Her eyes fell on an entry on the right-hand page, dated 21st March. There was the usual list of herbs written in pen, and underneath a pencilled entry in the same fastidious hand.

First day of spring, and so I have a one should any ask me for help with a-courting. And why not, for I do love the young, let them do, I being too old, well not so old but here it is, and it is the handfasting. Gardenia for harmony. Musk for passion. Jasmine for love. Rose geranium for protection. Yarrow for seven years' love and to stop all fear.

Maggie read it again. It was almost identical to the recipe given to her by Ash! Only the yarrow was different.

> *These being all essences, but for the yarrow, which wants the dried herb, a pinch mixed with these essences. Then pour off into two jars, and then each anoint the other from their own jar, by the moon, asking. And after the seventh night, the remaining poured into one jar and both jars be hidden in some secret place. And there's the handfasting.*

Maggie looked at the recipe sadly. It would be fun to try, she thought, but the idea of coaxing Alex to agree to join in a witch's love ritual, smearing each other with oil, depressed her. She might as well try to persuade him to fly from the bedroom window after their last spat. On the left-hand page of the diary, the previous day's entry, was another recipe:

> *Dwale. Now she is a harsh mistress. A. says she is my lady, as she has my name. She is from the valley of shadows, and she stalks those who would use her. Sleeping, madness and death. The leaves soaked in wine vinegar and pressed against the temples brings sleep and eases intolerable headaches and agues. Two of her beautiful berries might kill a small child. A. told me they once used her juice as cosmetic—well she can keep it. Deadens pain of childbirth. A. says now I must use her against my enemies. Dwale is sacred to Hecate and should be picked May eve.*
> *It is one for the flying, as last night I found out. God help me, for I may have come too far in this*

The entry seemed to have broken off. Underneath these words, and scrawled in another, barely literate hand, was a further entry. Maggie had to turn the diary on its side and squint hard to make it out.

> *Ha for there ain't no turning back*

It was curious. It had obviously been written by some person other than Bella, the author of the diary. Maggie had always assumed that the diary had been a very private thing; that she shared its exclusivity and sense of dark secrets only with its author. Here also were the first signs of the diarist's distress.

She closed the book and helped Sam to put on his coat.

Ash was fascinated by the diary. He ordered Maggie to make coffee while he leafed through its pages. Sam was allowed to play on the floor with the doll. "Dwale," he said, "is an old witchy word for deadly nightshade. You know, belladonna."

"That's why Bella says it has her name."

"Deadly is right. Don't be tempted to try any of this. There are easier ways to cure a headache. But who is this mysterious A.?"

"I don't know. She keeps cropping up, doesn't she? I can't tell if she's a friend or an enemy."

"That's right. Bella seems uncertain about it herself. I get the impression Bella is always looking over her shoulder at A. There are some interesting recipes in here. Would you mind if I copied them?"

Maggie did mind. She prickled. "No. Go ahead."

"Maybe you wouldn't mind lending it to me for a while."

She felt, not for the first time, the thrill of possessiveness. "No. That's not possible."

Ash looked up from the pages and into her eyes. "Not even for one night?"

"It's not possible."

Something told him not to push the matter. He nodded. "I'll make some notes. If that's all right by you."

They chatted about the contents of the diary as Ash scribbled down some of the formulae. Much was already familiar to him, but one or two concoctions took him by surprise. "Bella was into listening to the wind. Have you tried it?"

"I have," said Maggie.

He looked up again. "Tell me about it."

Sam was happily playing on the floor with his puppet. He wasn't dextrous enough to manipulate the strings, but he cheerfully dragged the wooden doll across the floor and gave it a half-formed voice. The doll told him it was sleepy, so he laid it on the floor beside him and felt sleepy himself. He could hear his mother and Ash murmuring at the back of the shop. Their soft, lilting voices retreated slowly, grew muffled and far-off, and the distance between him and them seemed to expand. Their presence diminished and grew cloudy, and his eyelids became heavy.

His arm holding the doll lifted slowly into the air. The strings were held taut, the doll's feet lightly brushing the floor. He felt a slight tug on the strings, and then another tug, in the direction of the door. The door stood ajar. Sam looked up at the tiny, silent bell. Then he looked out of the door and saw her.

It was the old woman. The old lady who had stolen the doll from him last time they came in here. She was outside on the catwalk, squatting, her back to the painted safety railings. She was looking directly at him. She held out her hand with her index finger crooked toward him. She made a trigger movement with her finger, and the puppet strings went taut again, and tugged in her direction. Sam looked from the puppet to the old woman. She repeated the gesture, and the doll seemed to want to walk toward her. Dragging the puppet, Sam left the shop and walked over to her. The sound of shoppers' activity on the level below echoed strangely in his ears. Sounds, shouts became frozen.

Her eyes seemed washed out, only vestigial traces of hazel color remaining. She waited until Sam approached her; then she moved her outstretched finger to her nose and pressed it. Her tongue shot out. Sam giggled. Then she grabbed the loose flesh under her chin, tugged it, and her tongue disappeared back into her mouth.

"Can you do it again?" said Sam.

She did it again. Sam was enchanted. Then the old woman straightened her back, beckoned him to follow her, cocked her leg over the safety railings, and jumped.

They were four levels up. Sam leapt at the railings and pressed his head to them. Down at ground level he could see dozens of tiny people walking to and fro. They were the size of his toy soldiers. He could also see the old woman. She was suspended in midair, only a few feet below the catwalk.

She took two steps, walking on air. She looked back at him, beckoning him to follow. Sam giggled, and climbed up on the railings.

Ash took a slurp of tea. "My wife and I are going to take a walk on Wigstone Heath on Saturday. Why don't you come? Bring the kids."

"That would be nice," Maggie said. "I'll ask Alex. Though I don't expect you'll have much in common."

"That doesn't matter. We can have a picnic if it's not too cold."

Maggie was delighted at the thought of new friends, what's more her *own* friends. Everyone she knew was connected through Alex. Maybe she would lend Ash the diary for a night after all.

There was a fluttering at the window that made her look up. It was a bird, fanning its wings and swooping at the window, as if it was trying to get inside. Its beak and claws tapped against the window as it hovered against the glass.

"Christ!" Ash shouted. He pointed at something outside and leapt to his feet. Maggie saw he wasn't pointing at the bird, but at Sam, who had cocked a leg over the railings on the catwalk, and was preparing to swing himself over the edge.

Ash vaulted the counter and rushed out. He flung himself at the rails and collected Sam in his arms just as the boy was about to let go. Maggie, coming up behind him, ran at the rails. She could see shoppers huddled on the ground fifty feet below, pointing up at them. The sight of the drop flashed like a blade, and she wanted to vomit. She looked up and saw the bird, fluttering at the windows roofing the arcade.

It was a blackbird. It escaped through the open skylight.

ELEVEN

De Sang was expecting her. His receptionist told Maggie to go right in. She pushed open the door to see the whitehaired psychologist lying facedown on the carpet, blowing out his cheeks and making slow progress across the floor with a breaststroke motion. Also blowing out his cheeks was Sam, happily swimming beside him.

"Come and join us," said De Sang. "We're having a race to see who can get to the other side the slowest."

"To the island," shouted Sam between gulps of air.

"I mean to the island."

Sam was having a great time. Maggie might even have joined them, but she'd put on a new skirt to come and collect Sam. "I don't want to get wet," she said.

De Sang didn't get up, so Maggie took a seat. She bit her nails. "Are you getting some clues to his character?"

"No," gulped De Sang. "We're just playing."

Maggie crossed her legs and looked around the room. On the walls hung a gray diploma, almost obscured by lots of kids' paintings in bold, primary colors. "Is this how you win their trust?" She was trying hard to sound friendly.

De Sang mouthed at her like something inside a glass tank. "No. Just playing."

"No talking!" Sam shouted.

De Sang reached the wall and got to his feet. "I win so I lose," he told Sam. "Time to go home."

"NO!" screamed Sam.

"Captain Hook," he said. Sam looked thoughtful and stared at the carpeted floor. "Swim outside and get your coat." Sam did as he was told, breaststroking toward the reception. De Sang was red in the face from his exertions. He perched on the edge of his desk, drying off. "Great exercise," he said.

Maggie watched Sam swimming out of the room and, against her preference, laughed. Then she became serious again. "So can you tell me why he tried to throw himself over the railings?"

"No idea. Can you?" He smiled.

"How much are we paying you?"

"Lots. Hope I'm worth it. Who is Mr. Ash?"

"The shop owner. The one who grabbed him in time. Ash saved his life." He looked at her. "No, I'm not having an affair with Ash."

"Good Lord. Did I suggest you were?"

"No, but you gave me a look. A *psychological* look."

"In that case I'll have to be more careful."

It was Maggie's turn to offer him a searching look. His face was wreathed with lines. He managed to make a virtue out of his scruffiness, and for this reason she thought she could like him after all. "Somehow we got off on the wrong foot, didn't we, Mr. De Sang? After all, we both want the same thing."

"We're making progress already." He smiled.

Alex declined to go walking with them on Wigstone Heath. It was a blustery day, and he preferred to curl up on the sofa in front of the TV, sipping lager from the tin. Maggie festooned the kids with hats and scarves and took Dot along with them to meet Ash at a prearranged spot. When they got there, he was sitting in his car alone. His wife, he explained, hadn't felt well enough to come. Maggie wished she'd left the children with Alex.

Wigstone Heath was a wind-blasted stretch of moorland, dotted with stunted bushes and outcrops of rock eroded into eerie shapes. A prehistoric stone circle called the Dancing Ladies commanded the elevated middle of the heath; and at some distance, leaning slightly into the wind, was a large single standing stone, the Wigstone from which the heath had taken its name. It was like a solitary broken tooth. They headed for the stone circle.

The wind was as sharp as a scythe. It made Maggie's ears ache. Dot, at least, seemed to enjoy herself, running ahead and sniffing the path in front of them. Maggie told Ash about De Sang.

"All he seems to do with Sam is play with him."

"So?"

"Well, I could do that."

"Then why don't you?"

Maggie wondered why she didn't.

The children ran round the stone circle, attempting to leap from one stone to another. Dot cocked her leg against one ancient megalith.

"What is it?" Amy wanted to know.

"It's a stone circle."

Amy sighed as if her mother was an idiot. "But what's it for?"

"It's a mystery," said Ash. "Sometimes it's more fun when we don't know the answer. Then it can be anything we want it to be." Amy looked less than impressed with this. "All right, I'll tell you the legend. There were these nine ladies. They were dancing naked here one midsummer night. And a wizard put a spell on them, so that if they were still dancing when the sun came up they'd be turned to stone. Well, the night was so short, it took them by surprise. But they were so beautiful the wizard couldn't take his eyes off the dancing ladies, and he got turned into stone too." Ash pointed over at the solitary standing stone across the heath. "There he is."

Amy counted the stones in the circle. They seemed to confirm Ash's story. She walked over to the single stone. "She's happier with that explanation," Maggie said.

"But it subtracts from the mystery, don't you think?"

"I'm sure there's some deep meaning to it."

"Yes," said Ash. "I'm sure there is."

They all sat in Ash's car and ate sandwiches and had tea from a flask.

"You didn't forget to bring the diary, did you?" Maggie asked him. It had been on her mind all day.

"No, I didn't forget." He produced it from the dashboard. "And I've got something to show you." He flicked open to a page which was blank but for a few herb names written on the first two lines. "What do you see?"

Maggie took the diary and held it up to the window. She could see nothing more than what was obvious. She shrugged.

"Watch." He took the book from her and pressed his palm down on the page. After a minute he took his hand away and half a page of faint pencil writing had appeared, barely decipherable.

"How?"

"Some trick with the pencil graphite and chemicals, I suppose. More successful at hiding it on some pages than on others."

"That explains why I kept finding stuff on pages I'd already looked at."

"You probably surfaced some of it just by keeping it in a warm, moist place, or by exposing the pages. You'll find more in there than you thought."

"Have you read all of it?"

"I haven't had it long enough. I was about to ask. Though I suppose you'll want it back for a while now I've showed you that little trick."

"I suppose I will," said Maggie, already engrossed in the phantom writing.

"Be careful with it," said Ash. "Strong stuff."
"Yes."

Be careful.

So why am I afraid? When I take such care?

Is it A. whom I fear? Or is it this craft that seduces me? When it steals my every thought? And though I have this and that to attend to, always I think the craft, the craft, and return to it, and when so many wonderful things are shewn to me that I cannot otherwise. Wonderful things, falling one upon the other.

And may I do good with it, that's the best of all.

But A. torments me and says I play and am not true to the path. Why do I let her abuse me? Why listen? But she says I have not yet come to my fork in the path, as all will and must, says A. Then she flatters me and says I must come to my fork in the path early because I am this and I am that. And it is at the fork I must make the DECISION.

In her few quiet moments Maggie read and reread the new pages of the diary as Ash had revealed them to her. Recipes for salves and ointments and healing herbs were numerous; but more mysterious were the diarist's outpourings over her misgivings, and the strange courtship with the unnamed A. Maggie did not understand the meaning of these fretful passages but felt in some way they were speaking to her. They were at times like an echo of her own doubts, and yet like the diarist she felt the irresistible seduction in the unfolding mysteries promised behind the words.

Certain passages made her blood quicken.

There is a fork in the path in the woods as I now see, and one is the way out, and one is bathed all in the blue light. This is the path of DECISION as I take it. But howsoever A. will have it, I say I am on the path of the blue shining, and the DECI-SION is made. But A. says I will never do at that.

No, I would not go naked. There's an end. I am resolved not to be put off, nor teased, nor threatened nor bullied no more by A. For now I see she wants me for her own uses, to do this or that EXTREME thing.

Though she struggled to assemble a coherent picture from these entries, Maggie had, at least, discovered some continuity.

In spite what I wrote a few days ago, today I went naked for the LISTENING, and there is an end to all talk of play. It was the blue lighted path, but not lighted in a common sense, and even A. says yes and how yes was the DECISION. And it is made. And it shut her mouth for a while, and I'm glad of a bit of peace so I am.

I'd just as lief not prove her right but it brings me such reward my heart hammers to tell of it. And dangers, there are dangers I never guessed, but such reward! My heart is like a scales, up, down, I don't know.

I am still afraid and A. says that is proper.

What was it that had pitched the diarist into such raptures? Maggie wanted to know what great step it was that appeared to have been taken. There was the *listening* mentioned again, which Maggie had already been seduced into sampling the afternoon she'd forgotten to collect the children. Extraordinary things had happened, in their small way, and certain emotions had been excited; but there were no blue lights or shining paths or spectacular decisions to be made.

Meanwhile she found a preparation for treating Amy's eczema; and an inhalant for treating her own sinus complaint, which she used with some success. She had an itch for the creativity of the thing, and she cast around for subjects. But it wasn't ointments and herb baths she wanted, it was more. The diarist's excitement infected her.

Maggie had never had an affair since marrying Alex, though she had once come close. But, in hiding her herb collection from him, in poring over her diary in secret moments, and in plotting snatched intervals away from her family, the entire enterprise felt a little like that. She was cagey about what she'd been doing and careful not to let anything slip. Meanwhile curiosity pulled like desire.

The diary was full of mysteries waiting to be undressed. Her work with oils was deeply sensuous; streaming with exciting, public perfumes and with private, arousing musky odors. Her secret world flowed with refreshed moods and new histories, and was charged with possibility. It was a potent, dangerous seduction; and Maggie was seducing herself.

One morning, about half an hour before dawn, Maggie woke up as indeed she'd asked herself to before falling asleep. She slipped out of bed and dressed hurriedly. Alex snorted and turned in his sleep but didn't waken.

In the kitchen she shredded and boiled her concoction of bay laurel, mugwort, and cinquefoil, inhaling the fumes before pouring the brew into her thermos flask and carefully disposing of the dregs. She got in the car and drove through the empty streets.

Gray light was peeling into dawn when she arrived at Osier's Wood. She parked the car and took her flask and a blanket. There was a heavy dew and mist, a will o' the wisp streaming from the woodland and across the distant meadow. The woods were eerily silent. Trees stood in dark ranks, prodding branches at her in strange, silent gestures. They enfolded her, tree trunks closing behind her like gates.

She found her way to the middle of the woods, dawn light creeping dimly through the fenestrations of the trees. She listened. There was nothing but the occasional drip of dew from a branch. Then the moistness of the trees and the leaves and the earth became a kind of sound to her, a dull harmony. Black and gray and green branches twisted and drew around her like an exotic alphabet she hadn't yet mastered, but which she could learn. She put down her flask and her blanket and took off her coat. The decision had been made. She glanced around her before starting to undress.

It was cold, October-dawn cold, but she stripped and stood naked, looking up at the trees, as if waiting for something. Leaf mold oozed between her toes, her nipples became erect. A shaft of light lit up the dew on the bark of a tall silver birch. She moved to it, collecting dew on her fingers and putting the droplets to her mouth as if they were honey. They tasted strangely sweet. The glinting silver birch took on a lavender hue. She put her tongue to the bark. She licked, inhaling the deep smells of the bark, the smells of moist, old wood, and the fungal odors.

A breeze rippled through the woods and she shivered. She threw the blanket round her shoulders and sat at the foot of an oak. Opening her flask, she inhaled the steam, and it made her feel drowsy. She ran a hand through her long hair, tossed back her head, and listened.

The wind in the tree told her many things.

It told her true things and false things.

It was a friend and a false friend. It told her secrets and lies.

It whispered what she must do to love her husband, and what she must do to kill him.

TWELVE

Alex, Amy, and Sam were sitting quietly round the table having breakfast when Maggie got back to the house. Dot slunk away as she entered the kitchen. She was greeted by silence.

"I've been for a lovely walk," she announced, a trifle too enthusiastically. "You should all do the same if you know what's good for you."

"Early start?" said Alex, buttering his toast.

"I figured it's the only time I can have to myself if I don't want to be accused of neglecting anyone."

"Shall we see," said Alex, "if we can get through an entire Sunday without having a bust-up?"

Amy looked at Maggie as if the decision was entirely up to her.

Alex went along to the Merry Fiddler for a lunchtime drink with his cronies. He always made a point of inviting Maggie, and she always made a point of declining to join him. Didn't she have the Sunday roast to think about?

The children vanished with Dot down into their converted cellar playroom while Maggie got busy. Not until pans were bubbling and steaming on the stove did she go down to check on the children.

They were playing quietly on the rug. Dot was scratching

herself in the corner. Alex had made a decent job of converting the cellar. He'd wood-chip-papered the walls and laid a floor of wooden tiles only six months earlier. Maggie noticed a rust-colored stain spreading from beneath the rug.

"Who spilled something?" she asked crossly. The children looked up with wide eyes. "Off the rug. Come on! Up! Up!"

Maggie pulled the rug aside to reveal a large, reddish-brown stain, four or five feet in diameter. It was dry. Someone had spilled paint, she guessed, and had tried to hide it with the rug. Only Dot looked vaguely guilty. Maggie fetched a bucket and a scrubbing brush. She scoured at the wood tiles, but the stain showed no sign of lifting. She scratched at it; it wasn't paint and she couldn't work out what it might be. So she tried a solvent, but that didn't lift it.

Amy, standing on the other side of the stain, said, "It's a face."

Maggie stood beside her and saw that she was right. The stain formed an inexact visage; features only half-formed in places, ugly, contorted, but nonetheless a face. Maggie covered it up again with the rug. She returned to the kitchen to attend to the roast.

"It's the lady," Sam told Amy after Maggie had gone.

"What lady?"

"The lady at the shop. And she's been in the garden. She has."

Amy tried to sound like her father. "Are you telling lies?"

"She has! She rides a rat! She's been in the garden!"

"All right. I'll lift up the rug and you spit on her face. Go on. You spit on her face."

"No, I'll lift up the rug, and you spit."

"You're scared."

"You spit, Amy. Go on."

So Sam lifted up the rug and Amy spat on the face. Then they put the rug back.

"Don't say anything," said Amy.

————

"Great dinner!" said Alex, wiping gravy from his mustache. "Tell Mum thank you for a great dinner, kids."

"Thank you for a great dinner," said Amy.

"Thank you for a great dinner," said Sam.

This was Alex's way of trying to make peace. The lunchtime beer had made him frothy and exuberant. He got down from the table and put a match to the fire he'd prepared earlier, picking up the Sunday newspaper before flinging himself on the sofa.

"Before you get too comfortable," said Maggie, "would you have a look at the playroom floor? I think there's damp coming up from underneath."

Alex looked at the fire, then at his newspaper. He let the paper slide to the floor. "Sure."

He went down into the playroom and checked out the tiles. That was his Sunday afternoon gone. He had just enough tiles in reserve to replace those ruined by the staining. Lifting out the old ones, he found no sign of damp. It was puzzling, but he simply relaid the new tiles. It took him the best part of two hours.

"Job done," he told Maggie, returning to his sofa minus the lunchtime cheer. "Probably something in the woodstain."

Ten minutes later the fire was roaring and Alex was snoring.

Maggie decided to make an effort herself. She was not so self-absorbed as to suppose her relationship with her husband would mend on its own. She knew that marriage was sometimes a job of work. It needed routine maintenance with full commitment and sleeves rolled up. If only she could find a way of blending that with her newfound interests.

Gardenia for harmony. Musk for passion. Jasmine for love. Rose geranium for protection. Yarrow for seven years' love and to stop all fear.

Harmony! Passion! Love!

She would be prepared to settle for the first and least of these, if only it were that simple. Yes, it was easy enough to make a pretence at harmony. Be sweet, Maggie! Be pliant! Save your spices for the family casserole and don't ask for more, Maggie!

But that wasn't harmony. That was the paralysis of a weak heart—when inside she was scalding.

Passion, once there had been plenty of that. There had been a time in the beginning when they'd been afraid to get out of bed for fear the other might not be there when they returned. Now there were times when, making up her face before a mirror, she might pause to remember some of that passion, and to stretch briefly like a cat, letting go a deep, sensual sigh. Love. Protection. Protection from what? From these adulterous fevers? Or from the fear that—even at that moment—invisible hairline cracks were appearing in the myth of cosy domesticity, a myth she'd never previously had time to challenge.

Maggie didn't want to lose any of it—Alex, the children, the family hearth. But she'd become terrified by a sense of how fragile the thing was, how a moment's inattention might break it. Seven years' love and to stop all fear. Well, they'd had seven years' love, and maybe they'd worn it out. That was her biggest fear of all, that something irreplaceable was already spent.

Earlier that day, before coming home, while still in the woods, she'd been gifted an inspirational message. Maggie, sitting under her tree, had been brought out of her reverie by the tiny quivering of some live thing. Its striped markings blended in so well with the leaf mold and the autumnal ferns that she hadn't noticed. A faint movement betrayed its presence, and she came to her senses, instantly recognizing the black and gray-brown chevrons delineating its length: adder.

No more than a yard from her bare foot, it had been sizing up a small bird alighted on a moss-rich, rotting log. Maggie couldn't understand why the bird didn't take flight. It was a tiny jenny-wren, close enough for her to see that it was looking at the adder. Then she realized it was hypnotized. It was paralyzed by the gaze of the snake.

The adder was a late hibernator. Most of its cousins would be settled in for their winter sleep, and for that reason Maggie felt that here was a significant moment. It was a gift for her; a message from Nature. Maggie had narrowed her eyes and stretched her neck. She made a low hissing noise. It seemed madness, but she'd thought she could project her will into the snake. "Leave it." She wasn't sure if she'd spoken these words or only thought them, but they emerged like a rattling breath caught in the back of her throat. The adder's eyes flickered from the bird to her. Maggie clapped her hands and the wren flew off. The adder slipped away into the ferns.

She'd gazed for a while at the spot where the adder had been, before suddenly feeling bitterly cold. She had no idea how long she'd been there. It was then that she'd dressed and made her way back to the car.

The hedgerows were ablaze with berries and wild fruit. Maggie felt as if her eyes had been stripped of scale. Black-red elder-berries jostled for her attention with poisonous ruby berries of black bryony, healthful hips, brilliant white-beam, blue juniper, wild crab apple, and the shining black pods of deadly nightshade. The season had delivered, and the bushes were an open treasure chest. She determined to come back later, to collect. But meanwhile in the image of the snake and the wren she'd been given an epiphany. Here was a cameo, an emblem, a compact of her marriage. It was a message in a language she was uncertain how to interpret.

She'd prepared her oils by the method of *enfleurage*, filling small jars with leaves or petals, immersing them in olive oil and leaving them for a day or two; then repeating the process several times, throwing away the old leaves and introducing fresh leaves into the same oil, until it became saturated with the fragrance.

Finally the oil was strained through filter paper into a bottle. A few drops of benzoin tincture were added as a preservative before the bottle was tightly stoppered.

She was becoming an adept enthusiast of the art, using both instinct and olfactory good sense to decide when an oil was ready. She blended her oils with the eyedropper and added a pinch of yarrow herb.

She sniffed the result. It made her smile. It wasn't exactly what she expected, but an irrational belief sat inside her like a guiding spirit. Any residual scepticism was no more than a skin stretched over the void. Old doubts were drying, cracking, sloughing off, freeing the bright, moist creature underneath.

Then pour off into two jars, and then each anoint the other from their own jar, by the moon, asking.

She poured the blended oil into two small, opaque bottles; one for him and one for her.

That night, she waited until they were undressing by the soft light of the bedside lamp. Alex sat on the bed unbuttoning his shirt. She knelt behind him and began to massage his neck. He was tense, his muscles stiff as hawsers.

"That's nice."

She dipped her fingers. He tried to look across his shoulders. "Keep still," she said softly. She ran a hand through his hair.

"Would you rub my neck, Alex? Just for a moment?" She slipped off her blouse, handing him a small jar. "Use this."

"Strong stuff." He kneaded it into her shoulders and into her back. The oil glistened along her spine and on her smooth, pale skin.

"That's enough. Come here." She took the bottle from him, held his hand, kissed it and wiped it across her own brow. Then she got up, set the two bottles on the windowsill to receive the moonlight, and switched off the lamp. She parted the curtains a little, to let in the soft rays of the waxing moon, and climbed into bed beside him.

"Do you love me?" she asked.

"You know I do."

"Swear by the moon."

"What?"

"Swear by the moon that you love me."

Alex snorted.

"I mean it," said Maggie. "I want you to."

"It's not Sam who needs a psychiatrist."

"Just do it. Say it."

"All right! I swear by the moon I love you. Can I go to sleep now?"

"Yes. You can go to sleep now."

THIRTEEN

Maggie decided that the children's playroom needed cheering up. She tossed out a couple of old, broken, hard-backed chairs and introduced two brightly colored bean bags. She also placed a few potted plants around the place: a parlor palm and a geranium brought indoors after a successful summer. She was placing the geranium on a low table when she was gripped by a strange notion.

A momentary giddiness swept over her, and as if caught in a flash photograph she saw Alex working at the castle dig.

"How could that be?" she said aloud. Sam looked up from his toys and smiled at her.

"He won't like that, will he, Sam?"

"Yes."

"Go and fetch your coat. We're going out."

The dig in the hollow outside the castle was underway as usual. For work, Alex wore Wellingtons, overalls, and a permanently knitted brow. He was directing a couple of students to set a series of level indicators. Round the perimeter of the dig area a wooden boardwalk had been constructed, to allow visitors an uninterrupted view of live archaeology. The public, however, had not been per-

suaded to desert the cinemas or the shopping malls or even their
armchairs in favor of live archaeology. The idea had not been a
vast commercial success, and it irked Alex to be on display to
schoolkids and the odd courting couple. But on this day he looked
up and saw Maggie marching Sam along the wooden planks toward him.

"Hullo. What's up?"

"Found anything?" asked Maggie.

"Not really."

"You haven't dug up anything interesting today?"

"Not even a button. Why?"

"Not even a button," Sam repeated.

Maggie stepped off the walkway and paced across the sward
to the far rim of the hollow. "Dig here."

"What?" Alex laughed.

"Just dig here."

"Why?"

"Because you'll find something."

"You can't just dig anywhere you like, can you, Sam? The
place would look like a rabbit warren, wouldn't it, Sam?"

"No," said Sam.

"Please yourself," said Maggie. "Come on. Sam." She swept
Sam up in her arms and walked back the way she'd come. "Say
bye-bye."

"Bye-bye," said Sam.

And they were gone. Alex looked at the spot Maggie had
indicated he should start burrowing. He shook his head and
turned back to the job of supervising the dig.

Back at the house, Maggie began to make a more systematic
study of the diary. She had begun to reread the entries day by
day, hoping to glean more information about its author, Bella. But
it was problematic. She wasn't convinced that the entries had been
made chronologically at all, and still some of the pages contained
nothing more than lists. Other pages needed raising, which she
did either by pressing them with the palm of her hand or, more

effectively, by applying a warm iron to them. Occasionally the heat failed to bring up an entry in full, but Maggie was learning more all the time.

Stinging nettles burn the finger to touch it. But to boil takes out the sting. Then it will do as a remedy against the poison of hemlock, mushrooms, quicksilver and henbane, and the oil of it takes away the sting that itself makes. Gather in July and August, and will also give you good protection.

Other entries were eccentric and inconsistent.

A. says white moths are the souls of the dead. But I say this is twaddle, and that we should separate these superstitiousnesses from the true knowledge.

On the following page was an entry which Maggie was unable to read in its entirety.

Now I take back what I said about the white moth for [missing] and was angry with me and showed me and told me that I should not gainsay my dark sister. My fear did [missing] I thought I should die. Why do I let my dark sister lead me? For we put the [missing] which use of the flying ointment I now abjure. Shred and powder the dwale and hemlock and [missing] and hellebore and steep in hogsfat. But that you should [missing] and go courting death, for Hecate, and I have seen her [missing] that you should fly and I am afraid to look upon her face [missing] and a warning for all who take that path. Why do I let my DARK SISTER lead me so?

Maggie did her best to recover the missing words, but she was unable to raise them on the page. Some oily substance had stained the paper there, and the full prescription was lost. Flying ointment she'd heard of before; but who was the dark sister, if not the mysterious A.?

Sam was enjoying himself in the cellar playroom, swimming like a slow fish. It was a good game, but better when there was someone else to play it with. When his friend the doctor was swimming, it was easier to hear the sound of the waves and the splash of the water. He liked the doctor.

Sam got up from the floor and looked around for something else to do. He had a crate of bright-colored plastic bricks in the corner, next to the potted geranium. He waddled over to the crate and tugged it away from the wall. Then he felt something wet splatter across his face.

It hit him sharply across the cheek. Someone had spat at him. He lifted his hand to his face and wiped at the spittle. It was slimy and cold. He looked around him, but there was no one else in the room.

He was still looking to see where the spit had come from when a second gob slapped him hard in the face. This time he knew where it was coming from. Sam wiped his face, backing slowly across the floor away from the low table bearing the potted geranium.

Maggie came down the steps to the cellar to check on Sam and found him crouched against the wall.

"Sam? What are you doing?"

"Nothing."

"Are you all right?" She picked him up.

"Yes."

But Maggie's nerve ends were prickling. She looked round the playroom. There was a disturbing smell in the air, a bitter tang, not strong, but pervasive. She looked at the pile of toys. She gazed hard at the potted geranium. She looked at the new bean bags. Then she noticed the stain seeping from under the rug.

She had a bad feeling. Sam was strangely subdued.

Still cradling Sam, she swept the rug aside with her foot. The peculiar discoloration of the wood tiles had returned. It had come back exactly as it had before. Maggie stooped to wipe a finger across the surface, but it was dry. The marks she'd previously identified as a face had reappeared. She kicked the rug back into position, recovering the offending stain.

"Tell me, Sam."

Sam didn't want to speak. His fear of earning disapproval for telling lies, Maggie knew, was bringing on an unhelpful reticence. He muttered something inaudible.

"What was that? Tell me, Sam. You can tell me anything."

"It was the lady."

Maggie shivered. "Come on, let's go upstairs and light a fire."

FOURTEEN

After three days, and against his better judgment, Alex got a dig going on the spot indicated by his wife. Truth be told, he had more helpers than he could usefully employ, and he set three volunteers on the task to keep them from under his feet. They roped off a square and set to work.

On the second day, Alex was as surprised as anyone when things started to turn up.

At first they hit what was a Norman wall forming part of the castle's foundations. These remains predated the main castle by a few hundred years, but were in no way remarkable. The medieval castle builders had simply capitalized on what was, after all, a prime defensive site. The volunteers were instructed to cut a section along the Norman wall and below it.

What was extraordinary was the unearthing of artifacts below the wall's remains: artifacts some five hundred years more recent than the building of the wall. Of the several explanations for this, Alex favored slippage of land. The "Maggie dig," as he came to call it, was after all adjacent to a hollow in the grass, and successive generations of coal mining immediately below the site had caused considerable subsidence over the years. But he later dismissed this and theorized that the new finds were some kind of intrusion on the site.

Apart from shards of pottery and glass, the first artifact to show up was a rusted dagger. It was ceremonial rather than martial, with a long blade and a cumbersome, wrought handle. The knob of the handle was a grinning gargoyle head, with half-folded wings projecting back. The implement was cast in a rough bronze material and studded with three tiny red stones, something like fire-garnet. It had no place among the debris of a Norman wall.

Then its twin turned up not three feet from the first. Alex temporarily abandoned the main venture and flung himself into the Maggie dig. He personally turned up half a tin plate and a few coins which were easy to date as sixteenth century.

Maggie crowed. "You should have listened to me in the first place." She glowed with pride: with deep, private satisfaction, and with secret vindication.

"A lucky guess." Alex laughed. "There's stuff littered all over that mound. How could you have known?"

"Instinct. Don't knock it. I just had this tremendous feeling about it."

Instinct? Maggie didn't know what to call it. But she accepted it as a gift from her recent handfasting ritual. She didn't want to compromise the gift with too many questions. It was an important confirmation that powers were aggregating to her.

"Well, I'm going to throw a couple more people into it tomorrow. See if there's anything worthwhile."

Alex was always easier to be with when his work was going well. And for that Maggie secretly thanked her handfasting oils (even at that moment drawing down the moon's soft rays). It was a circuitous means of recapturing affection, certainly, but she didn't mind how it worked. Alex wouldn't admit it, but he was grateful to Maggie for giving him a diversion from his otherwise unproductive dig.

He kissed her hand before getting up from the table, and she thought again of her jars of oil standing on the bedroom windowsill. Maggie felt she had learned something about the extraordinary lightness, and indirection, of magic.

"So it was a ritual knife?" Anita Suzman was fascinated. Alex and Maggie had asked the Suzmans over to dinner. Alex had been regaling them with accounts of the dig—the principal dig—and had broken off to tell them about his most recent discovery.

They all got down from the table and sat round the roaring fire. Alex shrugged. "Certainly looks like that to me. But for what kind of ritual, who can say?"

"What made you break off from the main dig?" Bill said, stroking Anita's arm.

Alex irritated Maggie by leaning back in his chair, thrusting his hands in his pockets and modelling an expression of sagacity. "There were impressions in the earth around that spot. Looked like it had been interfered with at some time, but not enough to he obvious."

"Was it what you people call a hunch?" said Anita. Maggie noticed how she couldn't take her eyes off Alex. Alex looked sheepish.

"More wine for anyone?" said Maggie.

"Actually, I'll have to come clean. It was Maggie who told us where to dig."

Anita and Bill's attentions swept to Maggie like the minute hand on a civic clock. "I can't explain it," she told them.

"Maggie's gone a bit fey lately."

"Fey?" Bill look puzzled.

"Oooh," Anita said, a teasing note. "Perhaps she is a witch after all." Maggie wondered what she meant by "after all." She glanced over at Alex.

The wine had reddened Bill's cheeks. His eyelids sagged. "Eye of toad," he said vapidly. "Wing of bat."

Maggie challenged him a little sharply. "What is eye of toad?"
"Eh?"

"I thought so. All those things like eye of toad are code names for different plants and herbs. Eye of toad is camomile. Bloody fingers are foxgloves. Beggar's buttons are just burdock. That's all. No big mystery. Except to the ignorant."

"Consider yourself told," Anita said.

"I do," said Bill.

"Our kitchen's like a herbalist's grotto these days," Alex offered glumly. No one said anything. "An alchemist's chamber."

Maggie got up. "I'll go and wash the dishes."

Anita followed her into the kitchen. She insisted on helping while the men swilled the last of the wine and chortled like schoolboys.

"I'd like to know something about herbs," she said.

"Oh." Maggie shrugged. "I don't know that much about it myself."

Anita flapped a tea towel and looked annoyed.

After the Suzmans had gone home, Maggie went upstairs and waited for Alex. It was after midnight of the seventh evening of the blending of the handfasting oils. The moon outside the window was strong and bright. She held one of the jars up to her eye, and the moonlight became a starburst in the opaque glass. Silver light ran from the bottle like drops of mercury.

"Yes," she breathed. "It might."

She poured the oil from this jar into a second. Then she took the empty one and hid it in her secret chest. After undressing in the moon's soft light, she anointed herself with some of the newly blended oil. She sniffed at the perfume still glistening on her skin; a deep, sensual draught. It thrummed her nerves and her muscles were treated to an involuntary spasm.

It affected her. She felt strong.

"What are you doing in the dark?" Alex said as he came into the bedroom.

"Don't put the light on."

He was slightly tipsy. The wine had made him perspire, and he smelled good. It was an attractive manly odor she thought she'd ceased to appreciate through familiarity. He stood against the bed, fumbling with the buttons on his shirt.

Maggie flung herself on him.

Alex gasped, bouncing against the mattress with Maggie astride him. She tore the shirt off his back, buttons bulleting across the room. Alex strangled a protest as she rained bites and kisses on him, pinning him by his arms. A strange noise was coming from her throat. It made him want to laugh. Giggling, he tried to throw her off, but she was amazingly strong. She was gulping loudly between biting and kissing and sucking at his neck and shoulders. Pinning his chest with one hand, she tore at his trousers with the other, scratching him with her sharp fingernails.

Then he was completely naked and she was stretched over him. It was as if someone had thrown open the door to a white-hot furnace. There was a roaring in his ears. Maggie was drenched in perspiration and some incredibly strong scent. Her moist skin glittered in the moonlight. Still a strange rasping came from her throat as she licked and kissed and sucked the length of his body, scalp to toe, her tongue rough like a cat's. It seemed to him she had momentarily lost awareness of who and where they were.

He was massively aroused by the fury and ardor of her attack. He tried to turn her over, to turn her on her knees so he could penetrate her from behind, but he couldn't find the strength to shift her.

"Maggie," he said. "Maggie!"

She slipped his cock inside her mouth and sucked until it hurt, drawing her sharp nails from his shoulders down to his feet. Energy crackled from her like a discharge of electricity. She settled herself with a shimmy, and he felt the furnace heat of her as she lowered herself onto him, flinging her head back as his full length went inside her. She convulsed at the penetration, her breasts shivering in the liquid light, nipples erect to the moon. There was an overpowering odor of sex and sweat and scent, and a moment when Alex thought he was going to pass out. She pressed her hands on him, cooling him with her fingers. She stretched herself across him and the contact of her nipples and her skin made him hallucinate briefly, seeing and feeling her as eels of warm light.

"What are you doing to me!"

She went on until he was exhausted, exhausted and sore. No one had ever performed on him like that. He lay back on the bed, panting, with Maggie still sitting astride him, herself panting, finished, the sweat gleaming on her back and on her flanks, drops of perspiration pearling the moonlight. Her face was in shadow, but her teeth were white and sharp. The whites of her eyes glittered with lunar light, flashing in the dark. She looked frightening, like a goddess, or a demon.

"Now," she said when she'd recovered. "How long have you been fucking Anita?"

FIFTEEN

Alex denied it. He told Maggie she was insane. What could she say? That the trees told her? That the wind in the bushes had whispered in her ear one day when she was naked in the woods? That she knew the trees sometimes lied in order to help, but that this time she believed them? She had no evidence with which to confront him, and nothing at all to go on other than her instincts.

But she was determined to find out.

"You be careful," said Ash. "You just be careful." He dropped the catch on the shop door to make sure Sam didn't find his way out onto the catwalk. He could live without a repetition of recent events.

"I've spent all my life being careful. That's the trouble."

"But you're getting into a dangerous game here. This isn't like making an herbal pillow."

"That's why I'm asking you to help me."

Ash looked hard at her. She looked pale. Her copper hair was drawn back fiercely into a Scandinavian plait; her blue eyes were damp. "This is not an under-the-counter sale you're talking about. I don't even stock these things. They're poisons."

"Listen to this." She read from the diary. "*All questions will be answered and all matters settled. Take care to gather only on the moons as I have said and make the banishments which A. assures will keep us from the harm of demons. Honour Hecate, she says, and she will love you for her own; abuse her and she will imperil your soul. And all this can I testify. All questions will be answered and all matters settled, but that you fly.*" She put down the diary. Sam was hanging from her arm, looking into Ash's eyes. "But you see it, don't you? This *flying ointment*. It's an aid to clairvoyance, isn't it? That's what they mean by flying! That's all it ever meant!"

"I know all that, Maggie, but what I'm telling you is the ingredients are all highly toxic, deadly even. I mean that's what all that stuff about Hecate is saying: Watch out, she'll kill you!"

"Not to those who treat her with respect." Maggie was urgent. Ash had never seen her so animated. "And anyway. You've done it yourself. Once or twice."

He was shocked. "How do you know that?"

She narrowed her eyes at him; a strange, seductive gesture. "The trees told me."

He looked away, his cheeks burning. Her intuition was strong, and it was correct. He had experimented with the flying ointment, and had singed his wings. But what made him blush was something else. If her intuition about him was so strong, then she would also have guessed his instincts toward her.

"Fly with me, Ash."

He turned his back on her, busying himself, aligning jars on shelves. He couldn't look her in the eye.

"You could show me how, Ash."

Alex went back to his dig and tried to shut the events of the previous night out of his mind. The discovery of the ritual daggers had been reported locally, producing a trickle of extra visitors to the site. The presence of these spectators only irritated him further. He marched along the specially erected boardwalks in his heavy, muddied Wellingtons, saying, "Excuse me," yet all but bundling the visitors out of his way.

He was conscious of the scratches and the bruises and the bites

Maggie had imprinted on his body. She'd acted like a wildcat; he'd never before seen her like that. She'd been possessed by uncanny strength. Plus there was her insistence about Anita. He'd denied it a dozen times, but she was implacable. For the first time in their marriage she'd done something that made him slightly afraid of her.

No, that was untrue. There had always been something in her to make him a little afraid. A reckless streak. A promiscuous gap in her integrity that he felt would one day be used to take her away from him. It was a demon-worm that had always gnawed at him over the years, despite his best efforts to deny its existence.

Some of the things she'd done to him last night made him marvel. It occurred to him she might have been taking lessons from someone else.

"No," said Ash, "I can't help you."

"Then I'll do it myself." Maggie tapped on the diary. "I've got all the information I need."

"It's dangerous. Leave it alone."

"That's why I asked you to help me."

"I'm not going to. Don't ask me again."

"Come on, Sam." Maggie slipped the diary into her bag and got up to go. She tried to open the door, but couldn't manage to release the catch. Ash had to open it for her.

"Wait. If you're serious about it, let me make a suggestion." He rushed back to the counter and took out his address book, copying something onto a scrap of paper. "Do you know the village of Church Haddon? There's someone there you might go and see. Old Liz. She's a strange soul but don't let her frighten you. At least she won't let you come to any harm. Just see what she's got to say, first. Please."

Maggie shrugged and put the address in her coat pocket. Ash watched her dragging Sam along the catwalk to the stairs, and felt sad.

SIXTEEN

Alex had been charged with collecting Sam from De Sang's clinic the following afternoon. De Sang maintained an open-door policy, so that parents need not feel excluded from some esoteric process going on behind lock and key. The receptionist smiled at Alex as he passed her desk and stepped inside De Sang's room.

De Sang was seated in a hard-backed chair in the middle of the room. His hands were tied in front of him, his face was painted an assortment of vivid colors, and his trousers were round his ankles. Sam, face also painted, was running round the chair whooping and waving a paperknife he'd found on De Sang's desk.

"Come in! Come in!" De Sang shouted. "Pull up another chair!"

Sam had already found a chair and, shrieking with delight, was drawing it alongside De Sang. Astonished, Alex dropped into the proffered seat. "Hands, Daddy! Hands!" shouted Sam. Alex looked at the psychologist.

"*Hands!*" Sam screamed angrily. He'd found more string.

"Better do as he says," said De Sang. "Looks like he's got us."

Sam looked furious with his father. Alex held out his hands, and Sam wound the string round them so many times he didn't need to tie a knot. "You don't mess with Peter Pan," said De Sang, in a stage whisper. His face was a garish patchwork.

"Peter Pan!" yelled Sam. "Peter Pan! *Trousers!*"

"Sam made a discovery while he was here today. He went to the toilet and was so eager to get back in here he forgot to pull up his trousers. Result: he fell over. We made it a learning experience: man with trousers round his ankles can't go anywhere."

Alex tried not to blink.

"*Trousers!*" bellowed Peter Pan.

"He's Peter Pan. I'm Smee."

"Who am I?" said Alex.

"Oh. Just one of the nasties."

Peter Pan picked up the paperknife and waved it menacingly. "Better do as he says," De Sang said again.

"How can I put my trousers down with my hands tied?" Alex was serious.

Sam looked disgusted. He put down the knife. "Come here, Daddy. And no tricks. *No tricks!*"

"He knows all the tricks by now," said Smee, "so there's no use trying anything."

Sam unwound the string from his father's hands. Alex lowered his trousers, sat down again, and allowed his hands to be bound once more. Armed with greasepaint pencils, Sam set to work on Alex's face.

Alex wasn't too comfortable about it all. "Made any progress today?" he tried to sound casual.

"Not really. We've been playing most of the time," De Sang said chattily. "Although we did have a little sleep earlier on, didn't we, Sam?"

"Sleep?" said Alex.

"*Keep still!*" Peter Pan bellowed.

Then Alex noticed, amid the children's paintings on the wall, a framed diploma qualifying De Sang as a hypnotherapist. "Oh," he said, realizing. "Look-into-my-eyes sleep."

"Pardon?"

"Hypnosis."

"Good Lord, no. I mean sleep sleep. I was a bit tired and so was Sam, so we lay down on the floor over there and had a ten-minute nap."

Alex felt stupid. "I mean, were you looking for dreams or . . . something."

"No, we just wanted a nap. Good lord, man," Alex could see De Sang's grin behind the swirling clouds of smudged color, "you don't hypnotize or dream-analyse a three-year-old. It's all there on the surface. It only gets buried as we get older. Good lord."

Alex wanted to ask what was there on the surface. He'd suddenly remembered how much he was paying De Sang for all of this when they were interrupted by the receptionist entering the room. If she was at all surprised by the sight of two men sitting with their trousers down, she made a good show of disguising it.

"Your next clients are here. You might want to wash your face."

"Thanks Sheila!" chimed De Sang. "Time to go home!"

"No!" shouted Peter Pan.

"Sam," said De Sang. "Captain Hook."

Sam looked hard into De Sang's eyes before cheerfully resigning himself, and unbound the psychologist's hands, grudgingly doing the same for his father. Without being asked, he trotted off to find his coat.

Alex and the psychologist pulled up their trousers.

"Are we making any progress?" said Alex.

"Early days." De Sang looked hard at him, smiling.

Under the pressure of this smiling gaze, Alex felt obliged to say something, anything. "He's been a bit better at home."

"Really? That's excellent." Alex wished the man would stop smiling from behind the greasepaint. Then De Sang touched Alex's elbow and stopped smiling. "Your wife, Maggie. She's a very clever, very intuitive lady. I think she's understimulated and I think she feels undervalued."

Alex suddenly felt some immense weight shifting on a delicate fulcrum; an entire burden of blame spilling his way. "So it's my fault, is it?"

"Stop. Stop there. Both you and Maggie, like most people, have this incredible ability both to apportion blame and to feel blame being apportioned to you. This is not about blame. This is about life. I'm telling you this as a friend might tell you."

"I thought this was going to be about Sam," Alex protested.

"Of course it's about Sam. Now: shall we go and wash this stuff off our faces?"

The next day Maggie had the freedom afforded by being able to leave Sam at the childminder's. She decided to pay a visit to Old Liz.

It was a fifteen-mile drive to Church Haddon. Maggie found the place easily enough, parking in the street and walking the hundred yards or so to a gray tile-roofed cottage at the bottom of a cinder pathway. An old collie came to bark at her from behind a half-closed gate, and she hesitated.

A few yards away, the door to the cottage stood partially open. Maggie waited for the commotion to summon the householder from the shadowy interior, but no one came. The dog barked furiously, blocking her way.

Maggie looked the collie in the eye. "Don't be silly," she said, and the dog stopped barking instantly, coming from behind the gate to lick at her heels. She scratched it behind the ears, and it followed her down the path.

In front of the house was a vegetable patch. The cottage door showed its original wood, graying beneath a coat of flaking green paint. A rusting horseshoe was nailed over the lintel, horns up. Maggie hovered nervously on the threshold. She had to fight an impulse to retreat down the path, get in her car, and drive home. She glanced over her shoulder before knocking softly on the door.

There was no answer. She tried to peer inside, but was unable to see past the gloom of the immediate shadows. Smells hovered in the doorway; kitchen smells of bottled jams, vinegar, yeasty odors. She knocked again, a little harder.

The door nudged open a further inch under the pressure of her knock. The shadows within seemed to deepen. Maggie waited. She set a foot on the stone threshold and took a decision to push open the door.

"You wants to be careful."

The voice from behind made Maggie spin round. An old woman stood square on the path not three yards away. She was leaning heavily on a stick, evidently having been watching Maggie for some moments.

"You wants to be careful, going places you've no rights to go."

Old Liz was a skinny, bespectacled woman, iron-gray hair tied back and folds of loose skin hanging from her face and neck, making her look like a turkey in need of fattening. She was chewing or sucking at something in her mouth. "Goin' in people's houses."

"I'm sorry. I wasn't going in, I was just . . ."

"I know what you was doing."

"I thought no one was in. I was just about to go."

The old woman said nothing. She leaned on her stick, chewing vigorously, eyeing Maggie. Her eyes were dull black beads behind the thick glass of her spectacles.

"Ash suggested that—"

"I knew you was a-coming."

"Oh? Did Ash tell you then?"

"Ash? You knows Ash, do you? No, Ash told me nothing."

"Oh?" Maggie said again.

When Maggie took a step toward her, Old Liz reached down smartly and pulled up a bit of grass or herb from alongside the path, crushing it and rubbing it between thumb and forefinger. The gesture stopped Maggie in her tracks. She felt bewildered. The old woman didn't take her eyes from her for a second. A taste of bile rose in her mouth. For some reason this awful old woman frightened her. What was Ash thinking of in sending her there? She wanted to go home.

Suddenly Old Liz seemed to relax. Then she was pointing her

stick at Maggie "I sees it. It's all there, it is. But you don't even know when-the-day! You don't! Heh heh!"

"Pardon?"

Old Liz fastened the garden gate and then pushed past Maggie to go inside. "Yes, we knew you was a-coming all right. But it's been a time, hasn't it!"

Maggie didn't know whether she was expected to follow, until Liz snapped at her, "Come in and shut the door behind you. You'll be lettin' all the heat out the house."

Liz slumped into an armchair underneath a grandmother clock. Maggie couldn't sense any heat to let out; in fact it was marginally colder inside than it was outdoors. There was no fire to see, and Liz wore what must have been five layers of woollens.

Maggie closed the door and turned to explain. "Ash, when I was in his shop in town, he told me—"

"Never mind all that," Liz said irritably, "get that kettle a-going." She waved her stick fractionally toward the stove. Maggie did as told.

The old woman had made the kitchen her living quarters. A door gave way on to another room behind, but it was firmly closed. Some kind of larder was curtained off near the sink where Maggie splashed water into an aluminium kettle. The kitchen had a musty smell, like bacon curing, plus another scent which Maggie quickly identified. She looked up and tied to the rafters were bunches and posies of herbs hanging to dry. There was a huge range oven in the corner of the kitchen, but it obviously wasn't operational. Maggie put the kettle on a gas stove.

"My grandmother had one of these ranges in her kitchen." Maggie tried to make conversation. "They're lovely. They really are."

"She did, did she?" said Liz, tapping her stick on a floor made up of offcuts and irregular lengths of ill-matching carpets. "Well, listen to this."

And she sang a verse of song in a cracked, tuneless voice, tapping her thigh occasionally with her free hand.

I'm a-going on me way, a-going on me way.
I sees this I sees that, I sees what I see.
I knows as I'll not tell a soul,
For it's nowt to do wi' me.

When she'd finished, Liz sat back. Maggie smiled, but Liz looked as if she didn't want her to smile. They sat in embarrassed silence. Maggie wished Ash had been there to make a proper introduction.

"Ash, that is the man at the shop, in town—"

"Never mind all that," said Liz. "Two beans, a bean and half a bean, another bean and half a bean again. How many?" Then she spat something from her mouth on to the rug in front of her. Maggie saw that it was, indeed, a bean.

"I'm sure I don't know."

"Not clever then, are you?"

"I'm afraid I'm not."

"Then there's those clever ones who pretend as they're not clever. You could be one o'they?"

Maggie tried to force a smile. Then the old woman leaned forward out of her chair.

"Two. You've two little ones. Now then, how do I know that?"

"I'm sure I've no idea. How did you know?"

"That kettle's a-boil," said Liz.

Maggie made the tea. The old woman got up and stood over her, supervising with silent but intense vigilance. For a second time Maggie thought she wanted to go home. "Ash thought you might help me."

"He's no good. He comes here, then as soon as he comes he goes away again. What's the use o' that? Eh?"

Maggie could think of nothing to say.

"How much will you give me?" said Liz suddenly. Maggie was taken aback by this directness. Liz chuckled. "I'm just kiddin' on. I always say that to Ash. Heh heh. How much will you give me? I always say. And he says, as much as you want. Heh heh, that's a good 'un ain't it? As much as you want. You can say it. Say: as much as you want."

"As much as you want."

"Heh heh heh!" Liz thought this was hilarious. Then she turned serious, and said sharply, "Listen here, missie; I've never had anything as I haven't earned. So you be careful."

Maggie didn't know what offense she might have given. "I am careful."

"Yes, you're a one, I can see that. Liz can see that, but it's clear you ain't all released. You don't know when-the-day."

"Sorry?'

"You ain't expressed at all. Not released. Though I sees you are a one."

"A one what?"

"Don't try and kid on at Liz, because you're just a girl. A slip."

Maggie relaxed for the first time since entering the cottage. "Do you mean—"

"Hoi!" Liz silenced her with a wave of her stick. "None o' that."

Liz's eccentricity made Maggie smile. She shook her head, as if trying to flick away the very charm of the old woman's strangeness. "All right. What do you mean by saying I'm not released?"

Liz dropped her stick and slowly put her arms round her own shoulders, hugging herself. She lifted up her knees and hugged them into herself as far as she could, old limbs parodying the younger woman opposite. Liz was grinning and blinking at Maggie from behind her spectacles.

"I'm doing my best!"

Liz unfolded herself. "Your best might not be enough for what's at call."

"And what is at call?"

"You tell me."

"Ash thought you might help me with the flying ointment."

"Pssshhttttt!" Liz dismissed her with a wave of the hand and looked away.

"Will you?" Maggie said after a while.

"Listen to this:

> *I'm a-going on me way, a-going on me way.*
> *I sees this I sees that, I sees what I see.*
> *I knows as I'll not tell a soul,*
> *For it's nowt to do wi' me."*

Liz sat back in her chair and closed her eyes. Within seconds she was asleep and snoring gently.

Maggie sipped her tea. The grandmother clock ticked on over Liz's head, the heavy pendulum swinging from side to side. Maggie felt extraordinarily drowsy herself. She had to resist a temptation to close her eyes. The old lady slept on in the chair, still grasping her walking stick. Maggie was tempted just to get up and leave, but thought it too ill-mannered. She sat, and waited silently.

Presently Liz opened one eye and looked at her. She roused herself in her chair. "If you draw that curtain back," she said indicating the larder, "you can pour us a glass of elderberry wine."

"I can't." Maggie looked at the clock. "I've got to pick up my little boy in half an hour or there'll be hell to pay."

"Eh? Got to go? What's the point of comin' 'ere at all if you've got to go?"

"Cant be helped." She stood up.

"You comin' again tomorrow?"

"Can't."

"Go on then. Bugger off," said Liz.

Maggie turned at the door. "Can I come back again next week?"

"You just bugger off," said Liz, looking hard at the wall.

Maggie let herself out. She stopped at the gate to take a breath before walking back to her car, uncertain whether to feel amused or irritated by the old woman. Certainly the meeting hadn't produced the help and guidance she was looking for.

She wasn't looking for an explanation necessarily, but for a context, a framework for understanding. The inspirational message about where to dig in the castle grounds had left her feeling a little too pleased with herself. She hadn't felt the need to question it. But the sexual frenzy of the other evening had astonished even her. It was not as if something had taken her over; she was not possessed. On the contrary, she'd remained ultimately in control of what was happening. But the ferocity of the power which had suddenly been made available to her had genuinely shocked her.

Liz had not been able to offer her anything. Old people want to talk, Maggie thought as she drove home, but they don't want to listen, or respond, or give. Liz wasn't so much different from many very elderly people she'd met, half senile, self-absorbed, cantankerous, demanding.

She resolved not to bother the old woman again.

SEVENTEEN

"I was talking to Mr. De Sang," said Alex.

"Oh, yes?"

"He's got some interesting views."

"Yes?" said Maggie. The children were in bed. The fire was dying in the grate and Dot commanded her usual position stretched before it, twitching occasionally in her dog dreams.

"He was talking about something he called *projection*. Do you know what that is?"

"You're about to tell me."

"When Sam feels upset by his mum and dad arguing, he naturally projects a threat to his security and happiness. He then deals with this projection by contradicting everything, or by bad behavior, in order to get the attention and security he really needs."

"It's a neat enough theory."

"Similarly," said Alex, "when Maggie feels unhappy, she contemplates separation or even infidelity. But she can't admit this to herself, so she projects this on her husband."

"De Sang told you that?"

"No. I'm just trying to work things out."

"I see. The name of the game is Alex has found a new word."

"Don't be angry. I'm trying to help."

"This is not a good way of doing it."

"Got a better idea?"

"Yes. Come for a walk with me. Now."

"It's after eleven!"

"All the more reason to go. When did we last take a midnight stroll? There's a beautiful new moon out. Can't you see how important it is to do new things? Walk under a new moon? Strip the scales off our eyes?"

"Why?"

"Because I want to show you things! You always used to be the one to show me things, and now I want to show you things. We need it. We need to share things. When did we stop sharing things? When did we stop caring about what's happening inside each other's head? When did we stop watching for each other's reactions?"

"We don't need to go outside to do that."

"Oh, come on, Alex! The world is a different place at midnight. There's a power to it."

"It's impossible! What about the kids?"

"Wake them up! We'll take 'em with us."

"What's the matter with you? Amy's got school in the morning."

"They'll both learn more this way. Life doesn't have to be lived by timetable!"

"For Christ's sake. I'm going to bed."

He left Maggie pleading to an empty room and went upstairs. Moments later he heard the front door click shut. He looked out of the window and saw her get into the car, accompanied by a sleepy but happy-looking Dot.

Maggie parked the car and the crescent of the new moon afforded enough light for her to pick a path through the woods, with Dot snuffling at the damp, leafy way ahead. She had an inventory of plants and herbs to gather from the hedgerows at the perimeter of the woods, but first she wanted to collect something more mercurial: a sensation of the trees at night, an impression of dark places.

The new moon glimpsed through the trees was white, waxy, and maiden. Her crescent was turned upwards, like a pair of horns; her light traced delicate patterns on the leaves of the trees, running moist between shadows. The wood was a plane of silver and black, a newly minted world. The cool night fanned Maggie's face. Her skin was silver, the dog was silver, and the east-facing boughs of the trees were illuminated, all half-plated with dull silver, generating a soft luster. Maggie encroached deeper into the woods.

There was no sound. The earth swallowed their footfalls, and even Dot trotted on in an envelope of shining silence. The absence of sound conferred a visual intensity: trees stood in ranks making outlandish gestures, like spectators arrayed along the path; huge fungi festooned along fallen trunks were pumped full of intoxicant night air; bracken heads coiled like snakes. The night was spinning something of itself on an unseen wheel, something fine, elusive. Maggie stopped and listened. Dot stopped.

There was a presence in the woods.

It was like a low breathing, of trees exhaling. Far off, a dog-fox barked, three times. Dot's hackles rose, and Maggie felt her own flesh ripple, and the hair stirred on her neck. It was like a signal, and her body was answering. A call, indicating they were in the presence of something magnificent, something holy and terrifying.

Maggie had been holding her breath. Her throat was constricted. She released a sigh, hardly daring to disturb the stillness. The trees rustled in answer; they shivered, and the rustle of leaves on the uppermost branches was like the swirl of a cape as the breathing came closer. Dot lay down on her belly and put her head between her legs. Maggie wanted to do the same: fling herself on the ground and hide her head. The hair on the nape of her neck bristled. Her skin crawled.

But she knew she must stand tall and win the respect of whatever was out there. A voice came into her head.

Just to look at you.

Then a perfume, streaming from the earth. Not merely the moist wood smells, the decay of leaf, of fungus and bark, not just that which was always there. Something else. A spice, some bright herb, a mother earth smell; a signal-scent, property of the presence arrayed in the woods before her, behind her, all about. A hot wave flushed over her, followed by a chill.

Maggie was paralyzed. The moonlight in the woods flared momentarily, became a ring of silver fire all around her. A drop of dew—one brilliant, tiny, concentrated sphere of moonlight—dropped from a leaf and splashed her forehead. She was anointed. She tipped back her head and opened her mouth, and a second drop, like a silver coin, was placed on her tongue.

A name came to her, and she knew now in whose presence she stood. It was a name she had come across in the diary. It rippled free from some place deep inside her and presented itself on her tongue.

It was a name which had meant little to her when she'd first seen it, but which now magically summarized the moment in all its fullness. To state the name was to state the nature. The tree branches swirling like a dark cape confirmed her presence. The moon's horned coronet. The earth-spiced perfume and the holy ring of silver flame. The anointing, the gift. She had been granted speech.

"Goddess," she breathed. "Hecate."

Alex sat up in bed pretending to read a novel. He was only feigning to himself. It was well after one o'clock and Maggie hadn't returned. He was both annoyed and concerned for her safety. Scrambling from his bed, he tugged back the curtain. Outside, a faint white moonlight issued from a cloudless sky. New moon, Maggie had said. He thought the moon had a diseased look.

He pulled on his dressing gown. There was something he wanted to check out while Maggie was gone.

The spare room...He was convinced Maggie had been storing things in there, hiding something from him. Perhaps it was the excessive interest she'd shown in wanting to restore the room to some sort of order, or maybe it was the way in which the door had only lately been kept clicked shut that had tipped him off. He'd intended to confront her about it directly. So why hadn't he?

The spare room, being no more than a tiny shoebox shape, was useful only as storage space. It had become a dump for old clothes, worn-out appliances, broken toys, boxes of books and papers—anything they couldn't bear to throw away. He went rummaging, unsure of what he was looking for exactly, but certain there was something to be found.

He cleared a lot of old shoes from the foot of the wardrobe to get to a large cardboard box underneath. He had an allergy to the dust he was disturbing. It brought on a sudden perspiration and a fit of sneezing. His temperature shot up, making him angry with the box he was endeavoring to wrestle out of the wardrobe. It was wedged against the wooden uprights, and he tore at it to release it. When he finally ripped open a corner to reveal a length of white lace, he realized it was only the container for Maggie's wedding dress. He stuffed the box back in the wardrobe, hurling shoes on top of it.

A kind of madness swept over him as he prowled the room, tossing clothes aside and tearing open sealed boxes of old archaeology journals and papers. Then he noticed the trunk. It was partly concealed by a pile of paperbacks stacked on top of its closed lid. He pawed the books to the floor and rattled the lid. It was locked. The key was normally left in the lock. He kicked the lid angrily.

He hurried downstairs and came back with a file, easily snapping the lock. The trunk was overspilling with photograph albums and wallets of snapshots. He lifted all of them out before convincing himself they were hiding nothing, slamming the lid back down on the trunk.

He was restacking the books on the trunk when another idea chased him back to the wardrobe. He lifted out the shoes and felt the weight of the wedding-dress box. He shook it. It rattled. He lifted it and something slid about inside. He had to stand the box on end before it would come out of the wardrobe.

The long, white silk and lace dress was folded in half and wrapped in delicate tissue paper. Alex lifted it from the box as if it might disintegrate in his hands. Underneath was what he was looking for.

The diary, plus a collection of other objects. There was the jar of handfasting oil—he failed to recognize it as the one from which Maggie had massaged him over a week ago. He took off the top, sniffed it, and stood it on the trunk. There were other items: a stone pestle and mortar; a wooden-handled knife; a brass incense pot; a wooden stick stripped of its bark; an enamel pot; a bottle of olive oil; a collection of colored candles (some partially burned); an eyedropper; needles and cloth; and assorted candle holders. Alex sighed.

In addition to all of this, and laid out in alphabetical order, were dozens of clear plastic sachets containing various herbs, all neatly labeled. There were also a number of miniature ceramic pots, stoppered and containing scented oils.

A tiny hand tapped him on the shoulder.

Alex leapt backwards in terror, scattering books and the jar of handfasting oil from the trunk. It tumbled to the floor, spilling its contents on the carpet. Amy stood in her pyjamas biting her thumb.

"How long have you been standing there?" Alex had to put a hand on his drumming heart.

"I was having a bad dream," said Amy. She looked about to cry.

He sighed again, but this time with relief. All of his anger and confusion was dissolved instantly by the apparition of his daughter. Nothing was more important to Alex than the happiness and security of his children. He saw his duties as a father as a sacred calling, and any dispute with Maggie was a detail, a secondary matter. It could all be worked out later. He spread out his arms to Amy. "A dream, my darling? Come here, let me cuddle you. Is that better? I'm here to chase away all bad dreams. Shall I carry you back to your bed? Here we go. Or do you want to come to our bed?"

"Your bed."

"Anything you want, my darling. Anything you want."

Alex carried Amy back to his room and tucked her into bed. He stroked her hair and promised to return to her in a few minutes. Then he went back to the spare room, replacing everything as he'd found it. He located the jar he'd knocked to the floor and cleaned up the mess. He even tried to disguise the accident by refilling the jar with a drop or two of the olive oil. The box was restored to the foot of the wardrobe and layered over with shoes. He switched off the light, returned to his own room, and climbed into bed beside Amy.

Maggie arrived half an hour later, by which time Amy was asleep. Alex also pretended to be asleep. She slipped into bed beside him, and he felt a wave of cold pass from her. A draft of woods and earth smells came from her hair.

EIGHTEEN

The Maggie dig turned up a third knife identical to the first two, and another half a tin plate. Alex was having to keep an eye on both archaeological efforts simultaneously. He didn't entirely trust his mainly volunteer crew to do a decent job. He needed to be in both places at once. He was afraid they might miss some vital but unspectacular piece of scientific information in their eagerness to turn up museum-quality artifacts.

"Just slow down, for God's sake!" he was always telling them. "It's the fine details that count." He'd started bawling people out, and never heard himself until it was too late.

When the third dagger and the second half-plate appeared, he marshaled the crew into working around the objects with a fine brush until he—and only he—could lift them out. The half-plate was a perfect match to the first, cleanly sliced down the middle. It was found at a distance of eighteen inches from its other half. The first two daggers had been set at approximately two feet apart. The third was two feet from the second dagger and four feet from the first.

Alex marked the points of each find and connected the markers with a line of tape. It produced an isosceles triangle, its equal sides each intersecting the position in which the half-plates had been found. Alex instructed the three student volunteers he'd assigned to the job to dig round the apex of the triangle.

"WHAT'S THAT?" he screamed at one of the students, a youth with his hair tied back in a ponytail.

"This?" said the student, holding up a delicate trowel.

"Yes! That, that, that stone-breaking implement! What is it?"

The boy looked at the object in his hand as if someone else had put it there. At length he said, "It's a trowel."

"This is not a fucking quarry! This is surgery! Use SOMETHING ELSE!"

Alex stormed back to his main dig, leaving the students to exchange looks.

In the playroom Maggie was prising up wooden tiles. Every evening Amy took a great delight in checking on the worsening stain under the rug and reporting back that it was taking on the semblance of a face more and more with each passing day. Maggie made a great show of scoffing at the idea to Amy, but admitted to herself that it was indeed easy to discern a face in the pattern of the staining.

She'd moved the rug aside herself from time to time and saw what was unmistakably a pair of eyes (though rather far apart), a nose (though set at something of an angle) and a mouth turned back in an expression of sadness and suffering.

Alex had already established that there was no damp rising through the floor. There was nothing spilled or running between the tiles. Now Maggie had decided to leave the stained area untiled. Beneath the tiles was the bare concrete which Alex had put down over the original cellar floor. She simply laid the rug across the exposed concrete and tossed the stained tiles in the bin.

While his mother was upstairs discarding the tiles, Sam charged around the playroom brandishing his plastic sword. He hacked and slashed at an opposing army, single-handedly putting them to flight, ran his sword through a few small enemies, and stabbed a bean bag for good measure. Then he slumped on the bean bag, recovering his breath while deciding what to do next.

Something moist struck him sharply on his cheek.

Something had spat at him.

He heard a hiss. He stood up from the bean bag and turned unsteadily. Slap. It struck him again, stinging and wet on the cheek. It burned like a smack to the face.

He knew where it was coming from. He turned to face the potted geranium.

Inside the plant was a living, full-sized face. An old woman's face. Sam recognized her. She leered at him and grinned, blinking her eyes. Her face was made of leaves, her skin green, wrinkled, and veined like the leaves of the geranium, her teeth yellow.

It was the old woman who had stolen his doll. Who had beckoned him along the catwalk at the Gilded Arcade. She hissed at him. She produced hands out of the branches of the plant, brown hands with cracked yellow fingernails. She hissed again and opened her mouth. Her long black venomous tongue unfolded from between her cracked lips, a foot long, like a snake, inching toward him.

Sam's screams brought Maggie running down the cellar steps. She found Sam stamping his feet, screaming in an hysterical high-pitched wail, sucking in air in huge gulps between screams, his eyes streaming. He was hacking violently at a plant on a low table with his plastic sword. Maggie scooped him up in her arms, but he did not stop screaming or swinging his plastic sword.

"What is it, Sam?"

He only shrieked more hysterically.

Maggie carried him out of the playroom and up the stairs. The leaves and broken branches of the geranium lay in an untidy scattering at the foot of the low table.

NINETEEN

"Never put a geranium where there's a child." This was Old Liz's advice.

Maggie had changed her mind about not visiting her again. It bothered her that there was simply no one to whom she could turn for support; at least no one who could remotely understand what she had to say, let alone help her to say it. Alex wouldn't begin to listen. Ash at the shop was sympathetic, but somehow always on guard. However senile or even lunatic the old woman had originally appeared, Maggie decided she was the nearest to a kindred spirit available.

If there was a conclusion to be drawn from that, Maggie had steered away from it and had returned to Old Liz's house to recount the episode with Sam and the plant. Ash had told her Liz had a taste for sherry, so Maggie had brought her a bottle. The old woman had accepted the bottle without a word, setting it down and withdrawing from her pantry a bottle of homemade elderberry wine. "As for geraniums, no child will thrive with one. I know that. And you should know that."

"Why should I know that?"

Liz took a sip of blueblood elderberry wine. "Why, she says?" tapping her stick on the rug. "Why? Because you're a one as knows, or says you are."

"I've never said anything!" Maggie protested.

Liz grinned and made the same melodramatic gesture she'd made on Maggie's first visit, hugging herself like some deeply repressed thing. "But," she said, dropping the pose, "I see you're opening. Like a flower."

Liz pulled such faces when she spoke that Maggie wanted to laugh. "Is that what you see?"

Liz became serious again. "A one's got to be open to the world if a one's goin' to find her way. That's why you've got a money box. Open to the world." Maggie smiled. She hadn't heard it called a money box since she was a girl. Liz uncrooked a finger and jabbed it at her, backwards and forwards. "Stick it in, stick it in, stick it in. That's all those fellas can do. Stick it in. Good for nowt else. That's why they don't know anything. They can't."

"Don't you get men who . . ." Maggie picked up Liz's circumspect language. "Who are ones. Can't men be ones?"

"Oh, you do get 'em. Oh you do. You do." The old woman leaned forward. "Some."

"Is Ash one?"

"Pssshhttt!!!" Liz waved her stick. "What you want to talk another for? Eh? You don't talk another! Eh?" She seemed quite angry.

The rebuke made Maggie feel like a little girl. She couldn't understand why Liz tolerated her when her presence so easily inflamed the old woman. And then her acid manner would dissolve instantly, with equal unpredictability. She began to suspect the old woman might be teasing, playing with her.

"I'm sorry—"

"Do you like it? I said do you like it?"

Maggie realized she was referring to the elderberry wine. "It's lovely. Do you make it every year?"

"Take one o' them bottles for that husband o' yorn."

"That's very . . ." Maggie tailed off. She'd suddenly spotted a way in. "Would you show me how to make it as good as this?"

"How much will you give me?" Liz said, in a flash.

"Whatever you want."

Liz rocked with laughter. She pulled a grubby handkerchief from her sleeve to wipe the tears from her eyes. "There's a good 'un! That's a good 'un, ain't it?" She laughed again, a high-pitched laugh. "That's what Ash says." She recovered. "I might show you. I might. There's a lot to know about the owd gal."

Old girl. That was a term Bella used for elder in the diary. Maggie took the diary from her handbag and tried to show it to Liz, but the old woman seemed to grow annoyed. She waved it away. "Books! You don't want books! Books'll do you no good at all, and no one any good. Them as write 'em is the worst, and them as read 'em; there's no good in any of 'em. Books!"

It seemed important to put up some kind of argument. "There must be some good books! What about the Bible?"

"Bible? Eh? That only gives the worst ones an excuse to argue. Did it mean this, did it mean t'other? No. We don't want these books."

Maggie slipped the diary back inside her handbag. "When do you pick the elder? For the wine, I mean."

"Owd gal, well now . . ."

The old woman was a fund of both lore and practical information regarding the virtues and vices of the magnificent elder. Not only concerning the making of wine, but also of jam, and a lot more besides. It was a plant, she observed more than once, "as runs both ways." Maggie took this to mean it could have both beneficial and malign properties, something Liz had also said of the geranium. She wouldn't have elder wood in her house, and said a child's cradle should never be made of elder. Maggie wondered if Mothercare knew about these things. But the leaves kept flies away from a house, Liz maintained, and were useful for toothache and depression. Pinned on a stable door it would stop any horse from being hag-ridden, and before Maggie could ask about that, Liz told her an elder cure for warts and a conciliatory rhyme used by woodcutters:

Owd gal give me some o' thy wood
And I'll give thee some o' mine
When I grow into a tree.

Maggie's head was spinning with information when the old woman surprised her by suggesting they go out and pick some from the hedgerows.

"Can you get about on your stick?"

Liz chuckled and pulled herself to her feet. "We'll see. Pull that door to behind. Let's look to the owd gal. Come on, what're you waiting for?"

Alex was fast losing patience with the volunteers at the dig. He claimed they were drifting from the precise spot where he'd instructed them to work. If he didn't supervise them on the original dig, they disturbed and confused his sophisticated system of depth markings; if he neglected to oversee them on the Maggie dig, they started hacking at the earth like navvies.

"You do understand plain English?" he'd shouted.

"Yes," said the boy with the ponytail, "I've secured a place at Oxford University to study the subject."

Alex glowered. The other students turned away to hide their smirks. He was livid, clenching his fists at his sides until his knuckles turned white. Someone came up behind him and said he was wanted on the telephone.

"What?"

"Said it was urgent." The man from the ticket office pointed across the site. "You'll have to take it in my pay box."

Alex had to walk fifty yards to the ticket office. He snatched up the phone. It was their childminder.

When they returned from the field, Maggie looked at the clock and let out a groan. "Oh no. I'm going to be late for Amy and Sam!" She laid her bag of elderberries on the table. "I'm going to have to fly!"

"Eh? But you've only just got here." Liz protested. "What's the use o' coming if you're going to go before you've arrived?"

"Can't be helped!" Maggie swept out of the door.

"Bugger off then," the old woman shouted.

She followed as far as the gate and watched Maggie scurry down the cinder path, climb into her car, and speed away. "Aye," she said to herself. "You might or you might not do."

When Maggie arrived home, Alex and the children were at the kitchen table, eating sandwiches.

"Sorry," said Maggie. Alex remained tight-lipped. She brushed Amy's hair from her eyes. "You all right?" she said. Amy nodded, holding a crescent of a sandwich to her mouth. Sam, too, was all right. Everyone was all right. Except Alex.

Maggie put a hand on his shoulder. "Alex, it's just that I met this wonderful old lady and she wanted me to go for a walk with her . . . I know I've let you down again."

Alex spoke so calmly, and in such measured sentences, it was obvious he was boiling inside. "I was summoned today, summoned, from my place of work, by no other than my son's childminder. I had to leave off the responsible task of supervising several incompetent and insolent layabouts, risking the project and thus my professional reputation, in order to mollify said angry childminder . . ."

"Alex—"

He held a finger in the air. ". . . in order to carry out one of the few simple tasks allotted to my wife in any working day. In the general ratio of distribution of tasks and workload in a relationship between two people, I must declare—no, protest—that this is just a *tad* unfair."

"Alex, I'm sorry. Look. I brought you a peace offering." Maggie handed him the bottle of elderberry wine.

Alex looked at the unlabeled bottle, stood up, and took it outside. There was the sound of it smashing in the yard. Alex disappeared past the kitchen window, looking intent on a visit to the Merry Fiddler. Maggie held her head in her hands.

"Daddy's angry," said Amy.

Sam smiled, because he thought it was all a kind of game.

TWENTY

Alex called his team together the following morning. He wanted to give them a pep talk. The dig was working out badly, discipline was awry and morale was plummeting. He felt responsible.

His normal style of managing a dig was through the device of what he called "pretend panics." If he felt things slipping, he would gather everyone together, tell them there was a threat of bogus authorities threatening to close the dig, call for greater commitment to prove everyone else wrong, and then hand round the cigarettes. It usually did the trick.

But this was different. He felt depressed about the work and about his relationship with his team. To the volunteer diggers and students alike he seemed as approachable as a pit of snakes. He got wind of the fact that they referred to him, in whispers, as Vlad the Impaler. He decided to do something he'd never done with subordinates before. He decided to take them into his confidence and be open and honest.

The team stood around in a loose half-circle at the site of the dig, bored and barely awake, waiting for him to say his piece and get it over with.

"Let's sit down a minute, shall we?" said Alex. He squatted on his haunches. They exchanged a few looks before following his example.

"I wanted to have a few words with you before we started work today. Things haven't been going well and I wanted to make an apology to you all." Faces that had been looking away suddenly stared at him. They'd been expecting a collective bollocking, an exhortation to work harder and laugh less often. "That's right, an apology. I've been behaving like an arsehole lately and I haven't been the help to you I should've been. At first I blamed them upstairs, because of some of the pressures on this dig to succeed. But that was only because I wasn't honest enough to admit to myself that I've got problems at home, and that's why I've been taking it out on you. So I apologize and it won't happen again, okay?"

A few people looked nervously at each other. Mostly they stared at the ground.

Alex smiled. "Just to show I mean it, I'm buying the beers at lunchtime for anyone who'll join me and Vlad the Impaler at the pub. That's all. Let's get on with it. Anyone want a ciggie before we start?"

Well, it worked, up to a point. The team rolled up their sleeves and went to work in a relaxed sort of way. One or two students came up to him with suggestions. Richard, the boy with the ponytail working on the Maggie dig, suggested they strike back from the marked triangle of daggers instead of away from the apex. Alex approved and offered advice.

He was good to his word and bought everyone foaming beers at the Malt Shovel. He laughed along with his crew in all the right places, and spread a bit of gossip about some of the local museum staff. By pretending to be relaxed, he could almost become relaxed. He enjoyed it; he was sitting next to a very pretty student called Tania, and the beer was going down well. When everyone started to shuffle and look at their watches, he extended the lunch break by calling in another round.

"Crush the leaf and the berry together. Then make an oil out o' that. Seven days."

"How much?"

"Much as you like."

"And the dwale?"

"Four or five berries crushed up, fresh, on the day."

She'd brought Sam with her to see Liz. The boy crawled on the floor as Maggie's inquiries took on a new note of seriousness. There was an urgency in her voice discomforting to Old Liz. Maggie was impatient. She wanted it all too quickly.

Maggie had all the information she needed from the diary, but what disturbed her, and why she sought some kind of sanction from Liz, was the ambivalence of the reports. Accounts of wonders were scrambled with dire warnings. Abuse Hecate and she will imperil your soul.

Maggie had hoped for approval, encouragement, advice from Old Liz. She wasn't getting it. Liz answered her questions directly, but with a pursed mouth and a firm neutrality that did nothing to ameliorate Maggie's fears. She stuck to the bare facts, the cold ingredients. She steered away from all discussion of effect, and refused to be drawn into talking about the diary's promise of revelations and terrors in equal measure. This was a speculation in which Maggie was on her own, with only the diarist's obscure accounts to excite her hopes and inflame her fears.

But it raise me up. Oh the wonder! And to have all questions answered. It raise me up and it break my heart. How terrible her wrath! Sleep, coma and death walk behind. Now there are toadstools in the woods, but A. cautioned me against, for they enfeeble the will for flying whereas I need all strength. I stuck to A's direction and stayed within her compass and I have A. to thank for saving me from ruin and demons. We must help one another, and I see a good side to her. I have A. to thank for the banishments, and here they are.

The diary contained an exact formula for the flying ointment, the proportions of deadly nightshade described as dwale, the wolfsbane, cinquefoil, and soot, mixed in a carefully described oil base. Hogsfat was mentioned. There were precise specifications of when to collect the herbs. Finally there was a string of words and phrases described as "banishments."

Beneath all of this was written: *Never abuse her. Never never never.*

A light passed from Liz's eyes. They reset like hard, black beads, fixed on the younger woman. Maggie felt probed. If ever she'd been underestimating Old Liz, it stopped there.

"I see as you's set on it, girl."

There was a moment of heavy silence. Maggie picked up where she'd left off. "So, the wolfsbane as you've said. What's this about hogsfat?"

"That's just for keeping warm, that's all that is." Liz suddenly stiffened and looked over at Sam. "Here! Call 'im out o' there! That's no place for little boys!"

Lifting her stick she jabbed it in Sam's direction. He'd managed to crawl over to the curtain closing off Liz's pantry. He was on his hands and knees, with his head behind the curtain, when Maggie lifted him out by his belt. Liz darted a hand down the side of her chair and pulled a humbug out of a grubby paper bag.

"Here," she said to him, "bit o' suck." Sam trotted over to her to collect the sweet, but Liz grabbed his outstretched hand. She put her face close to his. "Keep your nose out o' them lady's petticoats. You hear me? No place for a little boy to be lookin'. Them's lady's petticoats. You hear me?" She let him go. Sam was terrified. He skittered to the safety of his mother's side.

"Well, you shouldn't go nosing in other people's things," Maggie said.

"Rooting, he was. Does a little boy good to be frit anyhow, and it'll keep him down when he's older. Wouldn't hurt you to be frit, either."

"What do you mean?"

"I've looked at you, girl. You want it too quick. You wants it all now. Well, you can't have it now. Listen here, I've thought maybe I'll give you a bit of this and that. We all need a little sister. There's not many more years left in me, I know that. And maybe I shoulda done more in this, but it's the little sister as comes to you, that's the way it was with me, that's the way it is. And I need a little sister to give this and that before I moves on. But I look at you, girl, and, well, I just don't know.

"No, I just don't know." Liz shook her head. "You've got summat settled on your shoulder. And I wants to say, here! Knock it off! But it won't be knocked off easily. It's of your own making, and it might suck you dry afore you're through with it. So maybe you are the little sister, come as you 'ave to me, but I don't know."

Maggie was unable to answer any of this. Instead she offered Liz a determined look. "So this hogsfat, it's not necessary?"

Liz shook her head again, perhaps in exasperation. "You wants something as'll keep you warm if you're in your birthday suit."

"But what if you're indoors?"

"How you going to fly if you're indoors?" Liz chuckled. "How you going to do that?"

"But you don't really fly," said Maggie. "Not really. I know that much."

"Pssshhhhttt!!" said Liz.

Despite a late start, the afternoon went well. Nothing new was unearthed, but the mood of the dig had lightened. The day was unseasonably warm and the scent of disturbed soil streamed with history and broken clay. Alex was much happier now that he was able to share a joke or two with his team. He winked at Tania, and he made free with the smokes.

"Watch out for your fingers. Have a bowl of water to wash your hands clean. When you fly you get a tingling in your fingers, and they go into the mouth, and then you're in a mess. You take care and have that water by you."

"I'll remember," said Maggie.

"Rub it all over."

"Sky clad."

"Psshhtt! I never calls it that. Daft talk. Rub it all over."

Liz made a massaging motion at her temples and on her throat and wrists. "Here. And put some in your money box."

"How much time?"

"Oh. You want a full night."

"As much as that?"

"And a day to get over it. Oh yes."

"Oh," said Maggie. That was the kind of time she didn't have.

TWENTY-ONE

Find it! Find it! She had to find it!

She went back to the wedding-dress box and broke two fingernails trying to heave it clear of the bottom of the wardrobe. It wouldn't come free. She grabbed at the old shoes littering the foot of the wardrobe, slinging them angrily across her shoulder. Crack! They hit the far wall.

She stopped for breath, sucking at a broken fingernail. Then she reached inside the wardrobe and tore frantically at the cardboard until the lid ripped in half. She stripped out the soft tissue lining paper, flinging it aside before dragging out the wedding dress. She balled the dress and hurled it across the room, where it landed, draped like a weeping bride across the closed trunk. Then she tore the rest of the empty cardboard box to shreds.

She waited for a moment, listening, breathing heavily.

Scrambling across to the trunk, she flung open the lid, scattering books, toys, and the dress before proceeding to empty it of its contents. Files, photographs, and documents were scooped onto the floor.

Maggie wanted to cry with frustration, but she was in too much of a rage for tears. And she couldn't find the diary.

She thumped heavily down the stairs and marched into the lounge.

"What the hell have you done with it?"

Amy looked up. Sam looked up. Even Dot, sprawled before the fire, looked up. Alex, to whom Maggie's fury was addressed, did not look up. He didn't even let his newspaper dip.

"I said what have you done with it?"

"Done with what?"

Maggie lashed the newspaper out of his hands. "You know perfectly well what I'm talking about. I want to know where you've put it!"

Alex had been waiting for Maggie to make the discovery. It had only been a matter of time. He'd gone into the spare room, removed the box from the bottom of the wardrobe, and emptied its contents. He'd replaced only the wedding dress, so that a cursory glance might not betray the deed.

He neatly reassembled his newspaper, smoothing out the creases before answering. "I don't want it in the house."

"I don't care what you want or don't want, I asked you what you'd done with it." Maggie stood over him. The children watched.

"And I've told you, I don't want it in the house. It's not healthy for the kids. I've destroyed it. Don't bring anything else like it into the house, or I'll destroy that too."

"The diary? What about my diary?"

"I've told you. I burned the whole bloody lot. That's an end to the matter. Now stop shouting and give us all a break."

"Give you a break? After what you've done I wouldn't piss on you if you were on fire!" Maggie stormed upstairs. Moments later she clattered down the stairs again and went out. Alex heard the car drive off. He saw his children staring at him, and he hid his burning cheeks behind his newspaper.

Maggie drove blindly. It was a misty night, and she drove with her lights full up, ignoring the flashing headlamps of oncoming traffic. Her own rage at finding the diary removed had taken her by surprise. She'd panicked, actually panicked on discovering it had gone; then she'd lost control of herself when Alex said he'd destroyed it.

At times she'd thought this compulsion—to experiment, to probe, to push at the envelope—was motivated by a rebellion against Alex's heavy-handed control. But now she knew it was much more than that. She'd felt invaded, violated by the idea of Alex laying his hands on her secret store. The diary was hers, and hers alone. She wanted it back, wanted to feel its leather covers in her hand.

She drove with a growing sense of direction. And as she drove, she had to face something about herself for the very first time. This business with the diary. These experiments. Up until that moment she'd considered the enterprise to be a kind of flirtatiousness. Something to be dropped when a more interesting attraction came along. She'd been fooling herself, she now appreciated, for some time. It was real. It was serious. *She* was serious. For the first time in her life she felt utterly serious about something.

She didn't want to take her rage to the woods. It would pollute the place; it would rob it of its hitherto blameless associations. Instead she drove north, twenty-five miles, to Wigstone Heath where she'd walked with Ash and the children.

The fire in her head was still raging when she parked the car and got out. The moon was pale, obscured by fine mist hanging before her like delicate webbing. There was barely enough light to make out the path in front of her, but she had to walk. She passed the dark, hunched shapes of stunted bushes and the smooth-shouldered outcrops of rock, threading a route toward the Dancing Ladies.

She wandered off the path, reclaiming it again later. Her feet became sodden with the moisture from the grass, and as she put distance between herself and the car, so her anger began to blend with remorse. What Alex had done was unforgivable; but her words to him, for their children to hear, were possibly even worse.

She could imagine Sam repeating them to De Sang, or Amy using them at school. Words like sharp knives, given to small children to play with unsupervised. The words whispered back at her, razors inside her head, and what hurt her even more deeply was that at the moment she'd spoken those words to Alex, she'd meant every syllable.

She reached the Ladies, the dark stones leaning at angles, cold, damp, impassive as gravestones. Maggie leaned her back against one of the upright boulders and wept.

Alex, tight-lipped, a choking stone in his throat, put the children to bed. They knew that this evening was not a night to argue. They undressed and got into bed without fuss.

"Can we have a story?" Amy asked, so tentatively that Alex thought his heart would break. He read them a tale from an anthology of fairy stories, but mechanically, and without his usual fun and playfulness with the characters' voices. It was unsatisfactory, but he completed the story. He closed the book and looked at his two children. Far from being asleep, they stared at him wide-eyed.

They seemed distant from him, like someone else's children, or, worse, like offspring of another species, a life-form very similar to humans but not the same. Alex suddenly felt a terror for them and for the long lives stretching before them. "Go to sleep now," he said, switching off the light.

"Can we have the light on?" said Amy.

Alex conceded, switched the light back on, and closed the bedroom door behind him. He went downstairs and poured himself a large whisky. All he wanted was to protect his family. He worked hard for them; he wanted to love his wife and children and to be loved by them in turn. This was hardly, he was certain, a complicated set of aims.

He knew he'd provoked Maggie beyond measure, but he'd been astonished by her vehemence. She'd been angry with him before, sure enough, but Maggie's recent behavior had been surprising in many ways. He wondered who exactly had been teaching her these new tricks.

Tricks like choice phrases. Like a taste for midnight strolls from which she returned with clothes dishevelled and grass in her hair. Like afternoons spent in mysterious places which made her forget her responsibilities toward her children. And suddenly discovered tricks in bed. Most of all the tricks in bed.

Alex poured himself another hefty Scotch, and stared into the fire.

Maggie sat at the foot of one of the standing stones. Her head felt clearer. Sometimes weeping worked like a release of sexual tension, giving vent to energies which might otherwise go spiraling destructively inside. Or sex, looked at in a certain way, could seem like crying. And it seemed to her that the stones had wept in sympathy—not with tears, of course, but with the formations of moisture deposited on them by the mist. The clouds had parted slightly to give the moon a keener light, sparkling on the droplets collected on the stones. Nine ladies weeping.

A preternatural circle. Stones hominoid in shape. Certainly feminine. Dancing ladies. What were the names of the nine muses? She knew she could hang her unhappiness on them, or any other feeling for which she needed to find resolution. They would take it, dance with it, convert it, give it back. Was that their true purpose? To make a pool? A well you added to, or took something from?

But this feeling! Moonbathing, that's what she was doing. She was asking to be moonburned as she stalked round the circle. The moonbright droplets glittered on the east-facing shoulders of the stones.

Maggie retraced her steps to the car and returned with a plastic film canister she'd found in the glove compartment. She went from stone to stone, collecting tiny droplets of moisture from each one in the plastic container. The act was entirely whimsical, inspired by the moment. The droplets no more than covered the bottom of the canister, but it was nonetheless precious. Moon-blessed. Holy water.

She left the circle and paced out the distance to the solitary standing stone. Already she'd resolved to replace the collection of herbs and plants and oils destroyed by Alex. Everything could be restored. The diary was a great loss; that much was irreplaceable. But now she had Liz to help her, to see her through.

Everything was going to be all right, Maggie decided, as she approached the solitary standing stone, the eponymous Wigstone. Ash had explained to her the origin of the name. *Wikke* was the Anglo-Saxon word for the craft of the wise: witchcraft. It derived from the word for the willow tree, *wikker*, still used to describe basket and other woodcraft. The subtlety and pliability of the wicker branch paralleled the mental prowess and agility of the true witch: the ability to manipulate not by strength but by the subtle stroking and weaving of existing force. And here was the power stone, the Witch's Stone.

It was almost twice the height of the Nine Ladies, mysteriously connected, but distant, withdrawn and watchful. Maggie collected more moisture from the rough-hewn block, squeezing the beads of water into her canister. She was intimidated by a sense in which she was intruding, pillaging; but somehow felt it was all sanctioned. As if this theft was permitted.

Sanctioned? Permitted? By whom?

No sooner was the question considered than she began to feel the presence. *The presence.* It was unmistakable, a richness of moment, exactly like the time in Osier's Wood.

But stronger.

The voice inside the silence. The slender, teasing fingernail extending out of the darkness to touch her spine below the neck. The prickling of the skin which was her due. Maggie gasped. She slipped and reached to steady herself on the stone, accidentally scything her finger on a sharp flake of granite. The blood trickled into her canister.

There was a new stirring.

No accident.

Once again, words. Where did they come from? Was it her heart speaking?

As she turned away from the stone, the mist on the ground flapped like the hem of a long skirt, then settled. It formed in a circle round the Dancing Ladies. It rolled, slowly, like a living thing. A breeze picked up and brought in a smell of spice, a hint of incense.

Yes, stronger than the encounter in the woods. Maggie knew she had raised it with rage, with tears, and finally with resolution. It was terrifying to be able so to do. It was chilling. It was momentous.

"You are everywhere," said Maggie.

Again words came back to her: *Just to look at you.*

Words. Speaking from the back of her brain. Words soft and indistinct like the mist, but undeniably real, and insinuating. Maggie froze. Her flesh crawled. It was stronger than ever and she wasn't ready. Something was going to happen, and it was too soon. She was unprepared. Not ready, she thought. I'm not ready to see your face. Not yet.

The encircling mist wavered. Maggie moved away from the stone and ran across the brooding heath. She raced along the unlit path, careening into stunted shrubs, bouncing off boulders along the way. Her hair streamed out behind her. The muscles in her thighs seemed to lock, heavy as tree roots. She struggled to lift her legs. She ran in the direction of her car through the mist, panting with exhaustion and delirium.

She ran in terror, an involuntary strangled murmur emitting from her vocal chords. But through it all was a strange delight. When she reached the car she was almost giggling hysterically, the way a small child might if pursued by a grownup in some game.

The living-room light was still on when she got back to the house. She sat in the car for a moment, composing herself.

Letting herself in she went through to the lounge. Alex was seated with his back to her. He gazed into the dying red embers of the fire and was nursing a tumbler of whisky. An empty bottle stood on the mantelpiece.

Alex got up slowly, clutching his glass. He turned to face her and took a step toward her, swaying slightly. He tilted his head and smiled, almost genially, but Maggie recognized a warning in it. "Been with your lover?"

"Don't be silly, Alex."

"You look a bit flushed. Whyzat?" His head fell forward. "A good evening's fucking?"

"Alex, I—"

"You've got some nerve. Accusing me." He drained his tumbler and let it fall on the floor. It bounced harmlessly on the deep-pile carpet.

"Stupid thing to do."

"Stupid," Alex mimicked heavily. A high, mincing voice.

"Alex, I want to tell . . ."

But she wasn't allowed to finish. Alex drew back his fist and his first blow broke Maggie's nose. She reeled back into the wall. Next he crashed his fist into her eye and Maggie saw stars, not like in the cartoons, but white hot needles of light at the back of her vision. He had to pick her up off the floor to strike a third blow, and by the time he split her lip, her eye had already swollen shut.

Alex left her sprawled on the floor snuffling snot and blood, and went upstairs to bed.

TWENTY-TWO

"I wish you'd come to me first. If you'd been here the morning after he hit you I'd have had an injunction slapped on him that day, to keep away from both you and the house."

Alison Montague didn't look like Maggie's idea of a solicitor. She was pretty, under thirty, and she dressed in a suit so sharp you could have sliced your finger on it. She wore silver battle-axe earrings and she worked for Sedge and Sedge. Her room didn't look like Maggie's idea of a solicitor's office, either. It had floral curtains and a play area in the corner complete with toys, to amuse clients' children.

"As it is," Ms Montague arched her eyebrows, "you walked out on them, and that sets you at a disadvantage."

"I wasn't thinking about the consequences. I just wanted to get away."

Maggie's broken nose didn't look too bad, though the bruises round her eyes had changed hue from lavender to a dirty yellow. It was a matter of some relief that her loosened canines hadn't shown any sign of falling out, and the swelling had gone from her lips.

"I understand that. No woman should have to put up with domestic violence. How's this bedsit working out?"

Maggie shrugged. "It's not the house I want. It's the children."

"And you say he's asked you to go back?"

"Practically on his knees."

The morning following the violence, Maggie had slipped out of the house before Alex got up. She'd had no intention of facing him. She knew exactly what she was going to do.

After all, Alex had hit her. Struck her! The man who had never previously so much as raised his fist in anger. It had shocked her to the white root. She thought she knew the man she'd been living with for seven years. Where had he suddenly found this depth of violence? It was as if she'd slipped into a parallel universe, where the man she was living with was like Alex in every detail except this.

She was not so naive about the world as to be surprised by the notion of marital violence. A kick, a slap, and a punch was as common a feature of the average British marriage as the Sunday roast. But not theirs. That wasn't how they lived their lives. But now he'd placed the argument beyond her. When Alex had struck her, he'd punched a hole in the fabric of her idea of who she was in the world.

He'd hit her, but she knew how to punish him. Even if it meant suffering herself. She had to make a stand. Not for her new way of life—that was suddenly all secondary, mere detail at the periphery of the violent event—but for her integrity. For her sense of wholeness.

She would suffer over the children. But, she resolved, Alex wouldn't hit her again.

She had spent the morning in the casualty ward at the hospital, before returning to study postcard adverts in the post office and local newsagents' windows. Alex had indeed broken her nose, but the small fracture on the upper septum didn't require her nose to be reset. In any event, keeping her good looks was the last thing on her mind. She'd looked and felt terrible, shivering and wiping her painful nose with the back of her hand and squinting through a closing eye. But by afternoon she'd found a bedsit in the New Markets area of town, two miles from home. It wasn't particularly cheap, the room smelled damp, and the heating was coin-regulated by a ferociously hungry gas meter. The kitchen and toilet were shared with two other bedsits on the same floor, and the shared bathroom came complete with a toadstool growing in the corner.

But it was better than getting smashed in the face.

After telephoning to check no one was home, Maggie went back to collect a few essential belongings and then installed herself in her bedsit like someone preparing for a siege. She spent two nights there before calling Alex.

He begged her to come home. She refused. For one thing her face still looked like a Halloween pumpkin, and she didn't want the children to see her that way. Of course she could lie, but she had an idea they'd know. It wasn't possible they could have slept through the crashing violence. She also refused to tell him where she was living.

She spent a long time on the phone talking to Amy and Sam, and promised to phone again the following evening.

Alex had woken from one nightmare into another. That morning he didn't open his eyes to some slow realization of what he'd done; he woke up to an instant self-loathing, and a taste like wet sand in his mouth. He crept downstairs to look for Maggie, searching the house in vain.

He desperately wanted to cry, but he couldn't.

The implications of her absence hit him as soon as the children got out of bed. He readied Amy for school and dropped her off outside the gates. Then he returned to the house with Sam, stupidly hoping Maggie might have appeared. He was already late for work when he decided to take Sam with him. It would be a nuisance, but he could keep Sam close by while supervising the dig.

So he believed. Initially Sam thought it wonderful to be at Daddy's place of work. Alex carried him on his shoulders, and

Sam regarded this a wonderful game. For five minutes. Then he wanted to get down. Some of the diggers made a fuss of him for a while, incurring Alex's pleasure; then, realizing what a brat Sam could be, their interest cooled and they got on with their work. Sam demanded total attention from his father: the more complex and sophisticated Alex's instructions to or discussions with individuals on his team needed to be, the more desperately Sam wanted to disrupt them; the closer the supervision Alex needed to offer, the more Sam screamed to be included.

He yelled. He kicked. He cried. He spat.

After a fraught half-hour, Sam started pulling up carefully laid depth markers, and wailed when they were snatched from his hands. Later, while Alex was showing someone how to shore up a wall, Sam tumbled into a ditch containing a foot of clay-colored water.

Alex felt his anger swelling, that Maggie could leave him with these problems. Then he remembered what he'd done to create this situation. Sam, wet and howling, now had to be taken home for a drying out. Tania offered to help, and Alex was pathetically grateful.

On the fourth night Maggie agreed to have dinner with Alex. He wanted to book a table at the Grey Gables, but Maggie didn't want sweet wine and cut-glass. She stipulated the Pizza Palace and opted for mineral water. He was late because his babysitter was late. Maggie had covered her bruises with makeup, to spare his feelings.

"Come back. I'm desperately sorry."

"No. I'm not ready."

"Please, Maggie."

"I said no and I meant it. If you ask me again, I'll get up and walk out."

"But what do you want?"

"I just want to see the children."

"Who's stopping you? See them any time!"

"I mean without you. When you're not there."

"Anything. I'll make it easy for you."

A girl in a baseball cap and with a hole in her tights came to take their order, pencil poised. "Sharing or separate?"

"Separate," said Maggie.

Alex muddled through the first few days. He was able to make arrangements here and there. Anita Suzman helped out, and Tania took an afternoon off from the site to look after Sam at home. One session with Sam, however, proved more than enough for most, and Alex had to revise his arrangements with the child-minder.

"How long is it going to go on for?" Tania asked him at the site.

"No idea. We're like a weatherhouse couple. She comes to the house in the evening and I have to go out to the pub. She's very civil and all that, but as soon as I get back, she has to leave."

"Seems like she's having it all her way at the moment." Alex looked at her. "Well, she doesn't have to take any responsibility for the kids, but she hasn't lost the emotional contact."

"I hadn't thought of it like that. Maybe I should start making some conditions."

"No," said Tania. "That'd just be using the children for barter."

"Hey! Alex!" It was Richard calling him. He'd been working solidly on the Maggie dig. "Come over here!"

Alex let it run for a few nights before putting his foot down. He told Maggie that the present arrangement was causing too much distress. He told her the only way he would allow her to see the children was if she'd move back in with them.

Maggie went away furious. She felt tricked. She was supposed to be the one laying down the conditions, not Alex. Now that he'd seen how desperately she wanted to be with Sam and Amy, he'd called her bluff.

She wasn't frightened for her children, she knew they were in no danger, Alex's outburst notwithstanding; but the idea of not seeing them drove her to distraction. She found herself running through the events of the past weeks, wondering if she was asking too much, wanting to capitulate, talking herself out of it, then changing her mind over and over again in gymnastic flips.

She cried a lot. She felt she was disintegrating. But she refused to return on Alex's terms, and sought legal advice, looking for custody of the children.

"What I'll aim for," said Ms. Montague, eyes lustrous and earrings a-dangle, "and I'm not saying we'll get it automatically, is an injunction to get him out of the house and a residence order so that you have the children." She had a habit of inclining her head to one side as she spoke.

"It suddenly seems a bit unfair to Alex," said Maggie.

"Unfair?"

"I mean, I'm the one who started messing him around. I can see how it might have looked to him, me slipping off at night . . . I feel like I'm the one who started the trouble, and he'll end up without the house and without the kids."

"Sod that! He shouldn't be so ready with his fists!"

Maggie was startled. Ms. Montague's earrings were waggling a mite enthusiastically. "He's never done it before, you know."

"I'm more concerned he doesn't do it again. If you want me to make an application for a residence order, be ready to go to court some time in the next two weeks. Meanwhile I'll prepare an affidavit as to his behavior, which you'll have to swear is true."

"What happens to that?"

"You sign it and I have it filed at court."

Affidavits. Injunctions. Sworn truths filed at court. It all seemed so ritualistic and incantatory; so grave, and so monumental. Maggie nodded agreement.

She walked home from the offices of Sedge and Sedge to her depressing bedsit in New Markets. It was the last day in November, it was cold and damp, and it was already dark at five in the afternoon.

The house she'd found was three storeys high and her room was on the middle floor. Someone kept a motorbike, leaking oil from its crankcase, in the downstairs hallway. Another resident on the ground floor played solid thrash at volume from two P.M., presumably when they got out of bed, to two A.M., presumably when they went to bed. It was playing when Maggie turned the key to the front door.

In her room she switched on the gas fire and pushed coins into her meter. It was like having a pet; it needed feeding often. Unable to visit Amy and Sam, she faced another barren evening.

Making coffee in the shared kitchen facility was Kate, who occupied the next room. Kate looked like a figure from an Aubrey Beardsley drawing and wore the kind of makeup other people would only use for a pageant. She described herself as "late gothic," but she was really a friendly, chatty domestic Cleopatra in black denim, and though there were ten years between them, Maggie felt as if Kate was the elder of the two.

"Is he always like this?" asked Maggie, referring to the noise from downstairs.

"Never stops. I'm gonna firebomb his room one of these days."

"Don't. I'm directly above it."

"Perhaps I won't. Doing anything this evening?"

"No one to do anything with." Maggie smiled at her.

"Me neither," said Kate. "Fancy going somewhere?"

TWENTY-THREE

Richard had discovered a fourth dagger at the Maggie dig, ceremonial, bronze, identical to the others but snapped at the hilt. It
was rather obvious from its position where a fifth might appear.

"It's not a triangle at all," said Tania. "Another dagger over
there would make a circle. They've been placed in a ring."

Alex called in another couple of volunteers. They all worked
through their lunch break, and within a couple of hours the fifth
blade came to light. They marked out the exact location of the
blades with wooden stakes.

"Could there be more?" someone asked.

"I doubt it," said Alex. Everyone stood round the circle, hands
on hips, staring down at the wooden stakes.

"Why not?" Tania wanted to know.

Alex rubbed his chin. "I dunno. I just doubt it."

"What if—" said Richard, stepping over the stakes and removing the original triangle of white marker tape "—what if it
isn't a circle at all?"

He took a new length of marker tape, wound it round one
of the stakes and carried it across the diameter of the circle to a
second stake. Thence across the circle again to the stake adjacent
to his starting point, making two sides of a larger triangle. Instead

of closing the triangle, he crossed the circle again to the fourth point, then to the fifth, and back to his starting point.

He'd marked out a five-pointed star.

It was a good game. "What if you're both right?" said Alex, taking the tape from Richard's hands. He inserted a short stake between each of the dagger positions before unwinding the tape to complete a circle round the five-pointed star. Now they were all staring down at a classic pentagram.

"I think we'd better keep this quite for the time being," said Alex. "We don't want people to get stupid ideas."

Everyone nodded sagely. None of them wanted people to get stupid ideas.

But Alex found he had a problem keeping those self-same stupid ideas out of his head. He was thinking about Maggie, and about how she might have known where he should dig. He was still convinced you could pick almost anywhere on this site and unearth something, but the extraordinary nature of the discovery complicated things. He could deny it no longer.

He was trying to relate this discovery to other things about Maggie's recent behavior. He'd read enough of the diary to form a rough understanding of its contents. He could stop guessing about the other items he'd found alongside the diary, and about the sphere of her new interests. If she didn't have a lover (and he'd concluded after all that he'd been wrong, and she probably didn't) then what was it she'd been up to at ungodly hours of the night?

For the first time, he felt a nagging fear about the safety of his children. For the first time a question was raised in his mind about the stability of their mother. Because the stupid ideas just wouldn't go away.

Maggie was having a good time. She was having to shout to make herself heard above the band, and was throwing back a dirty concoction of lager and blackcurrant juice, a drink to which Kate had introduced her. It was standing room only at the Seven Stars. Gutbucket blues at maximum decibels and a fug of sweating bodies, writhing cigarette smoke and beery, frothblowing chatter. They were being corralled against the bar by two youths in black leather.

"What's he say?" Maggie shouted in Kate's ear.

"He says do we want a drink."

"I don't know. What do you think?"

Both youths held a pint glass in one hand and a crash helmet in the other. Kate beckoned to one and shouted in his ear, "Two lager and black, but you won't get a shag out of it."

Maggie's lager went up her nose. The boy grinned stupidly and went obediently to the bar. Maggie felt some of Kate's carefree youth rubbing off on her. Kate had lent Maggie a leather jacket after telling her she looked too prim for where they were going. She was learning a lot from Kate. Like the fact that if you take the piss out of men they come back for more of the same treatment.

"Thanks. Now get back on your Lambretta," she said to the youth when he handed her a red lager.

"I ain't gorra Lambretta. I've gorra Norton."

"That makes all the difference. That makes you a person with a Norton."

"A Norton?" said Maggie. "Isn't that a two-stroke?"

"Here Derek. She thinks a Norton is a two-stroke."

"This is great conversation, boys. I could talk about motorbikes all night."

"Here! Are you trying to take the piss?"

"Get back on your Lambretta."

Several red lagers later Maggie and Kate were on the back of the two motorbikes speeding through the freezing November night. They were heading toward Wigstone Heath at Maggie's insistence. Maggie was on the pillion of the lead bike. They'd taken a cross-country lane, and she was hugging her motorcyclist out of fear and exhilaration rather than any desire for intimacy.

It was cold on the bike, icy. But wrapped in her borrowed leathers she exulted in it. It was loud, deafening even; she relished the deep, throaty roar of the Norton as it climbed through the gears, and the lash of the wind in her face. Her arms clenched the waist of the stranger controlling the machine and her thighs gripped the vibrating saddle. She wanted a bike!

The rider turned his head and shouted, "Where now?" She heard his muffled words through the crash helmet.

"Keep going! Keep going!"

She turned to see the second bike and caught a wave from Kate. Maggie was highly aroused, even though she knew she was just using these boys for their engines, their machines. She could fold herself across them and they would take her where she wanted to go. The bike hit top gear as they found a flat stretch of road. Maggie sensed a change of gear inside herself as they neared Wigstone Heath.

She felt a growing awareness as they approached the heath. There were things in the passing shadows which began to take on a faint, shimmering luminosity. A boulder. A road sign. A twisted shrub. She was sure she saw a hare crouched in the hedgerow. She looked over her shoulder, and these things seemed to hold the light from the headlamps long after the bikes had passed. She felt strange. There was a growing disquiet as they got nearer to the heath. The initial giddy excitement of the ride was deserting her.

This began to seem less than a good idea. What were they going to do when they got there? It was wrong. She was playing with these boys. It was not for her to take them there. It was an abuse of privilege.

It gave her a bad feeling.

But she didn't know how to stop it. The bikes were cruising toward the heath, locked into a trajectory, moving forward in a steady drone. Then at a bend the motorcyclist dropped down through his gears and slowed to take a sharp corner, leaning the bike into the road. Maggie saw a huge black shadow step out of the hedgerow in front of them, and the next thing she knew she was sailing through the air.

Then Kate was picking her out of the hedgerow. "Maggie! Maggie!"

She was winded and scratched, but she was all right. Dazed, she got to her feet. The injured Norton lay on its side in the hedge, engine still squealing, back wheel spinning. Its rider staggered over to her. His leathers had been sliced open and there was a bloody gash on his forearm. His friend Derek silenced the squealing bike.

"There was something in the road! There was something there!"

"I saw it, too," said Maggie. But she was more interested in what she had grasped in her clenched fist. It was a branch of belladonna, deadly nightshade, black berries clustered and gleaming with a dull light. She looked up at the stars in the clear, cold sky. They were brilliant. "It's incredible! Dwale! Deadly nightshade! She's everywhere! Speaking to me!"

"What?" said Kate.

"She's amazing!"

"That girl's concussed," said Derek.

"Don't talk rot," said Maggie sharply.

He held up two fingers in front of her eyes. " 'Ow many fingers do you see?"

"Get away, you stupid sod. I'm as clear as a bell."

The evening finished there. After that, no one was in the mood for completing the journey. The front forks were twisted on the Norton. It was barely roadworthy. They returned at a steadier pace, and the boys said good-night and dropped them off back at the house.

Music thumped from the ground-floor room. Maggie made coffee, and she and Kate sat in her room. "That cut on his arm," she said fretfully. "If I had my stuff here I could have helped him. Really I could."

"What stuff?"

"Oh, herbs and stuff. Never mind. I'll sort it out. It was just a warning, you know. She didn't want me to take those lads up there."

Kate looked at her strangely, as if she might be concussed after all. "You know what you are, Maggie? Witchy."

"Yes," said Maggie. "And I'm sick of that fucking music."

The branch of deadly nightshade was still in her pocket. She took it out and handed the leather jacket back to Kate. Then she found a length of cotton and a pin.

"What are you doing?" said Kate.

"She gave me a warning tonight. I have a feeling, a feeling she might balance it with a gift."

"What are you on about? Where are you going?"

Maggie didn't answer. Kate followed her downstairs, to the door vibrating from the thrash music. Maggie pinned the cotton to the cross frame over the door so that the branch of deadly nightshade hung at roughly eye level. Then she hammered on the door, and without waiting for an answer, returned upstairs to her own room.

"What are you doing?" hissed Kate.

"I don't know, Kate. Sometimes I just feel guided."

"Guided by what?"

"I don't know. I honestly don't know. Listen."

They listened. After a few moments the music was silenced.

"It's stopped!" said Kate.

"Exactly."

TWENTY-FOUR

Morton Briggs, dispensing law for Moore, Bray and Toot, was the provincial English solicitor manifest. A tangy, residual nicotine smell roosted in the weft and warp of a suit shiny at elbow and butt; and the initial benumbed impression this created was perfectly complemented by a minutely knotted, egg-stained tie. A pair of tortoiseshell spectacles rested halfway along a large, puce-colored nose. The overall effect was of confidence and complacency imparted in equal measure. Alex felt somewhat reassured.

Briggs' office was lined with books so heavy they were obviously not designed for lifting from the bookcase. The last book on the shelf, *Law Reports 1967*, had a binding faded on a diagonal up to the point where the sun reached its finger on a daily basis. The gas fire of the unreconstructed Victorian office generated a warm fug, and so did the bulky presence of Briggs himself.

"No, I think we'll leave that for the time being," Briggs said, twisting a pencil in his huge pink hands. "We should save that for later. It might be our trump card."

"So you don't think she'll win custody at the hearing?"

Alex found Briggs' easy confidence infectious.

"Not at the initial hearing, I don't. *She* left *you*, don't forget that. We'll oppose the injunction on the grounds of the children's interests. The judge will have little option but to preserve the status quo while he asks for reports to be prepared by the Court Welfare Officer. Then the real battle starts."

The real battle. If Briggs imparted confidence, it didn't make Alex feel any less depressed. He'd been appalled by this latest development. To his utter astonishment, an apologetic stranger in a black raincoat had turned up at his door, and had pushed a summons into his hands.

Alex had never before received a court summons. "Do I have to accept this?" he'd spluttered, looking at the envelope in his hand as if it was coated with cyanide.

"I'm afraid you already have," said the process server over his shoulder, the hem of his raincoat flapping as he retreated down the path.

He'd immediately picked up the phone to tell Maggie what he thought of it. He regarded it as an almost irreversible step on a downward spiral. When they could only communicate with each other by employing professionals, they had nothing left.

He'd pleaded with her to no avail, and he went on pleading. He'd apologized for striking her until he was sick of hearing the wheedling sound of his own voice. He'd even heard himself offer, preposterously, to accompany her on midnight walks under a moon of her choice; though he'd qualified his pleading by insisting that she come home, live with them, and behave like what he called a "proper" mother.

But she had adopted a siege mentality, he'd decided, and the only way to deal with her was to starve her out. Starve her, that is, of family affection by proscribing all physical contact with the children. Then the solicitor's letter had landed on the mat, and stakes had been raised in a way he'd neither anticipated nor wanted.

"How long will that take?" Alex asked Briggs dolefully.

"For reports? Three months at least."

Alex looked at Briggs and Briggs looked back across the top of his spectacles. Then the solicitor laid down his pencil and pushed himself back in his chair an eighth of an inch. Alex realized it was a signal: audience over.

Briggs escorted him to the door. "I'll be in touch," he said.

"Hello, stranger!" said Ash, when the bell above his shop doorway tinkled. Maggie closed the door and as she turned the light fell on her face. "You look like you've been in a fight!" Ash laughed, seeing her fading bruises. Maggie just stared at him. Ash stopped laughing. "Oh, no. You *have* been in a fight."

Maggie sat down while he set the kettle to boil. She had to wait while he dealt with a brief flurry of custom before she could tell him. Ash took her hand, put it to his mouth, and kissed it.

"Bastard."

"Perhaps I deserved it, Ash."

"Don't say that. Victim's mentality. All you did was go for a walk."

"He still thinks I've got a lover."

"And you still think he has."

"What makes you say that?"

The bell tinkled and another customer came in. It was a young man who wanted to buy a set of Tibetan temple bells. "I'm a herbalist," Ash explained stiffly, "not a campanologist."

"I get a lot of that," he said after the young man had gone. But Maggie was still waiting for an answer to her question. "Liz. She's a clever old bird."

"You've been talking to Liz? But I never said anything to Liz about it."

"That's what I mean by clever. She picks up a lot about what's *not* said by listening to what *is* said."

"And what does she say?"

"She says you've got it."

"*It?* You mean the it we're not supposed to talk about?"

"That's the one. Tell me about this grotty bedsit you're living in."

"It's not so bad. I'm enjoying the freedom. I can do what I want for the first time in my life. I can please myself. That reminds me, I have to make a new collection, herbs, plants, oils, everything. From scratch. From the beginning. I've got loads to learn and lots of time. I want you to help me."

Ash did help her. He went walking with her. They collected what they could from the hedgerows, and he told her what she could expect in the spring. As for the more exotic herbs, he donated a quantity from his own stock and refused to accept payment. Maggie felt she was abusing his good nature, and in the end she forced him to accept a nominal sum.

He also helped her in the selection of her tools and implements. She'd lost everything when Alex had thrown out her equipment along with her herbs, so she needed a new knife, mortar and pestle and other practical equipment.

Ash suggested she do things properly. He pointed out that the equipment was represented by the Tarot suits: knife for swords, mortar and pestle for cups, wand for batons and a pentacle drawn on an altar cloth. Why not consecrate the full set at the same time?

Christmas was approaching. The city had been decorated with lights. A grand tree stood in the marketplace. Ash shut up Omega one afternoon so they could spend a couple of hours together shopping. The event made her miss her children. Every previous Christmas shopping expedition she'd cursed them for getting under her feet, yet now she wanted to fall over them.

But she also liked being with Ash. He was so unlike Alex, this tall man with the ready humor. Christmas shopping had always made Alex irritable and stressed; Ash turned it into a game, always ready with a quiverful of words for the people serving them. They might come across a griper or a complainer in the marketplace press of Christmas shoppers, and he could turn their mood with the right words. Not clever words, not smart words, but just the right words. Stroking words which would dispel provocation and restore perspective.

The approach of Christmas also meant the approach of Winter

Solstice, Ash explained. "The twenty-first of December. Shortest day. It's the same festival, when you think about it. Just older."

Maggie remembered Alex telling her that religion had its own archaeology, layers of different ages built on the same site.

"That's when we should consecrate all this stuff," said Ash, meaning the knife, mortar and pestle and other equipment.

"The twenty-first. That's the day of the custody hearing."

The custody hearing took place in the depressing precincts of the county court. Maggie was talking to her solicitor when she saw Alex come in with his.

"Is he any good?" said Maggie

"Bumbling and inefficient," said Ms. Montague, fiddling with an earring, "but quite nice."

Alex saw Maggie whispering to a woman in a dark suit in the waiting area. He stopped Briggs as they came through the door. "Is that her solicitor?"

"Montague? Yes."

"What's she like?"

"Arrogant and incompetent," said Briggs, pushing his spectacles back onto the bridge of his nose. "But otherwise a decent sort."

Despite this composite of incompetence and inefficiency, the court managed to deal with the issue in under six minutes. The judge would not uphold an injunction over the property but issued a restraining order "protecting" Maggie from further assault. He ruled for the status quo pending reports to be submitted by the Court Welfare Officer. A date would be fixed for another hearing. Maggie, declining the opportunity to return to the house, was granted access to the children on two days a week.

"What I told you," said Briggs to Alex, gathering his papers.

"What we expected," said Montague to Maggie, clipping her briefcase shut.

Leaving Maggie and Alex to wonder why they'd even bothered to attend. Maggie expected Alex to wait behind afterwards. She thought he'd at least want to talk. He didn't.

The six-minute experience tipped Maggie into a deep trough of depression.

Ash did his best to take her mind off it.

"Why the Winter Solstice?" Maggie asked as they drove. She stared bleakly through the passenger window into the pitch dark outside. Spots of rain dotted the windscreen.

"Because now the days will get lighter. It represents progression toward the light. A good time to consecrate these things."

"Can't you do it for me?"

"You make your own dedications."

"Who shall I dedicate them to?"

"Don't ask me things for which you already have the answer."

It was approaching midnight. They got out of the car and began walking across the shadowy heath. Low cloud obscured the moon. The wind screeched around the stunted bushes and buffeted the rocks. It flapped the hems of their coats.

"It's fucking freezing," said Maggie, stumbling along the path.

"You chose this place."

"I suppose I owe her one here. Doesn't your wife mind you running around the heath at this time of night?"

Ash treated the question as rhetorical. They reached the standing stones and it started to rain. Maggie laid out her equipment: altar cloth, knife, mortar and pestle, and the hazel wand she had cut and stripped from the hedgerow a few days earlier. Ash stood looking at his watch. He wouldn't let her start until midnight. "If we're going to do this at all, let's do it properly. I'm just glad there's no one here to see us."

At midnight Ash lit the paraffin-soaked brand he'd brought with him. It looked dramatic. It sent shadows running for cover behind the standing stones. Spots of rain hissed on the flame.

"What shall I say?" cried Maggie, her wet hair plastered to her head.

"Make it up," said Ash. "It really doesn't matter."

"Have I really got to say it aloud?"

"Oh, yes."

Maggie squatted. She reran the events of the day, and for the first time allowed her depressive feelings to roll over and through her, like a storm cloud passing over acres of fertile fields. Tears pricked her eyes, but somewhere in that moment she found words. Words of power. The rain battened on her tears as she offered up each piece of equipment in turn, each to the four points of the compass. She dedicated them and asked that they be imbued with power in return. Ash stood in the circle, patiently but self-consciously holding the flaming brand aloft until she'd completed the cycle.

She was drenched. The cold and the rain took hold of her. They penetrated her clothes and eased their way into her. They possessed her bones. It was like being entered by a spirit, but it was elemental cold and rain. She had a momentary sensation of damp heat at her lips, breasts, and vagina. She shivered. It was a deep, earth-charged spasm.

"Finished?"

She nodded. Ash put out the flame. Maggie collected up her equipment, wrapping them in the soaked altar cloth, then came over to stand beside Ash.

They stood in the silence, the rain still falling. Then it fell harder, very hard, bouncing high off the stones.

"Well," said Ash.

"What do we do now?"

"We go home, of course."

During the drive back, Maggie sat in silence.

"What is it?"

"Oh, I don't know. I'm disappointed," she said. "I expected something to happen. To feel something more. To see something. Anything. But she just wasn't there tonight."

"Oh no, she was there all right."

"Well, I didn't feel her."

"No. She takes her gifts very modestly. But she was there all the time. You'll see."

"How will I see?"

"Oh, I dunno. She'll give you something back in return."

Two days later, Alex agreed to let her have the children for an extra afternoon. He was taking them to his parents' house in Harrogate, where they would spend Christmas. She wanted to give them their presents before he spirited them away. She took them to a burger bar—which previously she'd always strictly refused to do—and bought them everything they asked for.

The time came for Alex to collect them. He piled the kids in the car and turned to her before leaving, pulling a gift from his coat pocket. Whatever it was, it was beautifully wraped in expensive red-and-green paper and trimmed with gold thread and a golden bow. It had a label: To Maggie, love from Alex xxx.

"Can I open it now?" said Maggie. She was battling not to let him see how upset she was about the children.

"I wish you would."

She tore open the wrapping paper. It was Bella's diary.

"I thought you'd burned it!"

"How could I—me, an archaeologist—burn something like that?"

"Thank you for giving it back to me. Happy Christmas."

"Happy Christmas, Maggie."

She cried after he drove away.

TWENTY-FIVE

Christmas Day was bleak. Maggie woke with a hangover and a palate like a carpet soaked in sticky liqueurs. She'd been out with Kate to a pub on Christmas Eve. A drunk with Jesus Christ hair and the smell of vomit in his beard had spent the night trying to kiss her. She'd turned down two offers of bed and one of salvation when the Church Army had arrived with collecting tins just before midnight.

Now all she had was the vengeance of the morning after in her dismal bedsit. Kate had gone home to her parents' house. Even the thrash music (which hadn't started up again since she'd left her calling card) would have been almost welcome. The house was as quiet and as chilly as a tomb.

Beginning to wish she'd taken up the offer to spend Christmas Day with Kate's family, she switched on her gas fire and went to wash in the bathroom. The fungus in the corner exuded malintent. When she returned to her room, the gas had died. She emptied her purse onto the table, finding not a single coin for the meter. She flicked on her portable TV set. Every channel seemed to be showing cartoons. She got back into bed.

And there she stayed until midday when there came a hammering on the front door. Maggie got out of bed and, tying the sash of her dressing gown, padded downstairs and along the cold corridor.

"Ash!" He was standing holding a gift-wrapped present. She hugged him, almost bowling him from the step in her enthusiasm. "Oh, Ash!"

"Didn't like to think of you here alone. Thought you might need cheering up."

She took him inside and made him wait in the kitchen while she dressed.

"Cold in here," he observed when he was allowed in the room.

"This is the worst Christmas Day of my life. You've no idea what it's like to be on your own for Christmas Day."

Ash looked at her strangely. "Put your coat on," he said. "Time you met the wife."

"I couldn't intrude, Ash. It's not fair."

"Do as you're told. You're not staying here all day."

So she let him bully her into spending Christmas Day at his place. She carried her still-wrapped gift to the car and climbed in beside him. It was a half-hour drive along roads that were almost empty.

Ash lived in a large, slightly gloomy detached house with rampant ivy trailing the facing wall. The lounge had a coal fire burning behind a brass fireguard. Ash moved the fireguard aside and she took advantage of the warmth. Maggie made a quick assessment as Ash poured them both a glass of sherry. It was a most conventional room, disappointingly so with its Dralon suite and velvet curtains and its brass ornaments grouped around the fire. She'd expected something more . . . bohemian, more eccentric.

"Cheers," said Ash, tipping back his sherry.

"Isn't your wife going to join us?"

"The wife. Right. Time for you to meet the wife. Come through to the study."

Ash tugged her by the wrist and led her down the hall to a room at the rear of the house. He opened the door and propelled her into the room ahead of him. "Maggie, meet the wife."

Maggie looked back at him, perplexed. There was no one. But every eccentric or bohemian detail she'd expected to be exhibited in Ash's house had been crammed into this room. It was indeed a study. There was a great leather-inlay desk the size of a sports field standing against the far wall. A winking word processor suggested he'd spent some of his Christmas morning at work. The walls were decked with large maps, studded with pins and colored ribbon connecting geographical positions. Otherwise framed prints covered all available wall space.

The room was heavy with the pungent smell of incense. And on shelves or on freestanding display tables was an extensive collection of figurines, statuary, carvings, and fragments of bas-relief. The room was a museum, but with the aura of a shrine.

"They're all—"

"That's right," said Ash. "The goddess, in all her different incarnations. I collect them. Actually I study them. It's my hobby when I'm not in the shop."

"And the maps?"

"I'm tracing her movements, across history. See? She started out here, in the Middle-East, and her influence spread to Africa, to Asia and to Europe. Then with the migration of the peoples . . . only her name gets changed, she doesn't change."

"It's incredible!" She lifted a figurine from a table.

"That's the Ephesian Artemis. And it's original, in case you were wondering. From somewhere in Asia Minor about 1000 B.C. You went straight to it. Clever lady; I'm impressed. Most of the things you see here are reproductions. Some I had specially made."

Maggie weighed it in her hand. The lifelike representation had a dozen mammary glands. "It must be worth a fortune!"

"Yep."

"But why do you . . ."

"Refer to it all as 'the wife'? Because it's here. It's a good excuse, if ever I want to get away from someone. And because I spend so much time with her. . . . Come on. Let's go back to the other room."

Maggie carefully replaced the figurine on the table. He closed the door softly on the goddess and poured them both another glass of sherry.

"So you're not married after all. You don't have a wife."

"I did have. She died in a motoring accident three years ago." Ash looked into the fire. This was the sadness Maggie had sensed in him from the beginning. "Actually there's another reason why I call all that 'the wife.' Janie—my real wife—started all that research. She was an academic, writing a book. I'm trying to finish it for her. I don't have her brilliance. It's taking a long time."

He was trying to make light of it, and he wasn't doing it very well. She could see he'd never let it out to anyone; intuition told her he'd choked it all back. "Do you know," he was saying, "people say time will help you get over it. Well, they're wrong. When you lose someone, the world becomes a changed place. And it's changed forever."

She wanted to hold him, but it wasn't possible.

"I'm being morbid!" he said brightly, suddenly.

"No, you're not."

"Yes, I am. Drink up! Open your present! There's a turkey cooking. Can you smell it?"

Oh, yes. Maggie could smell the bird cooking.

They pulled crackers and wore paper hats and drained two bottles of claret and had a jolly dinner. It was self-conscious jollity, but it was genuine. They were relaxed in each other's company, and they were both desperately relieved not to have to spend the day alone.

After dinner they sat through part of a lugubrious television church service, before Ash switched it off and put some music on instead.

"Don't you believe in the miracle of the Virgin birth?" Maggie asked, ironic.

"No more than I believe Santa Clause comes down that chimney with a roast chestnut up his arse."

"You don't like the Christian Church, do you? I could see while you were watching TV."

"No, I don't. I despise it. Look, Christ was possibly the greatest teacher ever. A healer, in more ways than one. But if he was here today he'd have nothing to do with the Christian Church."

She'd got him on his subject. "Take the Virgin Mary," he continued, "our most recent incarnation of the goddess. But what did they do, these old patriarchs? They took her sexuality away. The virgin mother. And that's how they took her *power* away. Who do you think is that second woman you always see standing at the crucifixion?"

"What? You mean Mary Magdalene?"

"That's right. The prostitute, so called. The demoniac cured by Christ. She's the same person, the same Mary. But they split off the two halves of the goddess. The Magdalene is the sexy half. The virgin's dark sister, if you like."

Dark sister. The phrase rang bells. "Why did you say that? *Dark sister?*"

"Isn't that what she is? A shadow, always in the background, but always present. Come to think of it, Jesus was probably married to Mary Magdalene."

"Where do you get these outrageous notions?"

Ash smiled and nodded toward the study. "From the wife. But what really makes my blood boil about the Christian Church is the slaughter. All of those women in medieval times, literally millions across Europe, who were tortured and slaughtered and burned. Wise women. Healers. Simple herbalists, some of them, like me. Some of them just lonely old antisocial women. All put to the torch. Actually, they used to hang witches in this country, not burn them. But no one in the Christian Church, even to this day, seems prepared to show the slightest remorse for this holocaust. And they're still trying to do it! Do you know they had a campaign against my shop, because of some of the books I sell?"

"I'd heard about that, yes."

Ash waved a hand through the air, as if he wanted to swat a barmy world.

In the evening they played a round of Scrabble and drank more claret and a few glasses of brandy. Then just to prove how committed to Christmas he was, in a deep down sort of way, Ash produced a packet of dates, and they were in such good spirits they ate them all.

It seemed perfectly natural they should snuggle on the couch to watch a late film on the television.

"Would you like to stay here?" Ash asked her sleepily. She nodded. "You can have my bed," he said. "I'll make a bed up on the couch."

"That's not necessary. I want you to sleep with me."

He kissed her lightly, but then looked at her hard. "I'll stay on the couch."

"Why?"

Ash vented a deep sigh. "Let me tell you something. One of the greatest, most remarkable pleasures for a man in this world is the secret pleasure of an erection. After my wife died, the goddess took that pleasure away from me. I'm waiting for her to give it back."

Maggie felt a surge of love for Ash. It effervesced in her, like something foaming at the lip of the vessel. She felt the need to hold him, to cradle him, to impart love.

"It's all right," she said. "I want you to sleep with me anyway. Just to be with you. Just to hold you."

Maggie knew Ash had some crying to do, and she wanted to help him do it.

TWENTY-SIX

Boxing Day blues.

Ash left to fulfill a promise to visit his dead wife's parents. He went around midday, and though he suggested Maggie should avail herself of the house, she found herself wandering back to her bedsit. The place was still empty apart from her; then in the afternoon the thrash music started up again from the ground floor.

Maggie telephoned Alex. Alex's mother answered stiffly before putting him on. He was amenable.

"What have they said? Have they taken your side?"

"What do you expect?" said Alex. "Let's not get into it, eh?"

"Have the kids been behaving?"

"Amy is queening it over everything and they're spoiling her to death; Sam has been a little swine since the moment he got here. He's crying for you all the time and he's smashing anything that's put in front of him. Mum and Dad bought him an indestructible toy truck and he threw it on the fire."

"Let me speak to them."

Maggie asked Amy to share her toys with Sam, and she asked Sam to be a good boy.

"How's your Christmas?" Alex said when he came back on the line.

"Quiet."

Maggie broke a long pause by asking, "When are you leaving there?"

"Couple more days. Will you be home when we get back?"

"No . . . Maybe. I'm thinking about it."

"Yes. Think about it." Alex put the phone down.

Maggie was thinking about it. She wanted her home back. She wanted her children back. About Alex she wasn't so sure. There was one particular question about Alex to which she wished she had an answer. She'd confronted him with her suspicions, but it wasn't enough. She wanted to know.

Maggie returned to her room and fed coins into her gas meter. She wanted the place to be warm for what she was about to do. First she set up her table with the altar cloth and the implements she'd consecrated on Wigstone heath. She unboxed her Christmas gift from Ash, three ornate brass incense burners, which she set out in a triangle around the room, and set cones of incense smouldering.

Then she proceeded to mix her flying ointment.

She operated partly on information from the diary, partly on the basis of warnings and tips delivered by Old Liz. Getting information out of Liz was never easy, in that it came either in fragments or sudden outpourings. Checking or recapitulating anything was out of the question. It was like trying to catch rainfall: you collected only what went straight into the vessel.

It scared her deeply. Yet she wanted to do it, had to do it. She needed more than ever to prove to herself she was not some feeble spirit to be fisted around the house. The recollection of Alex's stinging blows came to her. It gave her the strength to proceed.

Using a base of almond oil she mixed her quantities with the precision and care only fear could marshal. Her hands trembled; her throat was dry even as she used her mortar and pestle to grind the ingredients. She invoked the name of a protective spirit given to her by Ash.

Once, when she was a girl of twelve, she'd ascended the ladders to the top diving board at her local swimming pool. She'd never faced the top board before. Up there she found a short queue of dithering boys of her own age, all failing to pluck up the courage either to jump or make the dive. Two boys walked to the extremity of the board and came back. They couldn't do it.

The boys had turned and, shamefacedly, had parted for her. Followed by their eyes, she'd stepped to the edge of the board. The cries and the splashes in the pool below had become remarkably hollow, had seemed to come from another world. Aware of the shivering boys behind her she'd offered a secret prayer, not to God but to Mother Nature, before dropping off the board. Then she was slipping through the air, plunging, seemingly forever, toward the water.

Emboldened by her example, the dithering boys were now all leaping from the top board. On reaching the side of the pool, she'd felt a mercurial trickle inside herself. She climbed out of the pool and went immediately to the changing rooms. Her first menstrual period had started.

Now, whenever she was afraid of doing something new, she always replayed that moment.

She mixed belladonna, juice of wolfsbane, poplar leaves, wild celery, and cinquefoil. To this she added a tiny ball of black resin which Liz had given her, and followed Liz's advice that she compound a kind of cold cream rather than an oil. Liz had told her that she should blacken the cream by adding soot, though she hadn't explained why. Maggie did as instructed.

These were different waters, darker waters, and they scared her far more than that leap from the top board. Far more, even, than had the red, lissom trickle heralding a new phase of life. But now, as then, she was busy disguising her fears from herself.

Even though she'd had her oils awaiting *enfleurage*, the operation took her two hours. She placed a bowl of water and a towel beside her. Then she was ready.

She locked the door.

She undressed and sat naked on the floor, inside the triangle of incense burners. She sat with her eyes closed for ten minutes, trying to address her mind to the matter. Music thumped from the room below, but despite this distraction she found she could easily come back to her question. When she was satisfied, she opened her eyes and reached for the prepared ointment.

It wasn't easy, because she was afraid. Her stomach squeezed. Her hand shook. Her mouth was dry. *Why am I doing this?* she thought. *Why? Why?* She looked at the black paste she had spent so long mixing. The incense in the room hung in heavy, serpentine coils. She felt nauseated. The black pool beckoned. *Because you must,* came the answer from inside her head. It was a voice she'd heard before, in the woods, on the heath; female, intimate, insinuating. *Because you are what you are.*

She smeared the paste across her forehead, into her temples, on her throat and round her wrists. She massaged it thoroughly into her skin, but only at these precise points. Then, as Liz had insisted, she took a quantity of the paste on her fingers and pushed it up inside her vagina. It seemed a perverse act, but Maggie knew of other intravaginal treatments. She wiped her hands on her thighs, daubing them in the process with sooty streaks, before washing her hands in the bowl of water. Then she sat back to concentrate again on her question.

She was perspiring heavily; even though she was fully committed now, the fear had not diminished. Someone had once taught her to meditate; so she tried to slow her racing heart by closing her eyes and silently repeating a mantra to herself, without losing sight of her question.

The meditation technique relaxed her a little. She vented a huge sigh, a discharge of anxiety, and started to feel strangely languid. It was a pleasing sensation, almost a numbness, a distancing from her body. It lasted for ten or fifteen minutes, though she was already losing her sense of time.

Then suddenly her heart rate rocketed. It started knocking heavily inside her, and she was engulfed by a terrible, blinding headache. She opened her eyes and was astonished to see great blisters of sweat oozing from her body, the perspiration glittering like moonlight on frost. Her vagina was burning inside and her throat was parched. She instinctively reached for the bowl of water, then remembered having used it to wash her hands. She tried to get up, but the movement made her vomit. She was sick into the bowl of water, twice, three times, until she was retching, unable to produce anything and at the same time incapable of drawing breath.

Then the retching stopped, and a profound numbness swamped her body. The pain in her head receded, as did the burning in her throat and vagina. She was breathing heavily, feeling only overwhelming relief that the pain had gone. She drew herself upright, her legs folded under her, her eyes screwed shut. Although she was still panting heavily, the frightening heart rate was beginning to slow. Instinctively, as if to give her lungs more room in which to work, she thrust forward her chest and pushed her arms back behind her. Then she tried to open her eyes.

Light hit her like a slap in the face. The instant she tried to open her eyes, she felt as if she had been grabbed by two giant claws, one round her neck, one squeezing her buttocks, and flung up, up, up into blackness, hurtling against a hot cinnamon wind. It was like being shot out of a cannon. White hot sparks exploded and buffeted her as she traveled through the blackness, detonating behind her closed eyes. Her blood roared in her ears.

Then she suddenly came to a stop. She was suspended in midair. All pain had gone, all sense of heat and odor, all sound. This time she could open her eyes. She was in a gray corridor, unable to discern whether indoors or outside. All was muffled as she drifted slowly along the corridor. Gray or black shapes, ambiguous things, fracturing shadows, drifted by her with languid movements like fish in an aquarium. Sometimes the shapes stopped, disappeared, reappeared, moved on. They could be geometric in form, or irregular. Maggie felt confused, lost.

She reached out at one of the shapes, and as her hand passed into it, the shape folded, quit. It changed into a face, mouthing words at her, words she couldn't hear.

The face was very old, androgynous, perhaps female, Maggie couldn't be sure. It hovered close, mouthing silent words, chilling but not threatening. Maggie moved away, but the face followed at her shoulder. Trying to speak was useless. It took her an age simply to turn and look into the eyes of the hovering face; then a long stand-off as she looked back without result, without consequence. Again Maggie moved away, and again she was followed. The face mouthed its words again, and again, until slowly it penetrated. *What do you want? What do you want?* the face was asking her. It wanted to help her.

Maggie tried to remember her question. It seemed a long way from here. She'd forgotten it. She would have to go back to her room to remember her question, and it was too far . . . too far away.

Then she recalled the question. She deliberately brought it to mind. The face disappeared immediately, and in its place, like a parting in the fabric of the gray corridor, was a scene. Maggie drew closer.

An elegant pair of hands, jewelled hands, a woman's hands, were carefully wrapping a Christmas gift. All Maggie could see were the hands, the gift, and the wrapping paper. The paper was expensive, pretty green-and-red material shining and winking in the pearly light. The gift was Bella's diary. The hands finished wrapping the gift, and now Maggie could see to whom they belonged. Anita Suzman. She was talking to someone behind her. Anita was naked, spread across a bed, lying on her stomach. She waved the gift in the air looking across her shoulder as she spoke. A man's bare forearms slid under her stomach, lifting her from beneath her belly, raising her onto her knees. It was Alex. He parted her legs and Maggie could see his erection as he moved closer to Anita, slowly penetrating her as he leaned across her arched back. Anita's eyes closed and her head dropped forward in pleasure.

Anita slipped out her languorous tongue and licked the pretty bow decorating Alex's Christmas gift to Maggie as he took her from behind.

The sound of someone hammering on the door brought Maggie round. She came to on the floor, flat out on her back. She had her hand in a bowl of water and vomit. The gas fire had gone out and she felt cold.

"Maggie! Maggie! Are you in there?" The hammering got louder.

"Who is it?" Maggie croaked. She was beetled, unable to get off her back.

"It's Kate. What're you doing?"

Maggie hauled herself to her feet. She felt weak. She slipped on her dressing gown, sat on the bed and put her head between her knees.

"Maggie!"

"I'm all right!"

"Then open the door."

Maggie staggered over to the door and opened it a few inches.

"God! Look at you!" said Kate. Maggie suddenly remembered the sooty flying ointment.

"Run me a bath if you want to do something for me."

Kate did as ordered and stood back as Maggie staggered by with the bowl to tip its contents down the toilet.

"Must have been one hell of a party," Kate said nervously.

Maggie looked back at her through a stray curl, but with a baleful eye.

TWENTY-SEVEN

Alex softened a little in the New Year. He let Maggie have the children for an extra day a week. It was always Saturdays he wanted her to have them, which was convenient for him, but she was grateful for any contact. Sam's conjunctivitis had returned, so she made a repeat preparation of the eye lotion that had cured him before.

Maggie's savings were dwindling. She was going to have to do something about money. Meanwhile Ash paid her to run Omega two days a week. He said he was glad of the days off, but she didn't see how he could afford it. Business was less than brisk. Maggie persuaded him to broaden his stock. They started selling sets of tarot cards and handcrafted jewellery; she got him to take a wider range of books. He grumbled something about turning his herbal kiosk into an occult emporium, but let her have her head. Trade improved, and she felt she had at least done something to earn his generosity.

Entertaining the children every Saturday proved to be a drain on her scant resources. Previously it had been something she hadn't had to think about. So she started taking them to see Liz, which cost nothing.

"I know'd you was coming," Liz said, eyeing Amy, whom she'd not met before. Amy stared in fascination.

Liz's crablike hand scuttled down the side of her chair and proffered a humbug.

"Take it," said Maggie.

"Thank you," said Amy stepping forward. Liz clasped her tiny hand in arthritic fingers, but lightly, drawing her close and planting a kiss on her cheek. Amy showed none of the fear of Liz evinced by Sam.

"She's an angel," said Liz. "A little dove, a little pigeon. Pretty, eh?" Amy blushed.

"Me!" shouted Sam.

"Yes, here's a suck for you. I'm not leaving you out."

"Say thank you!" said Maggie. He wouldn't. Maggie put the kettle on to boil; she didn't have to ask. Liz had got her stove burning. Maggie was relieved because it was cold outside.

Liz saw her looking. "I told you, I know'd you was a-coming. So I got a good fire going."

"How did you know?" said Amy.

Liz leaned forward and tapped her nose. Amy turned and smiled at her mother. She sat on a hard-backed chair and gazed at Liz. Sam crawled under the table.

Maggie wanted to tell Liz about her flying experiments, but in words the children wouldn't understand.

"A little too much belladonna, I think, Liz."

Liz's stick tapped involuntarily. "Oh? Oh? When was this then? Now I sees it."

"Boxing Day."

"Boxing Day? Boxing Day? Where was the mistress on Boxing Day?"

Maggie hadn't thought about the moon at all. "I didn't—"

"You've got to look out for the mistress. She's to be waxing when you're mixing, and in one of the air or earth signs. Where did you do it?"

"In my room."

"Pssssshhhhtu!!!! That's not proper. You'll come to grief, you will."

"Yes, well, it was a bit messy. Still, I got what I wanted."

"You be grateful then."

"Liz, there was a face. It seemed like someone helping me."

"Oh, yes. How do you think we'd go on if we didn't have someone helping us? Help and be helped. That's it. We're here to help one another, mark that, Amy?" Amy nodded. The old woman seemed to drift off into some reverie sparked by her own words.

"Did you give her anything?" Old Liz said at length.

Maggie was confused. "Give what?"

"Oh, her'll not be pleased with you if you didn't give anything for her help. Her might not come to you again. You've to give something to your dark sister if her's to help you." Liz fumbled in her sweet packet and held out a humbug to Amy.

Amy took the humbug. Liz tossed another to Sam, who was playing happily under the table.

"So that's my dark sister? But what do you give? And how do you give it?"

"Any way you like. Give an offering. Flowers, they like flowers. Or give her the next pleasure you gets off a man!" Liz hooted with laughter and her stick slapped at the floor. "Her shall like that even better! He-he!"

Maggie waited until Liz's laughing fit had subsided.

"Speaking of that, have you got anything that can put the lead in a man's pencil?"

"Yes," Liz said, sharp, "and I know who you wants it for!"

Poor Ash, thought Maggie, to be spoken about like this. But she believed she could help, and Liz did have this uncanny intuition . . .

The talk of gifts reminded Maggie she'd brought a bottle of sherry for Liz. She'd left it in the car, so she sent Amy off to fetch it, while she herself went to use the lavatory, a cold, cobwebby brick outhouse at the bottom of the garden.

Sam crawled unnoticed behind the curtain into Liz's pantry. The dusty fabric of the curtain closed behind him, with a silent jingling of the brass rings suspending it from the rail. Liz had told him to keep out, he knew. But he wanted to take a look.

It was cool in the pantry. Cool and quiet. He sat on the stone floor and looked up from floor to ceiling. Layer after layer of shelves, groaning to capacity. Bottles and jars everywhere, innumerable, those nearest the ceiling gathering dust, those resting on the cold stone floor collecting cobwebs. There were glass jars and stone vessels; green bottles and brown; giant Kilner jars; enamel jugs and crock tubs; pots and demi-johns; urns, flasks and vases and open-topped cans; all jostling for position on the shelves.

Some were unlabeled, some hand-labeled, some with their original brand labels fading, peeling, sticky from spillage. Those glass jars whose contents he could see were stuffed with black and yellow beans, or jams or fruit preserves or exotic-colored powders and leaf branches.

Sam touched the stopper on a bottle resting on the floor. The stopper fell off and went rolling between his feet and along a phalanx of bottles standing at the back of the pantry. He moved to fetch it, but was distracted by a sharp odor issuing from the unstopped bottle. He put his nose to the bottle: it was like cherry pop, sweet, sugary, but it stung his nose like the smell of disinfectant. He took a tiny swig, but it tasted sour. It made his eyes water. He could see the scent streaming from the bottle: a brown ribbon coiling in the air, passing under his nose and moving slowly across the pantry.

And now the pantry was full of smells. There were both familiar smells and smells he didn't know; rich, pungent odors and sharp, spicy confections. Garlic and toffee. Vinegar and vanilla. Lemon and malt. Hundreds of smells, leaking from their glass jars and bottles. The air was full of dim-colored thin ribbons of scent, like party streamers traveling slowly through the air, looping, tangling, drifting . . .

Suddenly a movement, seen out of the corner of his eye. A scuffling in the back of the pantry. Sam turned to look. Peering from behind a stone bottle was a large gray rat.

It looked at him with shining black eyes. Deep black pools. It lifted its fat head into the air, vibrating its whiskers and baring cracked, yellow teeth for Sam to see. Sam got a whiff of the animal, a hot, dirty stink of rodent. He tried to turn his head away, but he was caught, mesmerized.

The rat moved forward from behind the stone bottle, and Sam recognized, riding on its back and brandishing a match of wood, a tiny lady he'd seen before. The one he'd seen in his garden riding the rat. The lady who'd stolen his doll. The lady who had called him over the balcony in the shopping arcade.

She had him. Sam wanted to call out, but he was too afraid to move. Where was his mother? Where had Amy gone? He was paralyzed. As soon as the lady appeared, there was a roaring in his ears, and a quivering in the airstream. The ribbons of scent, still visible, shivered and creased. The jars and the bottles on the shelves vibrated, thrumming with energy, inching precariously toward the edge. The entire bottled contents set up a din in his ears, until he looked up and saw shelf after shelf of trembling jars and jugs and flasks and bottles threatening to topple.

And the contents of the jars had been changed. The huge jar of black and yellow beans had become wedged full of live, angry, buzzing wasps. The jar of leaf branches had become a tangle of black centipedes waving their legs at him. A jar of fruit preserve had changed into a human face, a boy's face, squashed into the jar, its nose and lips rammed up against the glass like leeches, its eyes blinking slowly at him. They were all going to fall.

And fall they did. First a glass jar containing a white-hot star fell from the shelf and smashed on the stone floor, sizzling caustically before it died. Bottles toppled, spilling pools of bubbling, steaming blood. Then a jar smashed to the left of him, spreading little boys' penises near his feet. The whole pantry was coming down around his ears. The curtain behind him lashed open as the din got louder.

"Now then! Now then!"

It was Old Liz, standing over him. She sank her arthritic claws into Sam's shoulders. He looked up to see her above him, her tongue thrust forward at astonishing length. Instantly she retracted her tongue and spat something, a bean, with great velocity across the pantry. The bean struck the rat. Its rider vanished instantly and the rat scuttled away. The jars stopped vibrating, the colored ribbons of scent disappeared.

Sam was white with fear. His face was contorted in a scream he was too afraid to release. Liz pulled him to her and he hugged her, burying his head in the folds of her old skirts, setting up a wail and crying hysterically now.

"Hush then. Hush then. Now you knows. Now you knows what's in Liz's pantry." She brushed his hair gently. "And now *we* knows, don't we. We knows this little one is *overlooked*, don't we? But we won't say anything, will we? 'Cos she's got enough to be reckoning, your mother, now ain't she? Hush up now."

Sam pointed at the smashed jars of jam and fruit on the stone floor. "I didn't do it," he blubbered, "I didn't."

"We knows. We knows who did it. Hush up afore your mammy comes in."

Liz looked behind her and saw Amy staring at them. She was holding the bottle of sherry she'd fetched from the car.

"You saw?" said Liz.

Amy nodded.

"Well, you saw it done. Now you keep it hid, little miss. Keep it here," Liz tapped the side of her nose, "and not here," she said, tapping her lips.

Amy nodded again.

"And when the time comes, you just remember Old Liz, see?"

Maggie returned to find them standing over the mess in the pantry. "What's been going on here?"

"Nothing to worry on. We've had a little accident."

"Oh, Sam! Let me clear it up, Liz. For God's sake, Sam."

"Don't blame the lad. There's a rat in there as scared him."

She turned Maggie back with her hand. Maggie made to insist, but the astonishing strength of Liz's grip prevented her. "Any clearing up and I'll do it. You leave that alone."

Liz sat back in her chair under the clock, and Maggie was surprised to see how Sam was clinging to her. Within moments he'd fallen asleep in her arms and Amy was settled at her feet. Maggie had the feeling that events beyond the breaking of a few jars had happened, but she couldn't tell what.

"Where were we? I knows. We were talking about Ash," Liz said in a low voice. "And about the lead in his pencil."

"Yes," said Maggie.

TWENTY-EIGHT

Alex collected Sam from De Sang's clinic one afternoon, to be presented with an envelope which, De Sang assured him, contained his final report on the boy. Sam was sitting in the consulting room, drawing with wax crayons.

"Final?" said Alex.

"Sam doesn't need to spend any more time here. You'd only be wasting your money."

"But I thought his behavior had been improving lately."

De Sang looked skeptical. "Read the report. At this stage, a good childminder will work out a lot cheaper."

"But what are we supposed to do?"

"It's all in the report." Alex made to tear open the brown envelope. "I prefer you to discuss it with your wife," De Sang told him. "Then if nothing's clear, come back to me and I'll go through it with you. But you won't need to."

Alex was taken aback by the abruptness of it all. He didn't know what to say. De Sang called Sam over. "Captain Hook!" he said, and Sam happily waddled off to get his coat. "Of course," De Sang went on, "if you're keen to spend your money, we'll happily keep Sam—at the usual rates."

"No, no," said Alex, and within a few minutes he was walking away from the clinic with Sam trotting happily at his side, wondering whether De Sang had just abused him or done him a favor.

When he got home, he opened the envelope and pulled out the typed report. It said:

REPORT ON SAMUEL SANDERS PREPARED BY
Dr James De Sang

Playing games.

After observing Sam on a number of occasions I have arrived at the following understanding of his behavior.

Sam is a healthy little boy, who like all children enjoys playing games. Games are very important. For children they are the means by which they come to understand social behavior. Sam has reached the stage of development at which these social games come into being.

In this sense Sam is learning the rules that govern life. These rules and morality are actually the same thing. It's all about behavior which is acceptable, and behavior which is not. Morality is a game. It's distinct from play, but it's still a game.

Up until about the age of three children do not adhere to the rules. After this time, they might imitate rules without understanding them, and will often change them to suit their own interpretation of the game. By the time the child is seven, it will usually begin rigidly to adhere to the rules in a genuine social manner.

Sad, isn't it? Sad, I mean, that we lose this capacity simultaneously to interpret whatever's going on in a number of different ways.

But that's life. Sam, however, shows no sign of imitating the rules (the second stage I mentioned above). This is what his parents tell me.

Now, I find that when Sam is in my clinic, he is very happy to imitate the rules. Not only that, I find him a very bright, creative little boy willing to invent rules to be shared. These perfectly healthy signs lead me to conclude that his environment may not be providing him with the best model for behavior. Here in the clinic we PLAY THE GAME. We try to say what we mean and mean what we say to Sam. We find he responds well.

His unwillingness at home to imitate the rules and instead to display defiance, aggression, violence, and hysteria (again as his parents tell me) indicates to me that his model at home is of someone NOT PLAYING THE GAME.

Since it is important for Sam to at least imitate the rules, I suggest that his behavior at home would be improved if all were to PLAY THE GAME.

Hard, isn't it? But again, that's life.

I'm being as direct as I can here, because I know I'm addressing intelligent people. To do otherwise would, after all, be playing quite a different game.

De Sang had signed his name at the foot of the report. Also enclosed was an invoice.

Alex dropped the report on the table and ran a hand through his hair. He picked up the telephone and dialed. A strange voice came on the line, and he asked for Maggie to be fetched from her room. "Can you get over here?" he asked her.

Maggie read the report for a second time before folding it and handing it back to Alex. He snatched it from her and slung it across the room. "The man's a fucking lunatic! He's the one who should be certified! Running around with his trousers down for three months to come up with that! And do you see what he wants to charge? We're not paying, that's for sure."

"No," said Maggie, "we must pay."

"You're joking! He won't get a brass ring out of me. Who does the charlatan think he's trying to kid? He can whistle for it!"

"It's as clear as a bell. And of course we have to pay him."

"Clear? What's clear? What do you mean clear?"

"The report is precise. De Sang knows what he's talking about."

"I don't believe I'm hearing this. The man is just taking the piss! He's laughing in his sleeve!"

Maggie looked into the fire. "The man is speaking clearly and accurately from the heart," she said calmly. "He's telling us there's nothing wrong with Sam. He's saying you and I are the ones who have to grow up."

"Where are you going?"

"To the pub," said Maggie.

TWENTY-NINE

"I don't know what's wrong," said Alex. He buried his head in the pillow. Things weren't going well for him. He was under pressure.

Firstly there was the constant stress of having to get Amy ready for school and Sam to his full-time childminder, plus keeping them fed, clean, clothed, and living in a house fit for human habitation. The expense of paying childminders to look after Sam and to collect Amy from school was starting to make work look like a waste of effort. And work itself wasn't without its share of problems.

The archaeological dig at the castle had resumed in January. Alex needed to produce results from his original dig if he wanted the project to be extended. Funds were tight, as always, and he had to fight for resources merely to erect a rain cover over the diversionary Maggie dig. That small site had filled up with water over the Christmas period and had to be drained before work continued.

Maggie herself was still refusing to come home. The court hearing would be upon them in a few weeks, and that would incur heavy legal fees. His financial worries alone were enough to drive him to distraction. He was beginning to wonder if he were the one who needed a psychiatrist. Except that psychiatrists had already demonstrated their dubious abilities in the form of James De Sang. Alex was still fuming over that report, and the accompanying bill. He was going to have to find a way to pay it. He wondered if he could arrange some paid overtime at work.

But that raised the problem of looking after Amy and Sam. And as for extra time, he could hardly claim it when here he was taking extended lunch breaks for the occasional secret rendezvous between the sheets.

Anita gave up stroking Alex's flaccid cock. For her, too, it had been a disappointing session. She felt she was losing him somewhere. Lately he seemed less inclined to make the effort to see her. "Don't worry about it. Being anxious about it will only make it worse."

"Telling someone not to be anxious is guaranteed to make them anxious."

Anita was nettled. "Sorry, I'm sure."

Alex softened. "I didn't mean to take it out on you."

"Do you think she knows about us?"

"Who? Maggie?"

"Yes, Maggie."

"No, I don't think she knows about us."

Why did he lie to Anita? Was he afraid she might want to stop seeing him? Or was he just trying to keep his two worlds apart, so he could be a more accomplished liar should he have to face Maggie's accusations again?

Alex thought hard about it. He'd been careful not to do anything to arouse Maggie's suspicions, yet she'd confronted him forcefully, directly, on the night she'd ravished him. Ravished him? She'd comprehensively *fucked* him, before demanding to know what he was up to. He was still slightly dazed. Never had he been so completely overwhelmed. He couldn't have stopped it if he'd wanted to, no more than he could resist a hurricane. The force of it had utterly subdued him. It was like being staked out and flayed.

He didn't know that night whether something primal had

been given to or taken away from him. Perhaps, he reasoned, that's why the affair with Anita had begun, because Maggie had in some mysterious way unmanned him. Though there was, he admitted to himself, a disgraceful immaturity in the notion that he'd done all this to reassert himself.

Rationalizing, he thought; it's all rationalizing after the event! Just like Maggie's suspicions, powered by jealousy or maybe by intuition, it was all unfathomable, emotionally based, unknowable. She didn't know, she couldn't know. That's why he'd denied it, and went on denying it. And now here he was rationalizing away his adulterous relationship with Anita, when the thing had happened simply because she was *there*.

She'd always been there. He'd always been deeply aware of her. He scented her whenever she came into a room. It's simple. You observe the contract to pretend it doesn't exist and then *bang!* one day you're forced to admit it. It was a universal contract, in operation every day between women and men, a Devil's Contract, damned if you break it, damned if you don't. For there she was, coming round to his house smelling like a lynx, and always at the times when Maggie seemed most distant. Anita, shaking her platinum-and-golden hair; Anita, crossing and recrossing her long legs so that her nylons hissed, until his head was full of thoughts of her wearing nothing but her animal perfume.

And always between them this astonishing, fragile tension when they were alone for a few moments: the drying of the mouth, the involuntary stiffening of muscles. Like a spring coiling and tightening. So strong, this, and so dangerous to the two of them that it had to remain unspoken. Until finally it had to give. Only one act could break it.

When, one lunch break, he'd almost collided with her in the street, it seemed natural that they should decide to go to eat together. Anita was magnificent, he decided. She was one of those women who wear little or nothing in the way of rings, necklaces and accessories, yet who light up like a jeweller's window. Alex had long nursed an archaeologist's fantasy of gently uncovering fascinating layers of her perfumed clothing, ultimately to reveal the golden trove, which he would kiss. That day she was wearing a black, tight-fitting dress, black nylons and black heels. The sheen of her natural complexion and the precious-metal highlights of her hair contrasted provocatively with her carefully constructed lipstick pout. He wanted to eat her.

So when a decent table couldn't be found anywhere, at any price, it also seemed natural to go back to Anita's house for coffee and a sandwich. And when Anita's back was turned in brewing the coffee, Alex noticed her hands were trembling as much as his, so to stop his own hands from shaking he took a deep breath and put his arms around her from behind, letting his hands rest on her belly. Anita set down the jug she was holding and went very still. Neither of them spoke. Then she let her head tilt back on to his shoulder, and when he saw that her eyes had closed, he let his fingers splay across her thighs. He reached his hands under her dress. She moved to stop him, but ritually and without conviction. His cock was straining through his clothes, stabbing at her bottom. He felt her underarms perspiring heavily. She reached behind and pinched him savagely and he returned by probing inside her panties with his fingers, sliding a finger into her up to the second knuckle. Inside she was scalding. Then she grabbed his hand away and lifted it to her mouth, sucking the finger that had been inside her. She turned round, clasping her arms around his shoulders, locking her mouth against his and somehow *climbed* onto his hips, fastening her thighs around him.

She kissed him ferociously. He struggled to carry her that way—still kissing—through to the lounge, where he tipped her into an armchair and ripped away her shoes, her tights, and her panties. There was no archaeologist's fantasy of hidden treasure, it was too urgent, too hot. He pulled her dress up around her waist to reveal her soft, tanned belly, and when she loosed his trousers for him, his cock sprang out angry and engorged, swollen like a bee-stung thing.

He put his tongue inside her cunt until he was dizzy with the smell of her. She grabbed a fistful of his hair, drawing his head back, locking mouths with him again, as if wanting to taste herself on his mouth.

She spoke through the kiss. "Come into me."

That was the first time. It had all happened the day before Maggie had made her accusation. After that he'd met Anita for long, searching lunchtime sessions almost every second or third day. God, the potency of those afternoons, thought Alex wistfully.

Where had it gone?

He stroked Anita's hair. "No," he lied again. "Maggie hasn't got it in her to suspect."

"I'm not so sure about that." Alex looked at her. "Bill's got the . . . problem you have."

"What problem? Can't get it up, you mean?" He snorted. "What's that got to do with anything?"

"I wonder if it's Maggie's doing."

"What?"

"Something she's doing to me, I mean. Something she's working. She knows about us. She hates me."

Alex jumped out of bed and buttoned on his shirt. "Hocus. I've seen what she does. Herb tea and a couple of joss sticks." He thought about Maggie's "dig here" prediction. He kissed Anita. "I've got to go back to work."

That afternoon Maggie was at Omega, unpacking new merchandise she'd ordered for the shop. Here she had a collection of talisman jewelery—metal discs on thin chains, the discs engraved with obscure glyphs and symbols. The silver bell rang behind her, and she was surprised to see Anita, dressed, as usual, as if she was looking for a seat at the opera. "Heard I'd find you here," she said brightly.

"Anita!"

"Haven't seen you in ages. Thought you might like some company."

Maggie flashed back on her flying vision, saw Anita's pink rump thrust in the air. "You've taken me by surprise." She found herself offering Anita a chair and a cup of tea, much against her instincts.

"I've been worried about you, Maggie."

"Why should you be worried?" Maggie went back to unpacking her boxes.

"Not just you. Both of you. I saw Alex the other day and he doesn't look well. You don't look well either."

"Really? I feel great."

"I know he wants you back. And he's been seeing rather a lot of that student from his dig, the one who—"

"Tania? Nice girl. Looks after the kids sometimes."

"You should go back to Alex. You two were made for each other."

"To be honest, I'm enjoying the space. I'm not sure I want to go back."

"But you miss the children terribly."

Maggie bit her lip and opened another box of talismans. Anita, at least, knew when to change the subject. "They look interesting. What are they?"

"Talismans."

"Protective powers?"

"No, you're thinking of an amulet. Here, this is an amulet. But these are talismans. They're like batteries. You wear a talisman to increase your powers; an amulet to ward off powers."

"You're really into this, aren't you. What's this one mean?"

"It doesn't 'mean' anything. It's a love talisman. It's made of copper because that's the metal of Venus. This is the symbol of the planet, and this one is of its guardian spirit."

"Charming. Can I buy one?"

Maggie hadn't yet priced the stock. She'd thought of selling them at around ten pounds. "Handmade. Thirty pounds, seeing as I know you."

Anita took out her checkbook. "Not cheap, are they?"

Over the site of the Maggie dig, Alex had finally managed to erect a rickety shelter to keep off the rain, and to arrange for a ditch to be dug, to drain the water from the new hole. Tania had been put in charge of the Maggie dig. He didn't actually say it was a reward for occasionally babysitting his children.

Meanwhile he had enough worries over the original project. An unearthed wall had collapsed; vandals had appeared one night and moved the markers on an entire section; and the dearth of positive results of the project was clouding its future. Alex was scratching his head, his mind not on the job, when Tania came up behind him. She was about to say something when he asked her if she could babysit that evening.

"I can't do it every night, Alex."

"Sure. I know. I mean, think about it, will you?"

"I'll think about it. Anyway, we've found something. You'd better come and look."

They'd excavated a length of narrow-bore lead pipe inside the dagger circle. It was disintegrating, but so far it was still in one piece. About three inches in length had been uncovered.

"Is it old?"

Alex looked closely at the white layer of oxidation on the surface of the pipe. "Oh, yes," he said. "Oh, yes. Let's have it out."

"Can you give me a lift if I come round tonight?" said Tania.

"I'm still keen to learn a few things," Anita said after Maggie had seen out a customer. She didn't seem to want to leave, and Maggie couldn't think how to get rid of her.

"What things?"

Anita gestured at the rows of shelves. "These things. Herbalism. Talismans."

"What do you want to know?"

"Lots of things. How to attract someone. How to repel someone. How to know what another person is thinking."

Maggie looked at her. Anita had some question she desperately wanted to ask, but clearly couldn't. She gave the impression she was waiting for Maggie to open the subject. Well, she could wait. "Not easy, those things."

"But you do have some knowledge."

"Very little."

"Don't bullshit me, Maggie Sanders. I'm not completely without insight myself, you know." Anita's eyes fizzed. "I know what you do."

Maggie's laugh was like the silver bell above the door. "I don't know what you're talking about."

"Alex is one thing. Bill is another. You'd better lay off."

Maggie dropped what she was doing and turned round. "Anita, hadn't you better explain what you're talking about? Because I'm getting confused."

But Anita, if she was about to explain, didn't get the opportunity, because Ash came in at that moment. "Afternoon, ladies!" he said, in his vaguely ironic and proprietary voice. Maggie introduced them.

"I thought there would be someone," Anita said, getting up to leave.

"Pardon?" said Ash.

"On the scene." Ash looked at Maggie, and then back at Anita, who said, "Do you make magic together? Silly me. Of course you do. Well, this is nice, but I have to go." Anita turned and left the shop.

Ash stared after her.

"Alex's lover," said Maggie.

"Oh," said Ash, as if that explained everything. "Sexy lady."

"Some people think so," said Maggie.

She held up her new talismans for him to see.

THIRTY

Maggie didn't give up trying to persuade Ash to fly with her, but he resisted stubbornly. She also tried to get him to talk about his own experience of flying, but all he would say was that it differed for different people, and that it was an experience he was most reluctant to repeat.

She could understand that. Her own recent efforts had succeeded in poisoning her. Despite exercising great care, it had taken her two full days to recover properly from the effects of flying. The nausea, headaches, night sweats, and bowel disorders had been a grim toll. But she was convinced that the preparation had been fundamentally correct. What had failed, she suspected, was something in her mental preparation, some inability to *transform* the poisonous properties of the flying ointment. She thought it was something Ash might know about.

Maggie stayed at his house occasionally, though not often. She'd made the mistake one night of giving over her best efforts to cure Ash of his impotence. The undertaking failed. She sucked him and squeezed him and teased him with her sharp fingernails and licked him from head to toe with her darting tongue, all to no avail. Though he pretended otherwise, she knew he was mortified. All she succeeded in doing was augmenting his anguish.

The craft she kept in reserve. Liz had given her strict instructions on that, and Maggie was too afraid of seeing the craft fail to do otherwise. But she continued to press Liz on the use of the flying ointment. She was whipped on by overwhelming curiosity, yet too afraid to go it alone again. While Ash held out against her, she turned to the diary, where she found another of Bella's entries on the subject of flying. It was not helpful, and it only redoubled her store of anxieties.

> *Last eve I did fly again and survived, but by the skin of my teeth, thanks be to Hecate, and ere I got what I wanted I was out of it. A. forced me into it though I'd not a mind for it. Why do I let her bully me? I'll have done with A. if there's a way for it. I'll kill her off, my dark sister, so I will. And though I don't feel poorly, the banishments being correct, my hands are all a-tremble at what I did see.*
>
> *Now at least I have some knowledge on A. for I seen HER dark sister and HER dark sister and so on, all in a line like tied with May blossom or something of the sort which I couldn't make out. But I'm done, and I'll not fly again, no.*

Maggie decided that Bella was a witch of little resolve, for there was another entry a few days later.

> *I did fly again last eve though I'd said I'd not and I did intend but that I had A. tormenting tormenting tormenting me that I'd not SHIFT and I'd not used the flying ointment three times in the same moon, so since she was on her back but carrying water, the moon that is, I went along and did. A. left me alone a bit then, as she knows how I am towards her of late.*
>
> *A. says I'm not discreet enough and she says I'll pay. But things are not as they were.*

None of it was much help, except that the references to banishments were intriguing. There had been at least one earlier reference to banishments and something about "preservation from demons." Maggie understood these demons to represent the physical discomforts she'd endured, and put the question to Ash.

"Don't ask me. She's probably referring to the banishing rituals."

"What are the banishing rituals?"

"I'm not telling you. It only encourages you to go away and do something dangerous."

"Isn't it more dangerous if I don't know?"

"There are all kinds of banishing rituals. The idea is that the ritual keeps away any undesirable forces and influences. Some of them are complicated procedures where you have to wave a sword at the points of a star and so on; others are just about the time of day it's safe to work—dawn, midday, dusk."

"Can you make up your own?"

"You shouldn't underestimate these rituals. It's something about keeping your intentions pure, and your mind unclouded."

"I'm going to fly again. If you won't join me, will you at least watch over me?"

Ash groaned.

More artifacts were turning up at the archaeological dig, but they raised more questions than answers. Tania and her colleagues had found a metal handle with a back plate and screw holes. Then they unearthed another piece of metal, square-shaped, again a plate with screw holes, but with a circular hole in its middle.

"These things were probably screwed to something wooden which has rotted," Alex told them. "See if you can find the screws. Also, take a section of earth and see if you can find anything in the soil which might suggest an imprint left behind by a wooden casket or something. Take it slowly."

They found a second metal handle. It almost certainly belonged to a large box of some kind. The function of the other fragment, the holed metal plate, was more difficult to guess. Then Alex saw Tania troweling at the earth, her hair scraped back and tied in a ponytail, bending over in her tight jeans. He had a lewd thought. He packed her off to fetch the five-foot length of lead pipe they'd already unearthed. When she came back, the lead pipe fitted snugly inside the diameter of hole in the metal plate.

Alex was supposed to have a lunchtime rendezvous with Anita that day. Instead he invited Tania to join him for a drink at the Malt Shovel. She accepted, and if she was surprised that he didn't invite the others, she said nothing.

He bought her lunch and a glass of white wine. "Can you come round tonight?"

"I don't want to babysit for you again, Alex."

"Not babysitting. I thought you might like dinner at my place. We could open a bottle of wine and *speculate* about what these objects might be." He narrowed his eyes on the word.

Tania had wide-open brown eyes, and they didn't blink. "That would be nice," she said.

Alex planned to have the kids in bed by eight o'clock and Tania in bed by eleven. He hoped she could do for him what Anita, lately, couldn't. He wondered, with vague feelings of guilt and suspicion, what Maggie would be doing that evening.

Ash had agreed, under protest, to supervise Maggie's flying experiment that evening. He made his study available, knowing how uncomfortable her bedsit could be. He also told her what he knew about "banishments" and fashioned a ritual for her, half from memory, half invented, but in any case a precise order of events which they rehearsed twice in order to get clear.

They'd agreed to begin the process at dusk. The flying ointment was prepared. Incense was ignited in Ash's study, already smouldering in brass bowls as the sky began to darken outside. Maggie began to feel the itching, the claw squeezing at her bowels as the hour approached. Why am I doing this? she asked herself again. What's driving me? A bitter taste lined her palate, as if the memory of her first flying experience was a metallic dust secreted in her saliva. Deposits of anxiety. Ash felt her jitters.

"You don't have to, you know. No one's making you."

"I don't know why; but I must."

"I'll make you some herb tea. Settle your stomach."

Maggie saw her chance. "Good idea. You sit down. I'll do it."

She made the herb tea, but not one Ash had ever drunk before. This was one of Liz's. She sweetened it with honey.

"Mmmmm. Good. What is it?"

"My secret," said Maggie. "I'm going to take my bath."

"Don't be long. It's almost dusk."

Maggie took a perfumed bath. She knew enough about aromatherapy by now to scent the gardens of heaven. She'd made her own bathing mixture from sea salt, rosemary, frankincense, and cypress. After drying, she anointed herself with the protective oils of hyssop and basil.

Liz had also passed on a love scent. The old woman had made it up for her and had given it to her with a wicked smile and instructions to use it sparingly. Maggie had to beg her to reveal the formula. It contained jasmine, red rose, a minute quantity of lavender, a bit of musk, and ylang-ylang oils.

She came from the bathroom wearing her dressing gown. Ash was in the study wearing a loose-fitting jogging suit. He lit tall red and white candles. The incense was a specific compound of sandalwood and rosemary, pungent and sweet, streaming from the brass bowls and coiling in the air like snakes. He saw she was wearing one of her engraved copper talismanic charms.

On the rug Ash had made a large circle out of a length of clean, white rope. The circle was broken at the two ends of the rope. "Just remember," he told her, "that a rope on the floor is not a magic circle, it's just a rope. But it prompts you to maintain the circle in your mind." Outside the circle stood a bottle of mineral water to answer the ravaging dryness of Maggie's first experiment. Inside the circle was a bowl of water for washing and the jar of flying ointment. Maggie gave Ash a nervous smile, slipped off her dressing gown and stepped into the circle. She sat cross-legged on the rug, naked but for her talisman. Ash closed the circle behind her by overlapping the two ends of the rope.

Maggie composed herself. She dipped her finger in the water and touched her forehead. Repeating the words Ash had taught her, she made her dedications to Hecate and asked for protection: *I have purified myself and my heart is filled with joy. I bring gifts of incense and perfume. I anoint myself with unguents to make myself strong.*

Outside the circle, Ash watched, fascinated. The perfume from the censers hung heavy in the room. Her hair was like burnished copper in the flickering candle light and her skin flushed rose-pink from her scented bath. Her eyes were half-closed as she repeated the ritual dedications, a slight bloom of perspiration on her brow. She reached for the jar of flying ointment and began to massage it into her wrists. She rubbed it into her temples, her ankles, round her throat and finally put her fingers inside her vagina.

"Wait!" said Ash. He slipped off his tracksuit, opened the rope, entered the circle and closed it behind him. He crouched down beside her, dipping his hand in the water and touching it to his brow, exactly as she had done.

"Ash! What are you doing?"

"Wherever it is you're going, I'm coming with you."

He repeated the words, massaging the flying ointment into his ankles, wrists and throat: *Grant me the secret longings of my heart.*

"No cheating," said Maggie. She put her fingers in the jar of ointment and smeared it on his cock, then reached behind him and pushed her forefinger up his anus. Ash gasped. Then she kissed him full on the lips and smiled grimly. "Now wait."

They sat in complete silence for ten or fifteen minutes before she began to feel the faint dizziness and the perspiration on her brow. There was a taste somewhere in the back of her sinuses reminding her of her first experience. Again a burning, in her bowels and throat and inside her vagina, the dry heat which made her want to retch. But this time she saw the heat as a silver light climbing up the column of her spine. She visualized the heat as a silver sword, tip of the blade extending, as if she could control it, transform it, neutralize its poisonous properties, make it useful. The shimmering blade of light climbed up her spine and inserted itself into the tenderest lobes of her brain. Suddenly there was a wild knocking inside her—from her heart, it must be the heart—and then a strontium flash inside her brain, shock waves producing a profound numbness throughout her body.

Suddenly her head swelled, balloonlike, racing outwards at speed until it jerked to a stop, two inches from the ceiling and the walls of the room. She touched the ceiling and her fingers stuck to it like suction pads. She realized she was on the ceiling, not hanging from it, but on it, inflated massively. Her head and hands were so large, she could see nothing of the room. Ash? Where was Ash? She blinked and saw Ash, also on the ceiling with her. He was looking back at her with hugely dilated eyes. Their bodies were gargantuan, obstructing all view of the study. She put a hand on Ash's arm and instantly there was an explosion as he shot away, a distance of a million miles in a fraction of a second, leaving a laser trail of light like a spaceship from a science-fiction movie.

Then another explosion as he was back with her again. She looked into his eyes. They were stormy black holes, clouds racing across them chased by high winds, arcs of light, magnesium flares, moving landscapes. She went into them, passed through them, and he was already inside there, waiting for her. They held hands and went hurtling through lilac skies, buffeted by hot spice winds, until they came to an abrupt stop.

They were together in that gray corridor she had visited before. She tried to speak to Ash but couldn't make words come. Gray and black shapes drifted past her vision, dissolving, reforming. Then the familiar face was beside her, the face that had helped her before, questioning without words. Maggie told her she had a gift to offer.

The face disappeared and in its place was a familiar scene within a parting in the gray corridor. It was Alex, raising Anita to her knees. Maggie didn't want to witness the event a second time. She waved it away and it changed. Alex was still there. This time he was at home. He was lying on his back, in bed. Tania was with him.

Nothing was happening. Tania was also lying on her back, sheets drawn up to her waist, her doe-eyes gazing at the ceiling.

"Perhaps you're trying too hard," she said.

Alex turned over and bit the pillow. Tania's sympathy was even more provoking than Anita's

Hitherto, the evening had gone well. Tania had turned the kids on to something called "Cowboy's Glory", which was nothing more exotic than the beans on toast Alex could never get them to eat. The children, by now accustomed to Tania's presence, had gone to bed without too much fuss. Alex's party-piece lasagne had turned out well, and the first bottle of claret had given way to a second. Then Amy had come downstairs at the wrong moment to find her daddy removing Tania's blouse and sucking Tania's brown nipple.

"What are you doing?" Amy had wanted to know.

After Amy had been settled again, Tania and Alex removed to the master bedroom. But there, despite a lot of spirited wrestling and imaginative foreplay, the point had somewhere been lost. And though his body couldn't give him an erection, his mind was still ablaze with lust. Alex didn't want Tania's sympathetic clichés or her banalities, he wanted a night of deep sex. The kind of sex that went on until the early hours, and then even further, the kind of sex that left you sore. He wanted Tania to help him prove that

Anita had a problem and he didn't; that Anita was being passed over by the angels of lust and he wasn't; that where Anita exuded something dispiriting and deflatory, he was still clean.

At first he felt this was some kind of punishment cooked up for him by Anita. Then he changed his mind and thought it was all Maggie's doing. Then he wanted to blame Tania. He felt angry at her, lying there staring up at the ceiling, but he couldn't think why. So he settled for a compound resentment of all three women, lying in the dark in a sullen, curdled silence; but of the three, mostly he cursed his wife.

Maggie came to on the floor, lying on her side inside the circle. The censers had burned out but the scent was still heavy in the air. The candles had burned down. Ash was lying next to her, one arm round her. Her throat was dry. There was a slight tingling throughout her body. She reached outside the circle for the bottle of mineral water and gulped it back. Then she noticed something about Ash.

"Ash! Ash!" She put the bottle to his lips and trickled mineral water into his mouth. He coughed and came round, blinking at her. He groaned.

"You okay?" he asked.

"I feel fine. Weird but fine. Really. What about you?"

"A bit shaky. Otherwise fine."

"Was it like your last time?" said Maggie.

"Nothing like it."

"Ash haven't you noticed anything?" Ash looked puzzled as he drew himself up. Maggie nodded at his lap. Ash had a monster erection. His cock was pointing straight up at the ceiling, engorged, the swollen head bobbing slightly as he looked down at it.

"Goddess! You've come back to me!" He sat on the floor, looking delirious with happiness. Maggie got up and placed a hand on each of his shoulders. She hoisted herself over him. "I owe this one," she said, gently lowering herself down the length of his shaft, "as a gift."

"Goddess!" he said. "Goodness!"

THIRTY-ONE

Sam's nightmares wouldn't go away. There was a fat rat scuffling in his dreams. Waking from these nightmares, he would see the old lady lurking in his room. The rat-rider. For when he awoke it was as if he came back from these bad dreams clutching a black fragment, a ragged swatch of the dream itself, and that torn piece of dream was the old woman. She could appear anywhere in the shadows of the unlit room. As the coat draped over the back of a chair. As the lampstand in the corner. Among his box of toys. Under the bed. Oh, she would fade shortly after he'd woken up, too soon for him to wake anyone else, but not before she'd let him know she was there.

Amy had returned from one of her mother's visits to Liz with a vague sense that she must protect her brother. Liz had hinted and tapped her nose in a frightening way, leaving her with a feeling of responsibility. *Remember me*, Liz had whispered, *remember me*. When Sam became hysterical at the thought of sleeping another night alone, Amy had surprised her father by offering to let Sam into her room. Jealous of her space, like so many growing girls, Amy had up until now always refused Sam the opportunity of even *looking* in her room.

Alex moved Sam's bed into Amy's room. Then one night Amy was awakened by the sound of Sam crying and pleading in his sleep. She saw him sit up in bed and gaze across the room, eyes wide open. Amy looked over and saw an old woman in black clothes, firmly embedded in the wall. Only her head, hands and feet were visible, protruding from the wall. The rest of her torso was elsewhere, seemingly sunk behind the wallpaper and plaster as if it was made of Styrofoam. She was eyeing Sam with a vicious smile.

"Sam," Amy whispered.

The smile on the old woman's face turned into a sneer. She rotated her head slowly, until she was looking, her face green and rancorous, at Amy. Then she faded.

Amy got out of bed and put the light on. Sam was whimpering. She climbed into bed beside him and cuddled him until he fell asleep, just as her mother and father had done with her when she was smaller.

In the daytime, Sam would never set foot in the cellar playroom alone. If he did go down there, he would cling to his sister, and if she tired of him, he would cling to Dot's collar.

One day, in the excitement of a game with Amy, he almost forgot his troubles in the playroom. As he raced across the room, the rug slipped from under his feet and he cracked his head. The rug had shifted to reveal the face, more prominent than before, and more malevolent. The rust-colored stain bubbled moisture, glistening on the bare concrete as they looked on.

Amy touched the stained floor, and the rust color transferred to her finger. "It's wet," she said quietly.

She looked at Sam. He seemed very small.

"Wait here."

"No," said Sam.

"Dot's here. You'll be all right."

Sam hooked his hand under Dot's collar and slithered behind her. Amy ran up the stairs and into the kitchen. Sam heard her drawing a stool across the floor. Then he heard a cupboard opening, a rustling, and Amy climbing down from the stool. In a few moments she was back in the playroom.

She had something in her mouth. Sam and Dot watched as Amy stood before the face in the floor. She stood over it in silence, as if she was thinking hard. Her arms hung lifeless at her sides, her head was bowed slightly, drawn into her shoulders. She stayed like that for a long time.

Then she pushed her tongue out of her mouth. Sam glimpsed a small object sitting on her tongue, before she drew her head back and spat it violently at the face on the floor. The object landed in the middle of the face.

Nothing happened. Dot sneezed, but Amy stood her ground. Then the face began to blister and bubble in tiny spots. It peeled back, like old paint, and within five seconds the stain had disappeared. In the middle of the floor was a single dried bean.

"What did you do?" said Sam, still hanging onto Dot's collar.

Amy picked up the bean and settled the rug back into place.

Alex appeared in the doorway. "You kids are too quiet for my liking. Everything all right, Amy?"

"Yes," she said, pushing past him.

Sam followed her out, and so did Dot.

THIRTY-TWO

"Listen to this," said Maggie. She and Ash were lying in bed, candles flickering, empty wine bottles gathering in number, sound of wind and rain lashing at the window. She was reading to him from Bella's diary, pieces she'd read herself many times.

A. drives me, she drives me and drives me, my wicked dark sister. Always having me do the next thing and the next thing until I know I shall lose my wits. I'm out of patience with her but she's too strong for me, and knows it, and she does so keep on at me until she has her way. I am weak, for I know that without me she can do nothing. So why do I let her drive me?

Last night it was on the heath and I performed the shifting, and it has done nothing but left my wits in shreds and I can hardly hold this pen for trembling. No, I'll not talk of it, not even in this secret journal.

Only my dark sister knows.

Oh, the blackbird.

And A. says I'm too careless with my coming and going. But I say to her that she is the one who drives me hither and thither. A. says I'll pay for indiscretion, but I've told her if I pay, then she'll pay too, and she knows it.

All this because I give a herb scrying and a love simple to

one who lives near and came asking for it. What can we do,
when they ask us?

Maggie closed the diary. "Why was she so paranoid, do you
think?"

"Old Liz will tell you enough stories to answer that. There
was a wise woman near her who was thought to have dried up a
spring. When she died the villagers pulled her cottage down brick
by brick. This wasn't the middle ages, this was forty years ago.
She probably had reason to be paranoid."

"Who?" said Maggie. "Bella? Or the mysterious A.? You said
you thought of them as the same person."

"I do. A. is Bella's alter-ego, I assume. She gives her the excuse
to go and do the things she really wants to do. The dark stuff,
the things she can't face in herself."

"You mean Bella was a schizophrenic?"

"I suppose so. Something like that. Maybe not barking mad,
but certainly hiding behind this A. character she's always complaining about. See how she always blames what she does on A.?"

"I don't see it like that. I think A., whoever it was, was another witch. A separate person altogether. Leading Bella on."

"The way that diary leads you on?"

Maggie wasn't happy about that remark. "What are you getting at?"

"Never mind."

"No. Say what you were thinking."

"It was what we were saying about paranoia. You're steeping
yourself in a lot of heavy craft these days. If there's one thing I
do know, it's that the craft has also got a dark sister, and her name
is paranoia."

"I'm old enough to know the difference."

"Really? I know you've been working something against Anita
and Alex."

Maggie was surprised. "How did you know?"

Ash produced a strip of leather with five knots tied in it. Each of the knots was signed with a crude alphabetical representation. "These five letters wouldn't add up to the name of anyone we know?"

"Ash!" said Maggie, not at all annoyed. "You've been rooting through my handbag!"

"I'm getting very fond of you, Maggie, but ligatures? Just be careful. It's a wrong path."

Maggie looked away. The rain and the wind beat against the bedroom window.

Whatever Ash's objections, he swallowed them and indulged Maggie. She practically took over the business at Omega for him, and trade flourished in her hands. What could he say? If he lost some of his old customers, he gained three times as many new ones. Maggie also had a shrewd idea of how far Ash's integrity could be stretched. There was a lot of junk she could have stocked—bogus products carrying extravagant claims, miracle cures, lucky silver pixies—which she didn't. She respected his "what you see is what you get" philosophy on merchandising, and never tried to breach it.

He indulged her for what she'd done for him. And Maggie found in him a companion and lover who was excited by spontaneity. If they wanted to wake up at a ridiculous hour and go walking by a lake or in the woods, they did so. One time they drove in a thick night fog to a flight of canal locks, just to hear what the place sounded like when you couldn't see it. Dawn, midnight, and dusk. These were the goddess hours, the moments imbued with magic capability. Sometimes, however, even Ash balked. "No, Maggie, no! I'm not going out on the heath on a night like this. Listen to that wind!"

"But that's what Liz meant about flying indoors. It's why we felt like we were crashing into the ceiling. Next time we have to fly outside."

"Not in the middle of winter, we don't. Go back to sleep."

But Maggie lay in the dark quite unable to sleep. The wind outside, far from deterring her from a visit to the heath, only stirred something in her breast. She looked tenderly at Ash sleeping beside her, but she heard voices in the wind. Something was calling softly from the heath, and from the hills beyond the heath.

She did not know what was calling her, or if the voices were all inside her head. But it was beautiful, eerie, a low chorus of women's voices. One of us, they sang, you have always been one of us. It pulled her like the moon pulling on the tides. She was approaching her period; she felt the mysterious blood connection. How could she tell Ash? He was a man. How could she ever tell him about voices he couldn't possibly hear and was never meant to hear?

There was a rumble of thunder. She knew it was a night for her to go. She slipped out of bed and tiptoed to the window. Ash woke up, blinking sleepily at her. She kissed his lips. "I won't be long. Don't worry."

"Not flying, are you?"

"No. It's a Macbeth night. I just want to feel it a little."

Ash groped for his shirt. "I'll come." She wanted to tell him it was a girls' only night, but she was touched by his loyalty. It was the allegiance of a sleepwalker.

Ash drove steadily toward the heath through the rain. There was the first spear of lightning. The rains lit up against the headlights, swirling silver sparks.

"What is it?" said Maggie.

They were about halfway to the heath. Ash blinked into his rearview mirror. "For a minute I thought somebody had been following us. But it's nothing."

"And you said I was paranoid."

They reached the heath and parked the car. The trail was pitch-black, but by now they knew their way in the darkness. The rain had stopped. The storm had passed overhead, but there was still the distant rumble of thunder and the occasional fork of lightning. The afterbreath vapors of the fission and the smell of ozone touched everything. The earth was fingered with mist. Maggie breathed deep. She felt her powers magnified, quadrupled. She danced along the path ahead of Ash.

"The goddess! Hecate! All around us! She passed by this way! Smell her!"

The grass was heavy with rain. The standing stones were wet, glistening with water droplets, exuding their own granite odors. Maggie walked round the circumference of the circle, inside, brushing her hands against the nine stones. Then she stepped quickly out of her clothes. She pressed her naked shoulders and her thighs to the wet, erect granite, luxuriating in the suck of heat from skin to rough stone and the transmission of cold from stone to bone.

"Come on, Ash! Feel the rain between your toes!"

"It's fucking freezing!" he countered. But she was on him, pulling his sweater over his head. Giggling, the pair fell to the ground, rolling in the wet grass. Maggie got up and danced away. There was another feeble flash of lightning, seeming to come from behind one of the stones. Ash stood up and stared into the darkness.

"Did you see something, Ash?" Maggie was breathless. She put her hand on his arm.

Ash continued to gaze into the blackness. "I don't think that last flash was lightning."

"What do you mean?"

"I don't know."

THIRTY-THREE

It was the day of the custody hearing. Both parties had made their visits to the Court Welfare Officer, and both parties concluded that the Court Welfare Officer was biased against them. A report was duly compiled and a date set for the hearing in chambers. To attend, Alex dusted off the only suit he possessed and tied his tie in a strangling, tiny knot. Maggie put on too much makeup and wore high heels.

Briggs for Alex and Montague for Maggie. Morton Briggs exuded an easy confidence which Alex didn't share. Alice Montague did her best to put Maggie at ease. "Judge Bennett," she said. "That's very good for us." Each side was introduced to and interviewed by their respective barristers and the case was up and running by ten A.M.

While the Welfare Officer's inconclusive report was being read out to the court, Alice Montague, sitting next to Maggie, whispered in her ear, "Apparently your husband's not calling anyone as a witness. Any idea why?"

Maggie shrugged. She had no idea whether it was significant or otherwise. She herself was calling her childminder who, despite recent difficulties, had guaranteed to testify to Maggie's qualities as a fit parent. Maggie's worst fears were that Alex would drag in Anita Suzman, programmed to say hateful things about her ability as a mother; but it looked as though Alex was happy to proceed without witnesses.

However he may have looked, Alex was not happy about much at all. He was beginning to squirm at what he'd done since first receiving the summons, and he was even more nervous about the possible consequences of his actions. But Maggie had started this. She'd elected for the legal path! He'd pleaded, appealed, and begged; but she was not to be diverted.

So be it. Alex had actually uttered those archaic words aloud one day, an oath resonating with biblical weight. So be it.

It was, he'd decided, time to regain control. Things had got out of hand and now he was reining in. Emotional appeal had failed, familial affection had lost its way. He had a terrible feeling that Maggie's powers (and only now was he beginning to see them as powers, female, dissipatory, undisciplined) were on the ascendant, and their single tendency was disruptive. He knew he must meet her head-on with cold, hard logic. He saw how the brittle masculine lines of the law could serve him and not her.

Maggie, after all, had taken the decisive step on a road where he could match her yard for yard. He would fight to keep household and children by all means available. No, he wasn't happy about this. He wasn't *happy* about any of it. But he had switched off the emotional response and had abandoned himself to a close study of the rules of play.

And the rules of play had a habit of taking over from the original reasons for the engagement. Maggie soon realized why Alex wasn't troubling to call witnesses, and so did Alice Montague. Alex's barrister presented a large cardboard box containing a collection of small jars, bottles, and packets of herbs.

"Your Honor," said the barrister, "what we have here is a collection of herbs, hedgerow plants, oils, incenses—all of dubious medicinal value—which Mrs. Sanders gathered together when she became obsessed with notions of healing, witchcraft, and other practices which I can only describe as occult."

Maggie felt Alice Montague stiffen beside her. Alex had lied when he'd said he'd burned all of her herbs. She tried to look at him, but he was gazing straight ahead. The judge, who had not spoken a word and seemed not to be listening, took his spectacles off, as if the gesture would help him understand more clearly. "Occult?" he said.

"Yes, Your Honor, occult. It seems Mrs. Sanders discovered an old diary composed by some eccentric former occupant of the family home. She became obsessed with the bizarre remedies and treatments suggested by the diary, so much so that she began a campaign of experiments on her own children."

The judge put his spectacles on again and looked hard at Maggie. Then he began poking around in the cardboard box, sniffing at some of the containers almost theatrically. "You are married, aren't you, Mr. Boyers?" he said to Alex's barrister.

"As Your Honour knows."

"And doesn't your wife keep a spice rack in her kitchen?"

"Indeed she does, Your Honor, but—"

"And does that make her an inferior mother to your children, would you say?"

"Indeed not, Your Honor, though I must say—"

"And haven't you ever rubbed a dock leaf on a nettle sting, Mr. Boyers?"

"Most certainly I have, though—"

"Though what, Mr. Boyers?"

Maggie was astonished. The judge was teasing the barrister, giving him the run-around. She looked at her solicitor, and Alice Montague winked.

"Though what I would say, Your Honor, is that—"

"And did you not find the application of said dock leaf to said nettle sting an effective remedy?"

"Yes, Your Honor, most effective."

"And if your wife told your children to use this method of relief, would that make her a bad mother? No, Mr. Boyers, it won't do." The judge turned his nose up at the contents of the box and waved it away. "Can we have this removed?"

Alex's barrister lifted something else from his bench and handed it to one of the court ushers. "If Your Honor would care to study this, then I assure Your Honor that he might look at the contents of the box in a somewhat different light."

The case practically closed itself from that moment. What the barrister had given the judge was a photograph, taken at night, showing Maggie romping naked on the heath inside a stone circle. She appeared to be dancing, and the expression on her face suggested some delirium. In the background, smiling demoniacally (it might be assumed), was a bearded man, Ash, also partially naked.

The custody hearing which would normally be expected to last a full day was over by lunchtime. Alex was awarded a residence order, with no variation of the current contact arrangements.

"The bastard's been having me followed!" cried Maggie outside the courtroom.

"That's right," said Alice Montague. She was trying to comfort her.

"But isn't that illegal in itself? Following people?" Maggie's eye makeup had run. Her face was like a cracked painting. "Surely it's illegal to follow people."

Ms. Montague shook her head. "He must have commissioned a private investigator. That photograph—"

"It wasn't how it looked! We were only—"

"You don't have to explain anything to me, Maggie. At least try to comfort yourself with the fact that the judge awarded you good contact with the children."

"Isn't there anything I can do?"

"See your children as often as you can. Things might change. Maybe in the future you'll be able to work out some improved agreement."

"Agreement? After the way he's behaved today? I couldn't care if he stops breathing! You're married to someone all this time and you think you know the best and the worst of them. But you don't! You're living with a stranger. How could he have done this to me, whatever the arguments? It's unforgivable! I don't want an agreement! I want him dead for doing this!"

"Try not to be bitter, Maggie."

Bitterness. Bitterness was not something to be buttoned on and off like a coat. It was a cancerous spot, like a lump in the chest or a stone in the throat. It deposited a taste in the mouth which wouldn't wash away. Maggie shook hands with Alice Montague and left the building, her high heels clicking angrily down the stone steps to the busy street.

"Maggie." It was Alex, waiting outside for her.

She paused briefly and flashed him a look before marching away, her coat flapping in the wind. Alex was frightened by what he'd seen in her eyes.

"Try not to be bitter, Maggie." This time it was Ash, offering the same ineffective advice. Maggie had gone back to Omega, and he'd shut up shop to spare time to try and console her.

"Everyone tells me not to be bitter. But it's easy for you to say that."

Maggie sat looking oddly composed. But she didn't deceive herself. She knew if she didn't project a composure of sorts she would break something. She had to shut down her feelings, but even so she felt them working, agitating, trembling at hideous depth, like molten lava. Some rage inside her was loose and shifting, dissociating from herself.

"Yes, it's easy for me to say that," said Ash. "But it's also easy for you to give in to the kind of thoughts you're having right now."

"We can't all be so noble."

Ash let that one go. He handed her a cup and saucer. She hadn't looked him in the eye since she'd come into the shop. He was a little afraid of her. The appearance of her anger was too cold. "Look, you've lost a legal fight, but you've got access to the children. Think positive. There are other ways you can make this work for you."

"That's right." She suddenly turned to face him. "There are other ways."

"No," said Ash, realizing. "That's not what I meant. I was talking about using your access time creatively. Getting the most out of it. I know what you're thinking, and you'd better put away those ideas right now."

"A lot of other ways."

"I tell you, Maggie, it's a wrong path. A wrong path. It'll come back on you. Are you listening to me, Maggie? Maggie?"

THIRTY-FOUR

Liz was kneeling over her doorstep, whetting a wooden-handled knife on the stone threshold. It was a knife so old it had lost half its blade width on a lifetime's sharpening. A low, throaty singing emanated from her as she worked. Her voice wobbled with the vibrato of age, but Liz could still hold to a melody.

> *She become a rose*
> *A rose all in the wood*
> *And he become a bumblebee*
> *And kissed her where she stood*
>
> *She become a hare*
> *The hare run down the lane*
> *And he become a greyhound dog*
> *And fetched her home again.*

A shadow fell over her threshold and she looked up.
"Here she is."
"Here I am."
"Know'd you was coming." Liz went on whetting her knife on the step. "Where's that lovely little gel? Ain't you brung her to see me?"

Maggie stepped over her and went inside to make a brew. "I've lost her. I've lost both the children." Liz stopped what she was doing.

"Lost? What's all this talk of lost?"

Maggie bit her lip and explained the consequences of the court decision.

"Why," said Liz, "that's not lost. You proper turned me over when you said as they was lost. I thought they was dead. Nothing and no one's lost until they're dead."

"I want them back, Liz!"

"And so you shall have them back. But not by bleating about it, you won't."

"Will you help me?"

"I'll not."

"But you could, Liz. You could help me get my children back."

"And I've told you I'll not. I knows what you've got a mind to do, and it's nowt to do wi' me, but I'll tell you this: stay off of it."

"You don't know what I've got in mind. Why do you say you do?"

Liz straightened her bent back and waved the knife at Maggie. "I know more than you think. You mark it. More than you think. I knows what you put on that husband o' yours, and on his fancy woman. That's surprised you, hasn't it? And you think yourself clever; but never mind, because that was no more than justice. Justice. But this other, it's wrong path. Now I've told you and I'll say no more. But you mark it."

Maggie looked away. In one sense she was surprised by what Liz had known about her activities, but in another way she'd always recognized that Liz had a sight beyond her own.

"Did you mark it?" Liz demanded.

"Yes," said Maggie, like a sulky schoolgirl.

"Good. Now fetch my coat and we'll go for a blow in the

fields. For I don't like you coming in my house with all this on you. I don't like it one bit."

They walked along the edge of a sparse copse and across a field. Liz's old collie trotted ahead of them.

"Spring not far off," said Liz. "Smell it?"

"Yes. It's in the air."

"Not in the air. In the ground. In the growing. That's what you smell. Feel better for a blow?"

"Yes, I do feel better."

"Blow away some o' that what's a-settled on your shoulder." She pointed her stick at a plant with a yellow flower not unlike a dandelion head. "Coltsfoot. Earliest I ever seen coltsfoot. Weather's a-changing. Get me some o' that. Good for the lungs. Coughs. Very good."

Maggie stooped and picked the plant by the root. "What do you know about shapeshifting?"

"Psssshhhhttttt!" went Liz. She still hated anything mentioned openly.

Maggie ignored her. "That diary of mine, the one I told you about. It mentions it. It says that, well, it's the way to true power. Is that so?"

Liz walked on, tight-lipped.

"I mean, have you ever done it?"

Liz stopped. "Wouldn't tell you if I had. And there's an end to your questions, ain't it?"

"But why not?"

"I don't know who you might tell. You might be a blabber-mouth for all I know."

"Look here, Liz. All the time I've been coming to you I haven't said a word about anything to anyone. And if you know half what you claim to know, you'd know that."

Liz chuckled to herself, and flicked her stick in the direction of a wooden stile. "Let's head up there. You can collect me some firewood as we go."

Maggie was accustomed, and never objected, to being used as a packmule on these walks. She collected a few logs and stacked them under her arm.

"No no no," said Liz. "You still don't know your wood. That 'un won't burn. A one should know her wood. Here:

> *Oak shall warm you well*
> *That's old and dry*
> *Logs of pine do sweetly smell*
> *But sparks will fly*
> *Birch will burn too fast*
> *Chestnut scarce at all*
> *Hawthorn logs be good to last*
> *Cut them when leaves fall*
> *Holly log it burns like wax*
> *You may burn 'em green*
> *Elm logs like to smouldering flax*
> *No flame to be seen—*

Are you listening?"

"Yes, Liz."

"No you ain't. You're letting things play. And you ain't a-listening."

Liz leaned and Maggie hoisted herself on the stile, and they were quiet for a few minutes. Then Liz said something Maggie didn't understand.

"I was thinking how I might tell it you all. I was even thinking how I might give you the line when my time comes. And that can't be long. But I don't know, gel; there's a hardness in you of late. Today you're as tight as a drum, and I don't know." Liz looked off into the trees.

Maggie said, "But I only wanted to ask you if it was possible. This shapeshifting. To ask you if you'd ever . . ."

She tailed off because this time it was Liz who wasn't listening. She was gazing at a blackbird perched on an elm branch not six feet away. Perfectly still, its feathers were sleek and black, its beak a brilliant orange. Its head was cocked, its eye fixed on Liz's eye; or maybe Liz's brilliant gaze had skewered the bright eye of the bird. Nothing needed to be said. Maggie had her answer. The old woman had *shifted* in her time. She knew the way, and she had the wisdom of transcendent experience. She had tasted the flame many, many times.

The blackbird flew away.

"Put this thing out of your mind," said Liz, "and concentrate on them children o' yours. I'm worried you're bringing a shadow over them. Who knows. Maybe it's better if you don't see 'em for a while. But if you really want them back, then go and talk to him. Talk. That's the proper way. Folk must talk."

Liz moved off without looking back to see if Maggie was following. Maggie trailed at a short distance. They climbed the gentle incline of a hill, and Liz seemed lost in deep thought.

"Come to me on Saturday morning," she said at last, "and I'll give you what you need for the shifting."

"Shall I bring the children?"

"Leave 'em where they are."

"I thought you wanted to see Amy?"

"And I said not."

Maggie didn't argue.

THIRTY-FIVE

Fifteen miles. It was fifteen miles from Church Haddon to town, and then fifteen miles back again. That, she considered, was a tidy step, and with her arthritis it might even finish her off. But it had to be done.

Old Liz had already covered the first three miles and was stroking her stick through the hedgerow. "Come out, felon. Come out, old uncle harry." The mugwort was common, but not being in flower for some months yet, it was difficult to locate. She was in sore need of it, if she was going to survive this hike. "Come out, felon."

Three times already Liz had detected the plant, but she'd rejected each specimen. "There, there, uncle."

Liz had woken that morning, dawn's light breaking in through the uncurtained window, certain that Maggie's children were in danger. "Amy and Sam," she'd muttered, hauling herself out of bed. "We must look to Amy and Sam. Yes."

At times like these, she'd thought ruefully, she could have done with a ride in Ash's car, or even on someone's motorcycle. Those engines, she would have been the first to admit, were better than any amount of craft. Certainly she could have telephoned Ash; she had his number on a scrap of paper somewhere. But if she were to involve Ash, then he would tell Maggie, and all would know and all would be known and she might just as well stay at home.

No.

She would have to walk.

That fifteen miles and back would have been a trifling thing in her younger days. She would have taken it at a clip. But this arthritis and this bad hip, well, it held her up. And she didn't have a lot of time.

Old Liz didn't even consider the matter of breaking her appointment with Maggie. These other things were too important. Maggie could make her own way. Anyway, it wasn't for Maggie she was doing this, it was for those children. Liz had woken up vexed by what she'd seen in those children.

Liz had known Maggie would bring trouble from that very first afternoon she'd arrived at the house. What power she'd seen in her that day, Maggie hovering on the threshold, unaware that Liz was watching from behind, what potential! For a moment Liz had been afraid, surprised and afraid. She'd had to stoop down and pick a bit of something that day, to keep Maggie back until she'd got her full measure. Then she caught on how Maggie had no idea of her own capacity; it was all corked, but like a cork leaking under pressure of volatile, fizzing elements. For a moment Liz's heart had leaped, thinking Nature had sent her a little sister; but then she'd had to quiet herself with the realization it was impossible.

Maggie hadn't got a clue! And that made her a danger. One voice inside Liz told her to have nothing to do with the girl Ash had sent her; but another part of her had spoken up, and yes, she'd seen the fine qualities in Maggie; and didn't she herself have a need of at least someone?

A little sister, to make the pass? No, Maggie wouldn't do for that. But for Liz, there were no others of potential in sight. Not a one. And there was no greater crime, no uglier sin than to go to the grave without having passed on *the know*. This was sacred when all things were profane, and as Liz knew in her aching limbs and in the groaning of her joints, every day the Old Enemy drew ever nearer. No, Maggie could not be the one to take the pass, but there were other possibilities. The next best thing was to give her a bit of instruction. It wasn't enough, it wouldn't satisfy, but what else was there?

Liz was eighty-three years old. She didn't want to guess how many more years might be hers. But it had gnawed at her for a long time now that she might die never having found a little sister. Was it a punishment, she wondered, for the misdemeanors of her early years? She would rather have faced the torments of any Christian hell than allow that to happen.

So when Maggie had first appeared, Liz saw a rightness in it, a compromise, and also a sign that she herself was not much longer for this world, and she resigned herself to the idea. But then the shadow had crept over Maggie, and Liz had begun to have her doubts. *The know* was for those who struggle with purity of heart. Wasn't that how she'd been taught? The craft was not to be sullied by sourness of motive. Even with right intention, the path was fraught and dangerous.

But thankfully she was able to see past Maggie. Past and beyond. There was hope, like a crystal glimmering in the dark hedgerow shadows, and Liz could see it.

"Come out, felon herb!"

Liz found a young plant under the hedgerow. It was leaning northwards, a detail that had her nodding with satisfaction. She drew a sharp penknife from her pocket and unearthed the mugwort by the root. Then she sat down on the grass.

It was still early. The gray clouds were streaked with bands of white light, and the day could go either way. Liz stripped the fibrous roots from the plant with her knife and cleaned the stem with her spittle. Then she took a small vial of oil from her pocket. Pouring the yellow oil, she massaged it into the stem with her leathery fingers. The stem turned brown and the sap bubbled to the surface. Liz looked about her to make certain no one was watching, and kicked off her shoes.

She cut a chunk of the stem with a knife and put it in her mouth, chewing vigorously while removing her thick socks. Still chewing, she stripped the leaves and rubbed them vigorously into the soles of her feet. When this was done she stuffed the crushed leaves into her shoes, saving a few which she rammed into her pocket. Then she put her shoes and socks back on, stood up and set off again.

Maggie arrived at Liz's cottage at around ten o'clock. She pushed at the door handle, expecting it to swing open, but was surprised to find the door locked. Liz's collie barked at her from behind the door, but she knocked anyway. There was no answer.

Odd that Liz should have locked her door; Liz *never* locked her door. Even when she went out on one of her walks across the fields she tended to leave it ajar. She had no fear of burglars or intruders, and, as she said herself, she had "nothing worth pinching, 'cept a bucket of shit in the outhouse." Maggie knocked again. Getting no response, she stepped over to the window to take a peek inside.

It had been inconvenient for her to visit Liz this morning. The old woman had insisted she shouldn't bring the children with her, and this had necessitated a telephone conversation with Alex to change the standing arrangement. Since the hearing, Maggie had been stiff and formal with Alex, collecting and returning the children exactly as agreed, even though Alex claimed to want to be generous and flexible with the arrangement.

Alex, of course, now wanted them to be friends. He wanted everything to be civilized. Whenever she called at the house, Maggie accepted his invitations to have a coffee, but thwarted his efforts at conversation with the frozen hostility of perfect good manners. She answered his questions with the briefest of replies and deliberately failed to pose any of her own. She would look at her watch intermittently, and made transparent excuses in order

to leave. She played the part of the stranger who disguises bore-
dom with studied politesse.

Today she'd had to break the formality by asking Alex if he
would agree to changing her day with the children. Even though
he'd arranged to see Anita, Alex was perfectly amenable. He was
happy, he said, for Maggie to see the children any time she wanted.

Now Liz wasn't here. Maggie squinted through the windows
at the gloomy interior of the cottage. Her first thought was that
Liz might be ill, but Maggie could see her empty bed in the room
adjacent to the kitchen, its crocheted blankets folded neatly. Liz
never used the upper floor of the cottage; she slept in a bed downstairs to save her arthritic legs.

The dog continued to bark. No, Liz was out. Maggie went
back to her car. She would sit and wait. Liz had no transport; she
couldn't have gone far.

When Anita Suzman drove past the Sanders' home that morning
she was disappointed to see Amy, Sam, and Dot playing in the
driveway. Saturday was Maggie's time with the children; Anita
had arranged to spend an uncluttered hour or two with Alex. But
she was also puzzled to see an old woman, apparently watching
the children from the gateway. As she drove past, she felt an
irrational thrill of concern for Amy and Sam. Something seemed
amiss.

Anita was discreet enough always to park her conspicuous
bright red Cabriolet two streets away. She locked her car and
walked back to the house. As she approached, she could see the
old woman still in the gateway. Anita hung back to watch.

The grizzled old woman was beckoning to Sam. He didn't
seem to want to go at first, then he stepped over to her. Amy and
Dot had disappeared. The old woman stooped over Sam. She
placed her hands on his shoulders, and was whispering in his ear.
Then she produced something from the folds of her black skirts

and hung it round Sam's neck. Sam tried to lift it off, but she pressed it back on him, hiding it inside his T-shirt.

Anita didn't like the look of what was happening. She walked toward the gate, quickening her pace. The old woman, spotting her approach, stiffened and walked smartly away in the opposite direction. Anita watched her turn a corner and out of sight.

"Sam, come here."

Sam was playing with the string round his neck. Anita pulled it from inside his T-shirt. Dangling from the gray string was a neat little cloth sachet. Anita stretched out a hand, wanting to take a closer look, but Sam pulled away from her. "Amy!" he shouted, running back up the path in search of his sister. "Amy!"

Anita followed him round to the back of the house, and stepped in through the back door. She found Alex up to his elbows in washing-up suds. She brushed her lips against his cheek.

"Who was that old woman outside?"

"What woman?" said Alex, drying his hands.

"Outside the gate. Talking to Sam." She went through to the lounge and made herself at home.

"I've no idea. Shall I go and look?"

"She's gone. I think I chased her away."

"What was she doing?"

Anita never answered because the telephone rang. It was Maggie. She'd discovered she wasn't as busy as she'd expected, and wanted to know if she could have the kids after all.

"Sure," said Alex. "No problem at all. When do you want to pick them up? About an hour? Fine. See you then." He put the phone down. "That bitch is playing games with me."

"Why do you say that?" The old woman was forgotten.

"First she arranges to have the children today, which is why I said I could see you. Then she phones this morning, desperately sorry, can't have them. Now she wants them again. She's testing my patience."

"I'm sure she's not, Alex."

"Yes, she is. Every time she comes here she does it. Very polite. Nothing to say. No emotion. No talk. Nothing."

"What do you expect? She's still furious with you, and I don't blame her."

Alex looked at her. No matter what time of day it was, Anita always looked as if she was about to hit town. She was utterly desirable in her tight-fitting black dress, black tights and heels. Her lips were glossed and her eyes painted. She was fork-bendingly beautiful. He put a hand into her honey-blond hair and kissed her.

"You can hide upstairs when she comes," he said.

"No, I'm not staying. That's what I've come to talk to you about."

"What are you saying?"

"It's over. It has to be."

Alex looked away.

"Bill suspects something," Anita went on, "and I think we should quit while we're ahead. Anyway, you know it was running out of steam, don't say it wasn't."

Alex wasn't saying anything.

"It was good while it lasted, Alex. It was good, wasn't it? Wasn't it, Alex?"

THIRTY-SIX

Sunday morning Maggie was back at her bedsit. She was lying awake in bed, staring at the ceiling and thinking about Ash. The previous day, after failing to find Liz, she'd spent a few hours with the children before returning to Ash's house. There she'd made a big mistake.

"Ash, I intend to get my children back by any means."

"Please! Not again, Maggie."

"By any means."

Ash was making her a casserole. He stopped chopping vegetables. "I can't argue with you while I'm cooking. All that confusion, it goes straight into the cooking. And then you eat it. Did you know that?"

Maggie knew that. "You said to me you'd be a friend whatever happened, Ash. I believed you when you said that."

"And I meant it. And I always will. But to be a friend to you now is to tell you to drop this stupid idea. These methods will not bring your children back to you. They will only poison your own mind. If you want them back, you have to go and talk to Alex and work at it."

"I can't believe I'm hearing this!"

"Maggie, if you try to work something against Alex you might even succeed in hurting him. But you've forgotten the first principles of this business. It's wrong path. It will return on you three-fold. I believe that. It's the scariest thing about it."

"I don't intend any direct harm."

"I know exactly what you intend! You want to try this shapeshifting because you think it will bring you access to the children and some kind of special influence over them. I've been to the places your mind is going, Maggie! I know what I'm talking about!" Ash collected up the chopped vegetables and threw them all away. The meal was ruined before it had so much as simmered.

"It can't hurt anyone, Ash. I'm going to ask you one more time to help me."

"Are you deaf?"

"I need your help. Please don't let me down when I need you most."

"I said count me out!"

"Ash, if you're not with me, you're against me."

Ash looked stung. He grabbed her arm. "Don't try to lay that on me, Maggie. Don't you ever!"

It was their first dispute, and it was deeply acrimonious. She felt betrayed.

The door swung open and Kate entered the room. She was holding a copy of the *Sunday World*, a tabloid with a nasty editorial line and a high circulation. "Have you seen this?" Kate hissed.

Maggie sat up in bed as Kate laid the pages before her. It was a double-page spread, with a banner headline trumpeting COVENS OF ENGLAND. There was a large photograph of a smiling, pleasant but dotty-looking elderly woman in a Queen of the Nile headdress. She claimed to be—or the newspaper proclaimed her to be—Empress of the Witches of England. There were other photographs. One of them clearly depicted Maggie and Ash frolicking naked within a stone circle. Maggie was named, Ash was named, and Ash's shop in the Gilded Arcade was named.

"But where did they get the pictures?" Kate wanted to know.

Maggie groaned.

THIRTY-SEVEN

Spring Equinox, 21 March, a Monday morning. Alex was struggling to get the children ready for school and childminder, chivvying, coaxing, bullying, rummaging for clean clothes which weren't there because he hadn't washed them, dishing up a dog's breakfast because he hadn't shopped for a week, trying to let the real dog out and bring the milk in, to iron a blouse for Amy, pour a mug of tea for himself, find the minder's overdue cash, locate Amy's schoolbook which she couldn't go without . . .

Alex wasn't coping.

Anita had had enough of him. Tania, tired of playing the surrogate mother, had refused to help him all weekend. And the children's real mother had deserted him.

Maggie! Where are you, Maggie? For God's sake, Maggie!

Sam was being a brat, refusing to get out of his pyjamas, shouting and standing on a stool pressing the timer pads on the microwave oven. Alex could have cheerfully shut him inside it and switched to hi-power. Instead he dragged him off the stool and gave him a vicious slap across the leg. Sam started howling.

"Shut that before I really give you something to cry about," Alex growled. Sam obviously thought he'd already got something to cry about, because he didn't let up. Alex grabbed a pullover and took off Sam's pyjamas.

"What's this?" he demanded, spying for the first time the new, blue sachet hanging on a gray string round Sam's neck. "Did your mother put this dirty thing on you?"

"Noooooo hoooo hooo," howled Sam.

Alex showed him the back of his hand. "What have I told you about telling me lies? What have I told you?"

"Nooooohooo, she didn't."

"What? I said did your mother?"

"She didn't," said Amy.

"You shut up," said Alex sharply, and Amy shut up.

"Noooo," wailed Sam, and, seeing no way of avoiding another slap, wailed, "yes, nooooo, yes."

Alex pulled the string over Sam's head and tossed the sachet into the rubbish bin. Amy went to retrieve it until Alex shoved her roughly out of the kitchen. "Leave the filthy thing where it is. Go and get dressed before you get the next slap."

So Amy started crying too, and Dot came back in barking furiously at Alex, until Alex kicked her and she went whimpering into the garden. Alex looked around him at the detritus. The breakfast room was like a disaster area. He surveyed the failed breakfast and the piles of dirty laundry and his wailing children looking back at him through tears, and he felt like crying himself.

Amy defied her father and recovered the sachet from amid the rubbish. This time Alex ignored her. "Maggie," he said softly, "Maggie."

Spring Equinox, and Maggie was preparing. She was careful to combine all the elements of magic she'd learned with some she didn't understand. She was confused about the significance of planetary alignment (something Liz dismissed with a gesture), but with Venus exalted in Taurus, she blindly hoped this would offset her malefic intention.

For she admitted malefic intention. She wanted possession of her children, by any means. She wanted unhappiness and disgrace to fall on her husband. She believed that the rite of shapeshifting would confer on her the power to achieve these things.

After reading about herself in the newspaper, she'd returned to Liz's cottage. The old woman was again sharpening knives on the doorstep. Liz had been evasive about where she'd been the day before, saying only that she'd had an "errand" to run, something that couldn't be neglected. She had also seemed unwilling to let Maggie cross the threshold. She didn't want her in the house. It wasn't that she was in any way unfriendly; she just whistled up her collie and insisted that they go for a "blow" across the fields.

"Are you going to tell me what's to be done, or am I going to have to go it alone?" Maggie asked her, fearing further evasion.

"Oh, I'll tell you," Liz said, hobbling along the grass pathway with her stick. She said her feet were bad from having walked a "step." "Because it's in you, and it wants out. So we must have it. And it might be the only way."

"What do you mean, the only way?"

But Liz only pointed with her stick to a bush in the hedgerow. "Mistletoe. In flower. Cut a piece; you'll need some."

Maggie got that and other more complicated instructions, plus a new *oleum magicale*, different to the flying ointment. On the way back from visiting Liz, she called on Ash to show him the newspaper. He held his head in his hands.

"I'm sorry, Ash; I've brought this on you."

"No, you haven't," he said. "No, you haven't."

She returned to her bedsit, going to bed without eating. Liz had told her that the rite of shapeshifting required lengthy preparation and that she should fast for twenty-four hours.

Alex eventually dropped Amy at school and Sam at the childminder's. He arrived late at the site to find everyone in a state of excitement. There had been a spectacular find under the pentagram.

Tania and her crew had cleared the area of the staked circle. Initially the area close to the circumference of the circle had yielded nothing. But toward the center, by working more boldly across the diameter of the circle, they found what for some days now everyone had expected. It fulfilled certain fantasies of the type Alex had tried to suppress. They'd discovered human remains. First to come to light was a rib cage.

Everyone stopped working on the main dig and either joined the effort or stood around watching.

The archaeologists worked sideways, sweeping across from the rib cage, to mark the parameters of the find. Most of the skeleton was still firmly embedded in the earth. They dusted off extruding shoulder and knee bones. It was small enough to seem obvious what they were dealing with.

It's a child. The words swept around the group. *A child.*

Alex made them slow down the operation. There was too much excitement about the find, and he was afraid clumsy strokes might break up the skeletal pieces. He got everyone working with fine brushes. Those involved looked more like they were painting the bones than excavating them. Soon the watchers grew bored at the slow rate the thing was surfacing and went back to their own jobs.

The bones got nicknamed Minnie.

Alex supervised, fussily. By lunchtime they had exposed the entire flank of the rib cage, and Alex began to have doubts. The rib cage was too large to have been a child's, and he said so. There was something unnatural about the position in which other bones were coming to light. They were compressed into an extreme fetal position. The thigh bone was drawn up, and the skull, which they had just begun to touch, seemed slumped forward.

"I want an exact record of the position in which the skeleton is found. There's something odd about it. Go extra careful, please, this is not a sprint to the finish."

They proceeded now to work across the top of the remains, so as not to disturb the earth on which the bones rested.

Spring Equinox and Ash, as usual, took the lift to the fourth floor of the Gilded Arcade. On stepping out of the lift he realized some sort of commotion was going on outside his shop. There was a picket.

About nine ladies of pensionable age and a sad, solitary-looking gentleman in a dark suit crowded the doorway of his shop. Some held placards. One proclaimed NOT IN THIS TOWN. Their chatter generated a hubbub of excitement.

"Morning, ladies! Morning, sir!" Ash called cheerfully, gently shouldering his way through the white-haired scrum. The hubbub stopped. They moved aside for him and stood in a silent half-circle, watching as he took out his keys. No one said anything. Their eyes scoured him from head to toe, searching for the mark of the beast. At last Ash had the door open. He turned before going inside. "Bit of rain in the air," he said.

A tall woman with white cropped hair stepped forward. She had the sparkle of the mad evangelist in her eye. She carried a placard which read LEST YE FORGET. Ash, at least, couldn't remember the reference. "Satanist!" she said.

Ash smiled pleasantly. "Please. If you're going to call me names, can't you at least find some accurate ones?" He stepped inside and closed the door behind him.

Maggie spent the day preparing. She fasted, meditated, repeated her mantras, sipped water, brought her purpose to mind. She had decided that, when the time came, she would go out to Osier's Wood. She would have preferred to conduct the business within the safety of Ash's house, or even at her own bedsit, but she knew it wasn't possible. The woods had been the place where she'd had her first real scent of the possibilities within her; her first encounter with the spirit of the goddess. Her room constrained her; it had neither power nor resonance.

Hecate was choosy. Hecate was careful. Hecate preferred the seclusion and deep mystery of the woods.

At noon Maggie lit candles and incense and repeated the banishing ritual she had employed when flying with Ash. It had protected her then. She would repeat it again at dusk, when the moment was right.

She practiced mental projection of the things she expected to happen, exactly as Liz had told her.

At one o'clock she rehearsed relaxation and breathing exercises.

At two o'clock she drank a little saline water and gathered together everything she would need. Before leaving, she concocted her "listening" brew, and filled a thermos flask. She climbed into her car and drove out to the woods.

It was a dry, sunny day, warm for the time of year. She parked her car at a distance of half a mile from the woods and walked the rest of the way.

Deep in the woods, she found her spot, the hidden place she had discovered before, the tree-ringed tiny glade where Hecate had made her presence felt. She still had three hours before dusk. She settled down and spent half an hour practicing her visualization exercises. Then she opened her flask and inhaled the listening brew. It relaxed her, and she sat back to listen to the sound of the wind in the trees.

Alex had ordered a U-shaped trench to be dug round the skeleton so that it could be worked on from three sides. Now the bones stood out on a promontory of earth, a clay bed attended by a team working in hushed concentration. Something other than a dig now, the enterprise had become an operation of delicate flensing of the earth around and between the bones.

It had become clear that Minnie was not an infant or a child after all. It was an adult of small stature, whose awkward burial posture was due to having been squeezed into an unnaturally small space.

"Stop!" said Alex.

They all stopped.

"What is it?" asked Tania.

"What's up?" said Richard.

Alex stroked an imaginary beard and looked hard at the earth on one side of the remains. Then he walked round the other side, crouched, touched the soil, and then straightened his back. "Carry on," he said.

The delicate flensing resumed. Alex had an irritating habit of letting ideas boil inside his head. He distracted everyone by jogging from side to side, getting in close, stopping individuals with a gesture and then retiring without a word.

"Shit!" he said. "Stop! Everybody stop!"

Everyone let their brushes and implements hang at their sides. Alex got in close, eyeballing the earth near the still-covered skull.

Tania exploded on everyone's behalf. "For Christ's sake, Alex!"

Alex rubbed sweat from his eyes. "It's not your fault, it's my fault."

"WHAT isn't our fault?"

"Just nobody touch anything for a moment." He folded his arms and stared at the trench. Tania turned away and mouthed silent words at the sky. He saw her. "Come here. What's this?"

He pointed at the earth below the back of the skull. Tania got in close, everyone else huddled behind her. "I don't see anything."

"Exactly."

"What do you mean, 'exactly'?"

"I mean you can't see anything, but I can. I should have noticed it before. See this ragged pattern in the soil? The dark stain? It's the imprint left by rough-grained wood. Packed hard against the earth, see? Where wood has rotted and compacted into the soil. Everywhere else it's been broken up by worms and the like. But not here. Or here. And we've been so eager to get at the old bones we've ruined any traces of whatever it was buried in."

"Is that a tragedy?" said Tania.

Alex looked at her as though she were a child. "Minnie here was a full-grown adult squeezed into a small box. Some information about the box would have helped."

"We haven't disturbed the area behind the skull," Richard put in. "Or underneath. That might turn up some information."

"Let's hope so," Alex said glumly. It was true. He should have known better.

By late afternoon, another discovery was made. The set of bones was missing its left hand. Attention turned to the other side to reveal the right hand was also missing. The two feet had also been amputated before burial. They'd each been lopped off with blade strokes that cleanly severed bone.

At Omega, Ash was vainly trying to maintain an attitude of business as usual. It was difficult. The evangelists took it in turn to press their noses up against the window to see what he was doing. He was writing in a ledger, and this was clearly causing speculation outside. He deliberately affected a demonic grin, and made a great show of dipping his pen in the veins of his forearm; but he was actually preparing no more than his accounts.

Lunchtime had come and gone and not a single customer had passed through the picket. Then in the afternoon a young man braved the storm. He was so enthusiastically received by Ash that he went out and came in again.

Ash didn't know whether to close up and go home, or grit his teeth and stay on. He thought that closing would be giving in to them; on the other hand, by staying open he was only playing their game. By late afternoon he'd decided to close early, but to confuse them by leaving the window blinds up and the sign declaring the shop open.

He came out jangling his keys and the picket parted.

"Excuse me! Excuse me!" It was a plump, elderly lady addressing him, a woman with a heavy overcoat and a sweet, round face. "Would you be good enough to tell us if you're closing now, because we don't want to wait here unnecessarily."

Ash was astonished. Then he laughed out loud.

"Well, we can be civilized about it, can't we?" she said. Ash was about to reply when the glimmer of a silver brooch lying at her feet caught his eye. He picked it up.

"Is this yours?"

The old woman was taken aback. Then she smiled at him and gently rested a hand on his arm. "Do you know, my husband gave me that before he died. I must have dropped it and I'd have been heartbroken if I'd lost it. Heartbroken." She was beaming at him.

Ash pinned it back on her coat. "Well, at least one of you doesn't hate me."

The tall woman, "Lest Ye Forget," stepped forward. "You want to throw that brooch away, Mary, now he's touched it. It's tainted. You want nothing to do with it."

The sweet smile died on the plump lady's face. He saw her look from him to the interlocutor, and to the brooch. A tear began to form in her eye. He was outraged. He stepped toward the tall woman. "You," he said. "You'd have been there, wouldn't you? Cheering them on at the hangings and the burnings. It's how people like you enjoy yourself. It's good sex for people like you, isn't it? You'd have been at the front of the queue!"

Ash marched off along the catwalk, watched all the way by the silent picket.

Maggie had cleared an area to make a small, smoky fire, as instructed. Liz had told her to study the smoke from the fire before beginning the ritual. She followed this with a relaxation exercise, before commencing her serious preparation.

She unzipped and emptied her bag. First she laid out her circle with the long length of white rope leaving the ends open so that she could enter when the time was right.

She lit incense and repeated her banishing ritual.

Outside the circle she marked the four points of the compass. At north, at the station of Earth, she deposited a handful of soil she'd brought from the site of the Dancing Ladies, and she spoke the name of Uriel. South of the circle, at the station of Fire, she set a beeswax candle in a ceramic wind-protector. She lit the candle and invoked the name of Michael.

At the station of Water, at the eastern point, she set a jar of rain-water, earlier consecrated with salt. Here she spoke the name of Gabriel. The last point, on the western side of the circle, was the station of Air. Here she placed a sprig of mistletoe in flower. Liz had told her that the seasonal fruit of the mistletoe was preferred, but that if Maggie insisted on this particular time, then the mistletoe in flower would have to suffice. It was dedicated to Raphael.

She still had an hour or so before dusk. She sipped a little wine in which mistletoe had been steeped, and waited.

It was approaching five o'clock at the site of the Maggie dig, and everyone wanted to stay on. After discovering the absence of hands and feet on the skeleton, they'd pressed on to reveal that some kind of device was attached to the skull. Alex held up that part of the operation so that he might record the exact position in which it lay. Having done so, he was ready to give permission for them to uncover the device.

He was as eager as everyone else to stay on and work in the dark if necessary. But he had a problem.

"No, I won't," said Tania. "I'm not missing this. What do you take me for anyway?" She thought Alex was just using her.

"No, I can't," said his childminder when he telephoned. She thought it was high time Alex faced up to his responsibilities.

"No, I'm sorry," said Anita, when she too received his telephone call. She thought it was Alex's way of trying to rekindle things.

"Not even for old times' sake?" he pleaded.

"Especially not for old times' sake. Have to go; Bill's due back."

Amy had already been picked up from school by the child-minder and was waiting to be collected along with Sam. That was the arrangement. Alex was running out of options. In desperation he tried to ring Maggie. First he rang the telephone in the hall of her bedsit. Someone answered but told him Maggie was out. Then he looked up the number for Omega in the Gilded Arcade. There was no reply.

He went back to Tania.

"No, Alex. Absolutely not."

He drew her away from the others. "Please, Tania. I'm going to make a big media buzz out of this and I promise I'll tell them it was your dig. You'll get a job somewhere on the back of this. It'll look good for you. Think about it. Please help me out."

"I don't need this pressure, Alex."

"Please. I'll never ask you again." He held out the keys to his car. Tania looked back at the dig, and then at Alex. Her cheeks were burning. She snatched the keys from him.

"This is absolutely the last time." She was already marching away across the grass.

"You're a life-saver!"

"Fuck off, Alex," she shouted over her shoulder.

He turned back to his skull, rubbing his hands together in satisfaction.

Tania collected Amy and Sam from the childminder and drove them back to the house. At least she knew they'd become fond of her and were better behaved for her than ever they were for Alex.

"Can we have Cowboy's Glory?" Amy said, climbing out of the car.

"Yes, you can have Cowboy's Glory." Tania was too good-natured to dump her anger on the kids. So she opened cans and knocked out rounds of beans on toast. When they'd finished eating, she sent them off to play so she could get on with some clearing up. The house was a shambles. Sam reluctantly followed Amy down into the playroom.

Liz stood on the doorstep of her cottage. She was chewing something. Chewing, and staring out across the fields into the gathering dusk. The cottage door was flung wide open. Behind her, the old collie sat whimpering. Liz turned slowly, and silenced the dog with a look.

She was afraid for them. She'd worn herself out walking that great distance to the Sanders' house on Saturday, and then back again. It was too much at her age. She'd done her best to help Sam. But she'd been disturbed by the arrival of Alex's lover. That had been unfortunate. She just hoped that she'd done enough.

Liz turned her attention back to the gray horizon, across the fields, and to the graded advance of dusk.

Dusk came into the woods with stealth, insinuating itself into the smoke of her small fire. Maggie tied back her hair, slipped off her clothes, and stepped inside the rope, closing the circle behind her. It was cold, as she'd anticipated. In preference to the hogsfat mentioned in Bella's diary, she rubbed herself with an embrocation fluid, which numbed as well as warmed her. Liz had sanctioned this variation.

She performed her banishing ritual for the third and final time.

She unstoppered her new *oleum magicale*. It was filmier than the flying ointment, more opaque, highly scented with sandalwood and wisteria. She applied it to her body as before, to her temples, wrists, ankles, glandular points, intravaginally, but also a smear under her eyes, and a single drop on her tongue. Already the oil on her face stung her eyes. On contact with her skin it released strong vapors. She was forced to close her watering eyes as a bitter, acrid taste spread over her tongue, numbing her mouth and depositing a pellet of bile in her throat.

She struggled to open her eyes against the vapors. She needed to stay alert to what was happening in the physical world around her. Liz had told her that she must respond to the first thing to appear.

"What if nothing comes?" she'd asked.

"It will," Liz had said. "It will."

It could be an adder. It could be a bird. She would know when it approached the circle. But it would not enter the circle until she invited it in. She forced her eyes open against stinging tears. She waited, gazing at the smoke from her small fire as Liz had instructed her, visualizing forms rising from the smoke, weaving smoke and dusk into a single gray tapestry.

The most hideous feature of the discovery was not the amputation of limbs, but what was strapped to the skull's head.

Alex had decided to get the generator going and fix up a floodlight before allowing any more progress on the excavation. When everything was set up, they had returned to exposing the back of the skull and discovered the brank—a metal cap, fitting like a cage across the skull and face, with a cruel spike protruding from the brank into the open mouth. A V-shaped lip extruded a few inches from the brank at the other end of the spike.

With the skull itself half-bedded in the earth, Alex crouched down to take a close look. He'd seen a brank before, but not one quite so vicious as this. The floodlight scored stiff shadows on the white skull behind the bars of the brank.

"What's it for?" someone asked him.

"For keeping the victim quiet, I should think."

Turquoise light. Everywhere, turquoise light, shot through with deep blue veins. Maggie's heart hammered. A numbness coursed through her body, leaving only the sensation of a thrumming heart. Her body was anaesthetized, but her senses were keen. She had to keep her head still; any swift movement brought white-hot knives of pain. Despite the ethereal light, she could see every leaf, every branch, each blade of grass with absolute clarity. Details took on an artificial, plastic quality, an imprint of design, as if placed there by some unseen hand; but her eyes had been sharpened to the uniqueness of each leaf, each fern and log.

Waves. The woods were subjected to a gentle swell and fall like waves, a swell and fall she took to be the rhythm of her own breathing. The waves rippled in sympathy with her, as if part of her; she could no longer feel the extremities of her physical form. Her sensations extended as far as the range of her vision. She was what she could see. If an upper branch swayed in the wind, she felt the movement deep in her bowels. If a fern moved in a breeze, she felt a string drawn through her heart. The rotting of a log she savored as an infinitely slow burn somewhere inside her belly.

The upper fronds of the closest ferns waved, and she sensed a slow, sinuous progress along the earth toward her. A cold underbelly pressed to the leaf mold, moving closer. A sinuous rippling through the dead leaves. Would this be it? The first thing, Liz had said, the very first thing. The slippery, gliding sensation continued through the ferns, moving closer to the rope circle. Then it stopped, suddenly.

It had been beaten. Something else alighted outside the circle ahead of it.

It was a bird. A blackbird, but seeming brilliant blue in the turquoise light. Sleek feathers, still moist from the day the world was first made. It had stopped at the edge of the circle, head cocked, looking at her, eye to eye. Maggie knew this creature. She'd known it for a long time.

"Come in," she said.

The bird hopped inside the circle.

Maggie felt an unexpected wave of sadness inside her, and a hot, salt tear squeezed from her left eye, nestling on her cheek. She could see the moisture there, lensing turquoise light. The bird flew at her, hovering near, wings vibrating the air and fanning a wind at her face; beak dangerously close to her eye, it dipped and sucked the teardrop into its beak. Then it was gone.

Maggie stood up and looked around her, around the circle. The objects she had placed outside the circle remained in place, but there was no bird. It had gone, and with it, she thought, her chance. She felt unsteady on her feet, so she crouched down again, her knees drawn up to her ears.

A scorching pain racked her body and she had to spit a string of black bile from her mouth. Then an abdominal pain, of the type she'd not experienced since the birth of her son. She found she could relieve the pain by puffing her rib cage up and out and forcing her arms behind her back. Her body trembled violently. Sweat broke out on her brow and she couldn't stop the shivering. She puffed her chest out again and hawked another string of blue-black bile from her throat.

Then vomit. She was panting uncontrollably. Her chin retracted into her neck and she lost its shape. Her breathing was being constricted. She hawked again, trying to loosen the sensation of choking. She felt her feet scrabbling clawlike in the soft earth, trying to keep a foothold as her body convulsed. Suddenly she couldn't breathe. She gagged.

She panicked. She tried to shake her head out, shake it free of what was happening. But she was paralyzed. She was retching. Spit; if only she could spit she might loosen what was choking her air passage. But in the effort of spitting, her mouth puckered and extended outwards, her nose curving into a sharp point.

It was too ugly. She shook in terror. Then she felt a series of clicks in her joints, a sound like the cracking and resetting of bones. Please stop! She wanted it to stop! She tried in vain to reverse what was happening to her by dint of mental power. She felt her heart sink inside her into a tight ball, threatening to burst. Blood sang in her ears. Her skin flushed from scalp to toe, gooseflesh standing high, rippling across her body in a wave. Blue-black feathers erupted from her white skin as she scrabbled in the earth to keep her balance. She was turning in circles now, struggling against the metamorphosis, gagging for air. Stop! Oh stop!

Her wish was granted. The process was arrested halfway. She sobbed in relief, breathing heavily now. She'd managed to stop it. Then she tried to straighten her back, but was unable. She strained, but the effort only produced a cracking of bones and sickening pain. She waited. Tried again. She was unable to move.

Panic took her again. Liz! Ash! She wanted to cry out, but there was only a terrible gagging, and no one to answer. The metamorphosis wouldn't move forward, and she couldn't reverse it. She was stuck.

No air. A gagging in her throat. Her lungs compressed. Choking. Panic. She couldn't scream, she was unable to make any kind of noise.

Her eyes began to bleed. A jellylike substance formed across them. She was choking. She was paralyzed. She was going to die. Then she tried to relax. Think through what had happened. Think the process through from the beginning. She gave a final push, trying to heave herself into another world.

Only the brank was holding the skull in one piece. Alex identified a clasp at the side of the contraption, and attempted to clear the loose dirt from it with a fine hairbrush. The jaw of the skull gaped in a lopsided rictus. Alex put the brush aside, pursed his lips and blew delicately on the dust around the clasp. The metal cage of the brank fell apart. The lower jaw slipped from its bed of earth and bounced at the bottom of the trench, followed by half of the disintegrating brank.

Free. She was free. Free to fly in the turquoise light. Up, up, beyond the branches, above the trees. Into the ethereal light.

Two directions. There were two directions in which she could fly. The direction of space, of distance. And the direction of memory. She flew in the direction of memory.

Flying down the line. Down the ethereal light, turquoise yolk, unfolding, veined with brilliant blue. She flew into Far memory. Pain. Bella. Pain. A. Pain. Dark Sister. Understanding. The long line, understanding.

Far memory. Far memory. Far memory.

And returned. Flying now in the direction of distance. Ordinary blue space. Trees. Road. Cottages. Swoop on Church Haddon cottage, no, not there. Trees. Road. City. Castle, no, not there. Trees. Road. City. House. Find.

Far flying. Far flying. Far flying.

THIRTY-EIGHT

Amy sat at her desk in the cellar, coloring by numbers; Sam was arranging his soldiers and toy motors in a long procession, yard-long plastic trucks lining up behind a tailback of matchbox-sized models, with no sign of impatience. He played in his own world, happily naked but for a soiled white vest. The cellar playroom had one high window, looking out at ground level. Something brushed against the window and Amy looked up.

Twilight was yielding to darkness outside, a preternatural light, color-sucking. Amy turned to look at Sam, still intent on his serpentine procession of toys and tiny figures. An old woman stood over him.

Amy had never seen her before, but felt she knew her. The old woman was very old. She was dressed in black. Long skirts. Strange garments. Amy froze. She felt a cold wave peel her flesh open like a fruit. The old woman became aware of Amy's eyes on her. She turned her head slowly and mouthed silent words at Amy: *Stay back*. Her eyes were like the gray smoke Amy had seen coiling from a garden bonfire. They had fire in them, and imminent flame. The old woman turned her attention back to Sam.

Amy slipped her hand into her pocket.

Sam looked up from his snaking procession of toys and saw his mother standing over him. He smiled at her. She smiled back.

"Sam," said Maggie, "listen to me. Tell Amy to go away. Tell her, Sam."

Sam looked over at his sister. Amy was staring at them. There was something wrong with her. She was shrunk back against the desk. Her skin was white, all color drained from her cheeks. She looked sickly. She held her fist clenched tightly in her pocket.

"Tell her," Maggie said softly, smiling at him. "Tell her to go away."

Sam resorted to extending his carnival procession. "Amy, you have to go upstairs," he said without interest.

"No," Amy said, so sharply that Sam looked up at her again.

"Listen to me, Sam," Maggie whispered, but with more urgency. "Sam. Sam. Tell your sister to get out of this room. Tell her to get out."

"I told her."

"Well, tell her again!" Sam looked at his mother. She wasn't smiling anymore. Her faced seemed cracked, like a cheap mask. Then she smiled at him once more and everything seemed all right. "Sam. Tell her again!"

Amy darted up behind Sam and hung something round his neck. It was the herbal sachet Liz had made and given him and his father had torn from him; Amy had retrieved it from the bin.

The old woman rounded on Amy. She mouthed words, but seemed to have difficulty speaking. But her intention was clear. "Take it away from him!"

Amy cowered behind her brother. "No."

Sam was confused. He couldn't understand why Amy seemed so afraid or why his mother was screaming at her. He looked back at Maggie again. She smiled at him. "Sam, you don't want that dirty thing round your neck. Take it off."

Sam fingered the string.

"No," Amy shouted.

"Yes, take if off, Sam. And then you can come with me."

"Where?"

"Anywhere you want, Sam. But take it off."

Sam took the string with the sachet from round his neck and offered it to his mother. She stepped back. "Just throw it aside. That's all you have to do."

He let it fall to the floor. Maggie held out her hands to him.

Amy saw the old woman with her arms outstretched. She could see that Sam was going to her. She picked up the discarded sachet.

The old woman turned her head again, slowly, toward Amy. Her eyes were bitter gray smoke, full of loathing. She shook her head from side to side. Amy flung the sachet in her face, and the old woman disappeared.

"Where did Mummy go?" said Sam.

The playroom was silent. There was nothing. They looked at the desk where Amy had been sitting, her coloring-by-numbers exercise uncompleted. They looked at Sam's procession winding across the floor.

A snake was in its place. A fat, bloated, glistening serpent, with adder markings, its tongue flickering lazily. They backed away.

"Over here!" said a voice. The children wheeled round and crashed into the old woman, who had been standing immediately behind them.

This time Sam saw her exactly as Amy did. As he'd seen her before. Rider of rats. Stealer of dolls. Walker on air. The old woman in black, only now she held a tiny blade, a silver knife angled toward his genitals. Her eyes were smoke.

"All I want," she said, struggling to speak against a hoarse, cracked voice, "is my magic penny-purse. My moly-sack. My cursing pouch."

Sam's hand went instinctively down to protect his wrinkled, little-boy scrotum. The old woman nodded slowly.

Then she leapt, grabbing and twisting his vest, easily lifting him in the air with one hand and slamming him against the wall. Sam screamed and kicked his feet, thrashing against the wall as she angled the wicked blade toward his genitals.

Amy, too, screamed, and inside her scream she heard Liz saying, *Remember me, Amy, remember me.*

The herb sachet lay discarded on the floor. Amy grabbed it and tore it open, flinging a shower of desiccated leaves in the air above the old woman's head. She exhaled a foul jet of air at Amy and dropped Sam to the floor. Then she turned to face Amy, bringing her blade round in a sweeping, slashing arc.

Remember me. Amy threw her head backwards, narrowly avoiding the blade. Then it happened.

Sam saw Amy grow to full adult height. Her body expanded and reset. Her face changed, and where Sam had seen his sister he now saw Old Liz. The head Amy had flung back to escape the knife was now bearing down toward the old woman, tongue thrust forward, releasing a torrent of foul, watery substance at her. It was a jet stream of undigested beans, hard, white pellets traveling at bullet velocity, striking the old woman full in the face. The room trembled violently. There was a loud, painful, high-pitched ringing in Sam's ears. He put his hands over them and closed his eyes.

When he opened them again, Tania was picking him off the floor.

"What's all the screaming about?" she said. "What's going on?"

Sam looked around him. Amy was standing close by, unhurt, looking at him strangely. She looked white-faced, but normal again. There was no sign of the old woman, or of Liz. Where they'd both seen a snake, now there were only toys again.

"Oh, for God's sake." said Tania. She was looking at a pool of vomit on the floor. "Come on then, which one of you has been sick?"

Sam looked at his sister. "Amy," he said.

THIRTY-NINE

The following morning at the site, Alex was confidently holding a press conference. The local media were out in force, along with a few representatives of the national press. A small battery of photographers and cameramen grouped themselves round the site of the Maggie dig.

Tania was still at his house looking after Sam and Amy, listening to Alex pontificate live on local radio. She'd stayed overnight when Alex had returned late, praising his acuity over the conduct of the dig, consoling him over the mishap with the skull. She was a capable ego-masseuse.

It was a school holiday, and Alex had promised Tania that Maggie would collect the children at nine-thirty, and that she'd be able to join him at the site. It was now eleven-thirty, and no sign of Maggie.

"Obviously the burial was ritual in nature," Alex was saying on air, "we just don't know what kind of ritual was involved." He'd rounded off some of his vowels for radio and his voice indicated he was more than moderately pleased with himself. "We can deduce that the victim was a woman by the nature of the skeletal remains."

"And what is there to suggest that the victim was alive at the time of burial?" the radio journalist wanted to know.

"The brank was a medieval device for keeping people quiet, silencing them. There was also a length of pipe that fitted into a breather hole attached to the burial casket. I think the victim was squeezed into a tiny box and cruelly kept alive by the breather pipe. Water could be trickled into the victim's throat by means of the pipe and this curious attachment to the brank, prolonging her agony. It's some kind of oubliette, designed to keep the victim alive, at least for a while."

The journalist observed that this was a grisly find. Alex agreed that indeed it was. Tania, fidgeting in her chair, repeated the word *oubliette* like a black curse. The news report moved on to a feature about school dinners in the county.

She snapped off the radio. "Thanks for not mentioning me," she spat. "Get your coats on, kids. We're going up to the castle."

At the site, Alex was answering another journalist's questions. The reporter filled two and a half pages of his notepad and moved on. Tania arrived with Amy and Sam. Alex remembered he hadn't mentioned Tania in any of the publicity, as he'd promised.

"Hi!" he beamed. "How are we doing?"

"You're a lying bastard," said Tania.

"Don't start! Here, you can still get in on the act."

Another man drew up beside Alex and placed a hand on his arm. It was a tall, bearded man with thinning hair.

"Can I have a word, Mr. Sanders?"

"By all means. This is Tania. She's in charge of the dig."

"I'm not with any paper. My name's Ash. Your wife's in hospital."

Maggie had been found in the early hours of the morning, wandering naked along the fringes of Osier's Wood. She'd been reported by a passing motorist and picked up by the police, who'd taken her to the Royal Infirmary. Somehow they'd managed to get Ash's name and address out of her.

Ash drove Alex and the children to the hospital. He sat outside with Amy and Sam while Alex went in to see Maggie.

Alex choked when he saw Maggie lying in bed. She had a bloodless pallor and a bruised look. She was heavily sedated. She was hooked up to a saline drip, and a plastic tube was inserted into her nostril. He laid his head on her breast and cried, and she ran her hand through his hair saying, "It's all right. I'm all right. It's all right."

"How did we let it get to this, Maggie. How did we? When we love each other."

"It's all right. It's all right."

Alex emerged accompanied by a junior doctor fingering a paging device. Ash looked at the doctor, the children looked at Alex.

"She's dopey," the doctor was explaining, "because she's been injected with one hundred milligrams of Largactyl. It's a stiff dose. She may say a few strange things, but she'll be passive."

"Don't you want to keep her here? I mean for observation?"

"We'll arrange for your GP to make a domiciliary visit." Alex didn't respond. "Frankly," said the medic, "we need the beds."

Ash stood up. "Alex, it's time for you to take Maggie home with you."

Alex was in a daze.

"And I don't mean just for today. I mean home for good."

"Yes."

"I'm very fond of Maggie. She's helped me. But I know what she needs. She wants her family back. She wants her home and her children. She's going to need help. A lot of care and a lot of love."

"Yes."

The nurses got Maggie ready, and Ash drove the family home. He pulled up outside the house and kept the engine running. "You'll need to collect Maggie's things from the bedsit," he said to Alex when they climbed out of his car.

Maggie turned. "Ash . . ."

He wound his window down, but the wink he gave was a mite too rapid. "You'll be all right. Drop by the shop when you're feeling a bit better."

Ash drove away.

FORTY

Maggie did not not get better easily. The family GP made his visit, concluded she was out of danger, and left Alex with a prescription for Largactyl tablets to be used if her behavior became disturbed. She remained bedbound for several days, and even though there seemed little—at least outwardly—that ailed her, she showed no sign of wanting to come downstairs. Mostly she sat with a pillow propping up her head, her long, red hair combed in waves against the white slip on either side of her, and stared at the wall.

Alex fussed, cupped her hands, talked to her softly, asked her what he could get for her. She answered, faintly, briefly, always offering up a weak smile, but she never wanted anything. She ate little. "It's all right," she said. "It's all right."

Alex took days off work, washed, cooked, kept the children in order, saw they were well turned out. Supervision of the dig had to be placed in the hands of a subordinate; care of Maggie was Alex's immediate priority. Anita and Bill Suzman visited and brought a ridiculously lavish basket of flowers and fruit. Kate from the bedsit came with a gift of an outrageous pair of dangling earrings to cheer her. Ash dropped by and spent an hour holding her hand. But she had very little to say to any of them.

Worst of all was the lack of recognition she showed her children. There was no warmth, no affection, no interest, nothing. Alex tried to make them spend time in their mother's company, but it was pointless, even counterproductive. He stopped trying and simply made sure they kissed her good-night each evening before going to bed, but even that was a mechanical act. Once she looked at Amy and recoiled slightly, but otherwise they were like strangers. Alex despaired.

The GP arranged a visit by a psychologist. He stayed for forty minutes, gave Alex some banner words like "traumatic neurasthenia" to think about and prescribed a course of antidepressants which came in pink-and-white capsules.

One evening when Alex was talking to her, she turned to him and said, "Why do you call me Maggie? My name is Bella." Alex was so astonished he simply stared at her, saying nothing. Her voice was changed, it was softer, wheedling. Bella. Bella. He suddenly remembered it was the name of the diarist. "Where's your diary?" he asked.

"Hidden."

He kissed her gently and closed the door behind him. He knew the diary wasn't hidden at all. It was among the things he'd recovered from her bedsit. He found it immediately, and sat down to read it before the open fire.

The pages were filled with entries he hadn't seen before. He thought they must be Maggie's work, though they were written in the same copperplate hand as the original entries. He leafed through, toward the end of the diary.

Now they are whispering about me. A. said it would come to this. All of them even those I have helped. There's P. B. and R. S. and all I've to reckon with. This is how I am to be repaid.
   Oh, why did I not heed my dark sister?

It meant nothing to Alex. He turned over a page.

P. B. has lost her infant and puts it about that she must be over-looked and I'm the one. If this is gratitude. And all I did was to help this one and this other one. A. laughs in my face at that and tells me they will come for me. And yesterday a pantry window broken by lads hurling stones, and that no accident. A. says I must shift if I am to get a purchase on them, though that above all things makes me afraid down to my bowels that I lose my wits. What shall I therefore do?

I know I must hide this journal. Hide it, for it has all I know. For if they were to come and take this, then it would give them all they want, and there would be an end to it. I know a place where none will look, and I'll have a board made to keep it. Let them come and take me, they won't have this, for as long as this survives, I do too.

And then again:

Gerard come and he makes my board for me for the hearth, for he is a kind soul and I done this and that for him and all the children of his and he says he fears for me. He warns me they are after doing something, he has heard all the talk and they turn on any as try to speak up for me now. And he tells me it were better if I should go but where can I? At my age, and with what little I have, there is no place for me to go.

I have only this house and what little else besides.

Gerard tried to comfort me, but there's no comfort. I should have hearkened to A. who predicted all this, and never been a help to no one if this is how I am to be repaid. Where does all this hating one another come from?

And in the night I hear a scuffling and I come down to find a blaze in my hall. They have soaked a rag and pushed it through the letter flap and it catch at the curtains at the door and who knows what if I hadn't put it out. And what next?

Will they torch everything they don't understand? And is it be-

*cause I know this and that one among them? That I know all their
affairs and their transgressions and wrongdoings when they come
here and tell me? Help me get with child by him, help me lose that
child with that one. Is it because I know them all? When all I ever
did was to be a soft bird among them with a brave heart, a blackbird, to help them along here and there. A. spat and call me a fool,
and she tell me there is only one way out. Tonight I'll go with A.
and I'll shift, whatever the consequences.*

There was one final entry in the journal. The fine copperplate
writing was distended. There was a lack of the usual continuity.
It suggested a note of hysteria in the diarist.

> *I have taste the flame*
> *I have taste the flame and it burn my breath*
> *It scorch away my words I have none No words*
> *I have taste the flame*

This was Bella's final entry in the journal. Only blank pages
followed. There was no more information about her fate. Alex
closed the diary and put it aside. He looked at the dull red fire
shifting in the grate below the chimney where they'd first found
the diary. It seemed to him a long time ago.

One day Maggie got out of her bed and came downstairs. Without
saying a word she flung herself into housework, cleaning floors,
washing clothes, wiping paintwork.

"You don't have to do that," said Alex.

"I know, Alex. But I've got to do something to snap out of
it. If I lie in bed any longer, I'll lose my mind."

He nodded. At least it was a glimpse of the old Maggie; but
she looked so frail and ill he just wanted her to rest.

"You've got work to do at the castle. Go back to your job, if
you still have one. You've got a family to support."

She made a show of eating again, though it was only a show; and Alex allowed himself to be persuaded to return to work. Maggie was still distant from her children, particularly Amy. Alex would catch her staring hard at them while they played or were preoccupied in some activity. He would distract her and she would come to with a start. But the children detected an unexpressed hostility in her, and kept their own distance.

"Nimble be Jack quick be Jack," she murmured one time.

"Sorry?" said Alex.

"What?"

"Did you say something?"

"I don't think so."

Maggie gazed into the fire. The children were in bed and Alex was beside her on the sofa.

Alex had been meaning to bring up an old question. There was something lying around the house which still bothered him. "All those old herbs and things, Maggie. Maybe we should throw them out."

Maggie jerked her head toward him. Her lip twisted and her face contorted into a sneer. She barked at him like a dog. "SHE HASN'T GOT IT IN HER TO SUSPECT!" It was something he'd once said to Anita, but how could Maggie know? And then, barking still, "GOOD, WASN'T IT, ALEX? WASN'T IT? WASN'T IT?" Her eyes trickled with fire and her face had distorted. The voice was nothing like her own.

Alex looked at her in astonishment. Then her hand went to her mouth, and she was Maggie again.

"Maggie?"

She was trembling. "Alex, I'm sorry, I don't know where these things come from. I swear it."

But it wasn't like the first time, when Maggie had thought she was Bella, and had spoken in that gentle, wheedling voice. This was coarse and violent.

"Maggie, it's happened before."

"I remember. It takes me over. Then I remember. Hold me, Alex."

"You're not going to bark at me again?"

"Just hold me."

But it happened at other times. In a rare moment Maggie was chatting playfully to Sam when suddenly she barked at him, "SAM! MAMMY WHORE DADDY WHORE WHO'S FUCK-ING WHO?" The boy was terrorstruck. Amy, seeing it, took his hand and Maggie instantly snapped out of it. She wept to see him so afraid of her. She gathered him up in her arms. "I'm sorry, Sam! Mummy's sorry! Mummy's not well! Do you understand? Not well!" But Sam didn't understand, and her anguish and her tears only frightened and confused him further. Amy, watching it all, was also frightened and confused.

That night as they lay in bed, Maggie told Alex about the episode. He held her and tried to comfort her, but she was afraid she would one day lose control and do something harmful to the children. She felt a hovering presence; she described it as being like a lift rising inside her, its doors threatening to open on reaching the top to reveal the unspeakable. It was always there, always waiting. He couldn't understand, and there was nothing he could do but hold her and try to reassure her. He kissed her tears away.

But in truth Alex was hanging on to her by his fingernails. He was terrified. He was burdened by pieces of a jigsaw he was too afraid to push together. Indeed, he felt his survival, the survival of all of them, depended on keeping the things apart in his own mind. The Maggie dig, the experiments of which he knew, the diary, her shocking outbursts: they stood like a hooded figure on the horizon beckoning him toward some dreadful conclusion. But it was as if the hooded figure couldn't really exist unless it estab-lished clear eye contact, unless it *knew* that he *knew*. It skirted at the periphery of his vision, making signs, bidding for attention, wanting him to *look up*.

But he would not look up. He would resist. This was not the

Maggie he knew, but he hoped if only he could pretend for long enough that things were creeping back to normal, then the hooded figure on the horizon might fade into the shadows. All he had to do was avoid looking up.

He hadn't dared to touch Maggie since her illness, but one night he brushed her lips with his and let his tongue probe inside her mouth. She stiffened, and then bit hard into his tongue. Alex jumped back, spitting blood. The bite had sunk deep. Maggie's face was contorted and ugly. "HOW DO YOU LIKE FEEL OF BRANK THE BRANK THE BRANK?"

Just as suddenly she realized what she'd done, and was sobbing hysterically and reaching out for him. But Alex was out of his depth and drowning.

Later, lying awake in the dark, Maggie said, "I want De Sang. He can help me."

"What? That fraud? What can he do for us?"

"I've told you. He can help me."

"We'll get proper psychiatric help."

"No. I want De Sang."

"He won't help us, Maggie." Alex despaired at the idea. "I didn't even pay his bill."

Maggie made an appointment to call on De Sang the following afternoon. She took Sam. He ran into De Sang's consulting rooms and flung himself at the man, embracing the trunk of his legs. "Well, well, well! And how are you, young man?" De Sang stooped down beside Sam and spoke quietly to him, as though confiding the biggest secret in the world. "I want to have a talk with your mummy. Do you think you can keep Captain Hook tied up in that hallway for a while?"

Sam shuffled out of the room.

"My receptionist will keep an eye on him," De Sang said, offering her a chair.

"I've just paid her," said Maggie. De Sang glanced away.

"So," he said after she'd outlined her story. "There's Maggie, and there's Bella, and there's . . ."

"There's A."

"And you don't know her name?"

"No. But I think Bella does."

"And why do you think I can get Bella to tell us?"

Maggie pointed to the hypnotherapy diploma peeping from behind children's paintings on the wall. "I want you to conduct a regression. Isn't that the word?"

De Sang shook his head. "That isn't an everyday use of hypnotherapy."

"No. But then you're not an everyday kind of psychologist."

He smiled at her. Then he moved over to his couch, kicked off his shoes and lay down, as if he were the patient. "Let's you and me have a talk, Maggie." He settled his head against the pillow. "Just us witches."

FORTY-ONE

De Sang agreed to try something. He argued that the sessions should be conducted at Maggie's home. Her psychological difficulties had been generated in the home, he pointed out, and should be resolved there.

Alex made a point of being out.

De Sang arrived, and asked Maggie to make herself comfortable in the living room. He took off his jacket. "I want you to be very relaxed. The fact that I know you trust me is going to make this a lot easier," he said. She nodded.

"Maggie, have you been thinking about that word I gave you? I'm going to speak that word now. I'm going to say the word, and you'll remember it just how I showed you the other day. All right?" Again Maggie nodded. "And the word is, the word is, Maggie, what I told you . . . Wait. Before I tell you the word again, Maggie, I want you to get comfortable. Come on, let's shift these cushions around, that's better. Now take a deep breath, because I'm going to say the word, deep breath, good, that's good, and another, and the word is . . ."

De Sang had lowered his voice. He was almost murmuring. There was a cadence to his speech, a compelling rhythm, and even though he was saying very little, it was like a spool unwinding. "Maggie, I'm ready now to say the word, it's just a question of saying the word. Maggie would say the word herself but you can't, Maggie. You can try, but it's too difficult, isn't that right. Maggie? You buried the word so deep you can't bring yourself to say it now, can you? Isn't that right?" Maggie nodded drowsily. De Sang gently took one of her hands in his. "But it won't matter because I'm going to say the word for you. That's why I'm here, to say the word. I'm going to whisper the word to you, Maggie, and the word is *delphi*." Whereupon De Sang jerked Maggie's hand violently toward him in a short, snapping motion. Maggie's head lolled to the side, her eyes closed.

De Sang nodded in satisfaction.

"Such feelings of relaxation; you'd like to keep your eyes closed and remain relaxed, exactly as you are, why not, trusting me implicitly, knowing you're safe, quite safe, and I'm going to count to three and repeat our secret word and you are going to go deeper, all the while remaining aware of the sound of my voice, knowing you're completely safe, one, two . . ."

This time there was no sudden movement, but the sound of Maggie's deep breathing amplified, until it became almost like the purring of a cat. De Sang repeated this process, and then again a third time. Noiselessly, he got up and prowled softly around the room. Maggie sat with her head back, a slight rasping issuing from her throat in time with the rise and fall of her breathing.

At last De Sang stopped, leaned over her and said, quietly, "You can come to any time you want. Any time you want."

Maggie stirred. She lifted her head, rotated her neck as if to ease stiff muscles, and then opened her eyes. She looked directly at De Sang. *As easy as that*, De Sang thought. *She wants it.* "Hello, Bella."

Maggie held his gaze. "I don't know you."

"Yes, you do, Bella. You know me. I'm De Sang. I want you to trust me."

She looked suspicious. "Have you come to take me away?"

"No, Bella. I'm here to help you."

She started to weep. "They took me away. They put me in that place. I didn't do anything. They took me away."

"Don't cry. Bella, please don't cry." De Sang took her hand again and sat on the arm of the chair. "I promise you I'll help you."

"They hurt me."

"What did they do, Bella? What did they do?"

"They came for me. They said I was wicked. They put me in an asylum. I only tried to help them. But they didn't find my secrets. I hid them. They're coming for you! Hide them, said A. Hide! Hide! Hide! I hid them." She became subdued and weepy again. "They hurt me."

"You lived here, didn't you, Bella? This was your house?" She nodded, yes.

Go straight for the split, thought De Sang. "Do you know whose house this is now?"

She looked around her wildly. "This is my house."

"Yes, Bella. But can you tell me who lives here now?"

"I live here!"

"You did live here, Bella. But that was in the past. Someone else lives here now. Do you know her name?"

She flung herself forward in the chair, eyes wild, barking at him like a dog. "DON'T HURT DARK SISTER!"

De Sang stepped back a pace. *Too fast. Fool.*

"It's all right, Bella, it's all right. Relax, just relax. I want to help you. I promise they'll never take you back to that place. I promise you." She relaxed back into her chair. "Your secrets, Bella. You hid them. You were right to hide them."

"Yes, hide."

"You hid them up the chimney, didn't you?"

She stiffened. "Yes."

"They're safe. We found them. No one can hurt you now. Bella? Are you the dark sister?"

She looked confused again. The mention of these words

seemed to disorient her. "Dark sister? No . . ." She started to tremble.

"It's all right. I'm helping you. Like A. helps you. A. helps you, doesn't she, Bella?"

"No!"

"Is she your dark sister? This A.? Is A. your dark sister?"

"No . . ." She was trembling, shaking her head weakly from side to side.

"Bella. Who is A.? Tell us who she is."

She leapt up again, hissing in De Sang's face, "DON'T! DON'T HURT DARK SISTER! DON'T DARK SISTER! DON'T DARK SISTER! DON'T! HURT! DARK! SISTER!"

She was shaking uncontrollably, thrashing her arms and screaming at De Sang. Blood appeared at the corner of her mouth.

She's having a fit! "Bella," De Sang shouted above her screams, "I'm going to touch your head and you are going to go to sleep!"

He touched her brow and instantly she fell back onto the cushions. De Sang examined her. She'd bitten her tongue. She'd also wet herself: *petit mal.*

He brought her out of her hypnotic state.

Maggie was distressed and embarrassed on realizing what had happened. She was concerned that nothing should be said to Alex about her minor fit. He would have chased De Sang out of the house.

"Do you remember anything?"

"Turquoise light," said Maggie. "That's all."

"I met Bella."

"And A.?"

"Briefly, I think. But that's something much more volatile."

"What did I tell you?"

"Nothing you couldn't have told me from reading the diary. But that's not the point. Bella's only a screen. To stop me, or you, from getting to A."

"I'm not deliberately screening her."

"Not consciously. Maggie, I'm afraid I pushed it too far too soon. Let me see your tongue."

He examined the self-inflicted bite.

"It's the mark of the brank," said Maggie.

"What?"

"Never mind. Sometimes I say things and I don't know what they mean. Promise me you'll try again, whatever happens."

De Sang did try again.

He adopted the same routine, relaxing Maggie, evoking his keyword, applying the powers of suggestion, surfacing the persona they referred to as Bella. Only Bella was proving less communicative.

"Aren't you speaking to me today, Bella?" She shook her head, no. "Don't you trust me anymore, Bella? Has someone told you not to talk to me?"

She looked away.

"Is it her? Has she told you not to talk to me? That's it, isn't it? Your dark sister. She's told you to have nothing to do with me, hasn't she?"

"No." She pushed out her bottom lip in a pout, looking like a child, except that her face was wreathed in lines of pain and suffering.

"Why would that be? Why would your dark sister not want you to have anything to do with me? She's not afraid of me, is she?"

"She's not afraid of YOU."

"Can I speak to her?"

"She'll tell you to get to hell."

"I'd like to talk to her. Has she said anything to you about me?" No answer. She was refusing even to look at him. "Is she a healer, too? A healer like you, Bella?"

"She *was*."

"I want you to give her a message, Bella. Next time she speaks to you. Tell her my name is De Sang. Tell her I'm also a healer."

"She'll spit in your eye."

"Tell her. Tell her I can help her."

Suddenly she turned and looked at him for the first time that day. Her face was transformed. It was no longer the pouting baby. It was the sneering face again, animated, more energized than the deadpan of Bella, a cold sparkle in the eyes. It was a new personality. She threw her head back and said, "HA!"

De Sang stared at her for a long time. "Thank you for coming," he said at last.

FORTY-TWO

Alex was cultivating serious doubts about the value of De Sang's treatment. He tried to stay back as far as was practical, but since the psychologist insisted on conducting these sessions at the family home, it was impossible to keep things at arm's length. He was resentful of Maggie's implicit faith in the man. He was also irritated by the way De Sang let Sam climb all over him. Beyond all that he believed these sessions were making Maggie, if anything, more withdrawn from her family. He managed to smother all these misgivings with a stiff civility. He offered De Sang a glass of vodka.

"Who is this other . . . personality you're trying to get through to?" Alex wanted to know.

"It's the A. of the diary. That's all I can tell you. Bella haunts Maggie, and A. haunts Bella. A. manipulates Maggie through Bella, and uses her as a shield to stop me getting near her."

"But are they—were they—real people?"

"Maggie's the only real person."

Alex looked exasperated. "I'm out of my depth."

"No, you're not. Just think of it as archaeology. Ruins built over other ruins." De Sang drained his glass and declined a refill. "If only I had something on A. I could get to her. Provoke her. If I had her name, for example."

"When is Mummy going to play with me again?" said Sam. He and Amy were seated at the dining table, drawing with colored pens. Their behavior was always impeccable whenever De Sang was around, as if they sensed how important it was to cooperate.

De Sang sat down beside them, reached for a piece of paper, and began drawing along with the children. "When she gets better."

"Is she tired?"

"She's very tired," said De Sang. "What's that you're doing Amy?"

"Secret writing."

"Show me."

Amy offered De Sang a special pen she had. "You write on this, but you can't see anything. Then you press it on the radiator and then you can see it." She showed him a piece of paper on which she had written her name. "It's a spy-pen."

"That's clever. Where did you get it?"

"Mummy bought it from the toy shop."

De Sang studied Amy's graphics on the paper as if they were letters chiseled in marble over the oracle at Delphi. "Can I borrow this pen, if I promise to give it back to you?"

It was true, the sessions did sometimes make Maggie increasingly withdrawn and uncommunicative. She had her good moments and her bad spells. De Sang was afraid to push Bella too far about her dark sister: the initial hysterical reaction, the *petit mal*, all of these things made him anxious about the frail condition of Maggie's psyche. He was genuinely afraid her presiding personality might become completely swamped. In psychological terms, there was the danger of triggering a true psychosis.

But she was still seriously unwell. Physically her condition was so alarming he felt it necessary to prescribe a course of steroids.

A few days later De Sang decided to make his move. "Hello, Bella," he said. Maggie was responding more easily to the suggestion with each session. "I've come to talk to you again. Have you gone quiet on me?"

There was no answer. She blinked and looked away.

"I'm worried about Maggie."

As he'd expected, the name produced a look of confusion, a disorientation. He pressed on. "We might have to have her taken away."

Bella's bottom lip protruded. Her chin tucked into her neck and her eyes filled with water.

"You wouldn't like that, would you, Bella? You wouldn't wish that on anyone. Not again."

"They hurt me." Little girl's voice.

"No one's going to hurt you anymore. And no one's going to hurt Maggie. If you help me. Will you help me?"

"How?"

"Don't pretend you don't know, Bella. There's someone I have to talk to. Only, you've got to let her in."

Bella shook her head violently.

"If you won't help me, then Maggie will be taken away. And you'll see it. Because you are Maggie, aren't you, Bella?" She was still shaking her head violently. De Sang was afraid of another fit. But he knew he had to force the split. "Shall I call you Maggie, Bella? Or shall I call you Bella? Or shall I call you by your other name?"

Still she shook her head. De Sang reached into his pocket and pulled out a scrap of paper. The paper had at some time obviously been screwed into a tight ball, but he had folded it neatly. When De Sang had originally left the paper overnight by Maggie's bedside it had been in pristine condition, and blank. He'd also left Amy's toy pen alongside the sheet of paper.

"Someone was good enough to give me a name," De Sang said. "Look at what's written here. Is that your name? Shall I call you *Annis*?"

Her head stopped shaking and she flung herself back into the chair, arms out wide, cruciform. She'd blanked out.

De Sang was sweating profusely. He wiped his face with a handkerchief before proceeding. "Bella. Bella, I know you can hear me. I want you to listen to me, listen to my voice. You know I'm here to help. Bella, I'm going to count to five, and on the count of five I'm going to touch you and you'll become relaxed. One, two, three, four, five."

He touched her brow and she vented a deep, deep sigh, her eyes remaining closed. "That's good, Bella, that's very good. Now stay with my voice. I'm going to take you even deeper. Deeper. Because I want you to remember. I think it's before your time, Bella, long before your time. Remember before your time. How it was. And when I bring you back it will not be as Bella, and not as Maggie. You will remember."

"Yes."

The sudden response took De Sang by surprise. The voice was barely more than a whisper. Her eyes remained closed, but her head shifted slightly on the cushion. Her tongue licked at her lips and she swallowed hard.

"Annis?"

She didn't answer; continued to lick her lips and swallow uncomfortably, as if with difficulty. Then, "Yes."

"Annis. You've led us a dance."

"Dance?" Still a whisper.

"Who are you?"

"I am Annis. I am only a small bird."

"You've been frightening people. Little Sam."

She continued swallowing with difficulty.

"You hurt people, Annis."

She opened her eyes and looked at him. Some splinter of light in them made him afraid. "They are the ones who hurt. They hurt me." She gasped.

"Are you thirsty, Annis?"

She nodded, and he gave her a glass of water. She crooked her fingers round the glass and sipped the water painfully.

"Who are you, Annis?"

"Healer. Harm none. The priests. They came for me."

"Like Bella."

"Bella is weak." Her eyes closed again. He took the glass from her.

"Annis? Annis? Listen to me, Annis."

But she didn't respond. Her breast rose and fell with her heavy breathing, a soft rattle issuing from her throat.

Then she said, "You are a priest."

"No," said De Sang. "I'm a healer. Like you."

"No; you are a priest. New words. New gods."

"I don't think you can know me, Annis."

"Yes. I know you. You were there. You were the priest."

And Annis was gone, and Maggie was awake, shivering, shivering intensely.

FORTY-THREE

Ash had been brooding. His visits to Maggie, grudgingly allowed by Alex, had not convinced him she was getting better. On that issue, he and Alex saw eye to eye. He paid a visit to Liz, because he had no one else to talk to. He poured it out to her in a state of such agitation his fingers trembled round his teacup.

"It's a do," Liz said when he'd finished. She sat under her grandmother clock, the pendulum swinging from side to side, its soft ticking sweeping back the silence. She chewed at her inner cheek and stroked her dog. "Yes, it's a do. You're missing her bad, ain't you?" she said. "Why did you give her up so easy?"

"It wasn't easy, Liz. But it was her kids. It was destroying her to be apart from them. And deep down she loves Alex, I know she does. And though she didn't see it like that, I was standing in the way."

"You're too good, Ash. Some people are just too good for their own selves."

"She's ill. Very ill."

"What about this one that's seeing her? What do you say to him?"

"The psychologist? I don't know. She trusts him. But it may not be enough."

"She trusts him, eh?" Liz looked thoughtful at that.

"What do you know, Liz?"

"What'll you give me for it?" Liz laughed. Ash chuckled, but she saw there was no mirth in it. She got up stiffly and took his teacup from him. "I'm still aching from a step out I took." Then she lifted a bottle from her pantry and poured them both a glass of elderberry wine. "I knows," she said, "of this one as is grabbing hold of her and won't let go. I've seen 'er."

"Seen her? What do you mean 'seen her'?"

"She been hooking on to them children. She were in my pantry one day. I seen her all right."

"Do you mean the one they're calling Annis?"

"We don't say no names, do we? You should know *that* if you know anything. We don't say no names, but yes, that's the one. I been looking out for them children, so I been . . . agin her . . . as you might say."

Ash stroked his beard. "Is it—she—like a spirit trying to get possession of Maggie?"

Liz waved a hand through the air. "Soft. You're soft, Ash. You know nothing. She ain't a spirit as is trying to get in. She's a spirit as is trying to get out. How you ever going to understand anything when you're so soft?"

"What about the one called Bella?"

"Same."

Ash shook his head. "Maggie told me it all started with a bird. A blackbird."

"Aye, and she told me that story. And she were like you, soft, couldn't understand this, didn't know that. Talk it on for ever, she would. I says to her, no, the bird wasn't trying to get in you, it were trying to get out of you, but she couldn't see it."

"The familiar?"

"Whatever you wants to call it. The bird, then this one she's got trapped on her shoulder now, then the other one . . ."

"Annis and Bella."

"And more, as much power as you've got. All in you. And will come out, if you're a one. All for you to use. But if you're careless and choose wrong path, why, they'll want to use you, won't they?"

"But why does Annis attack the children?"

"Who else is taking Mammy's time and her wherewithal? It's all her vital, draining off to the children. So she don't want that, this one doesn't. She wants 'em out of the way so she can draw more vital for herself. Particularly the lad. He's taking a lot of her. So she goes for the lad. And there's something about that lovely gal she's afeared of."

"Amy?" Ash's head was swimming.

"That story with the blackbird. When it all started. Maggie breathed its spirit back to life. Now I never done nor seen that. But I believe it. Because, mark my words, there were more than just Maggie's power in the air that day."

"You're losing me, Liz."

Liz took a swig of elderberry wine and smacked her lips. "That's because you're soft. You want it all laid out in a line for you. And then it's not the thing it is."

"Go on."

"No. I'm proper talked out now." She stared down at the rug under her feet.

After a while, with nothing more said between them, Liz closed her eyes. Ash could tell from her breathing she'd drifted off to sleep. The clock ticked on. Once or twice she smacked her lips in her sleep; at one point she snored, in a sawing kind of way.

Ash gazed at the floor, and then at Liz's collie lying at her feet. Its ears pricked up and it looked back at him with sympathetic but helpless eyes. He thought he should get up and leave Liz to her snooze; she wasn't going to come up with anything for them. Then a sharp spasm went through him, and Liz opened her eyes.

Her stick had fallen to the floor. She leaned over and picked it up. "Yes, you'd best be on your way," she said, getting to her feet to see him out. Ash was a little surprised. Normally he had to endure Liz's abuse whenever he wanted to leave.

"She lost something, Ash. When she was shifting. When she went a-flying. She lost some of herself and her's got to find it again."

"Where to look?"

"What did your mammy tell you whenever you lost something? Look where you lost it."

Liz came as far as the gate with him. "Tell that one," she said, "to ask her about the Singing Chain."

"The Singing Chain?"

"That's it. And the Death Lullaby. Ask that."

"What are they?"

Liz looked cross with him. She raised her stick. "It's nowt to do wi' you. And you shouldn't even know. Now get off and ask him."

"Just one more thing, Liz. All this talk of a dark sister. Is Annis the dark sister? Or Bella? Or these spirits she sees when she's flying? Or is it the Hecate she talks about?" Or even you, he thought. "I mean, I'm lost."

"Is it because you're a man you're so soft?" said Liz. "These are all her dark sister. Coming out in different clothes. But there's only one real dark sister," and she tapped the side of her head, "and she lives in here."

Ash shook his head and walked to his car. He got in, turned the key in the ignition, and looked at the rearview mirror. Liz stood at her gate gazing after him, her collie at her side. She was pointing her stick at him.

Ash reported all of this to De Sang at his clinic. He got a frankly skeptical response.

"So far, all the information we've been working on has been internal to the workings of Maggie's mind. Bella is a character from a journal Maggie knows practically by heart. Annis is a similar story. Alex says she wrote most of the diary herself and is just using bits of information emerging from his archaeological dig at the castle."

"And what do you think?"

"What difference does it make? Her behavior and her health are what counts. But she wants to get well. That's why she gave me Annis' name with Amy's pen. That's an indication of the mind's natural subconscious will to heal itself."

Ash shook his head. "There's more to it. I know you think she's just weaving a story around herself. But don't you think this spirit of Annis might somehow have a life of its own?"

De Sang looked hard at him. "I'm a psychologist," he said, "not a fucking mystic."

But De Sang was running out of ideas. His sessions were hitting the same impassable bedrock. His aim in surfacing the persona of Annis through hypnosis was to achieve integration of Maggie, Bella, Annis all. And he was willing to try anything. He attempted a long session, hoping tiredness might offer some subtle change in the subject's response.

"Annis," said De Sang. "I want to talk to you again. I want to ask you some questions."

"Always questions."

It was after midnight, and De Sang was struggling to keep the weariness and hint of desperation from his voice. He'd been working with Maggie since early afternoon, unable to get beyond or away from Annis.

"You've told me, Annis, that you mean no harm. But I don't believe you. You frighten Bella. You've terrified Sam. Now you're threatening Maggie's life. Healers don't do this. Why, Annis?"

"The brank of time."

"So you've told me. But what does that mean?"

She sighed deeply and looked at De Sang from under heavy, drooping eyelids. "Then tell me why you want to hurt Sam. Tell me that."

"Because of his mother's love. It drains us. Makes us weak. Her love makes us all weak. She put balm on his eyes; he saw me, and I was in."

"In where?"

"Your world."

"She put balm on his eyes? Meaning Sam's mother?" No answer. No recognition. "What of Amy? You didn't attack Amy."

"The girl? She is . . . is a one. She has the know."

De Sang prowled the room, parking his bottom in turn on the windowsill, the table, and against the mantelpiece. Finally he dropped to his haunches in front of her before playing his wild card. "Annis, what is the Singing Chain?"

Her eyes flared open. She looked astonished. De Sang himself couldn't hide his own surprise at her reaction, and when she registered that, she relaxed again. "If you know of that, then you must know what it is."

"I also know of the Death Lullaby."

She shook her head complacently. "*That* you can *never* know."

"Then tell me about the Singing Chain."

"Let me sleep."

"If you tell me."

She snorted. "The Chain. It is the passing on of power from a one to another one. That's all. When we are dying, we find a one and give them our power, our hopes. The Singing Chain. My Chain is very long. As long as life itself."

"But how is the Chain passed on?"

"By the singing of the Death Lullaby. The most powerful of our many songs of power."

"Sing it to me."

Again she snorted with contempt. "No man was ever given this song. It is the property and chain of the wise women. Healers. And besides, to sing the Death Lullaby is to invite death. It is Hecate's song."

"If you sang it to me, I would die?"

"Fool. You are not a one. I would die. I. It is for the passing on, to a one. Now I want to sleep. I am weary of this."

"But tell me, Annis. Why didn't you pass on the Singing Chain? Why didn't you die?"

"My time was taken from me." A fat tear welled in her eye. "They broke a Chain of two thousand years. My little sisters of two thousand years!" Then she snarled, suddenly nasty again. "Let me sleep, you priest!"

"But you want to die, Annis! You said you wanted to pass on the Singing Chain! You told me that. Why not give the chain to Maggie! Then you could die and leave her alone, and the Chain would survive. Why not, Annis? Why not?"

Her eyes closed. "Here," she beckoned feebly. "Closer." She was whispering. De Sang put his ear to her mouth. "Closer. I will spit out the brank. Come closer."

He was ready for her to tell him. She grasped his lapel. Without warning she sat upright, launching an agonizing high-pitched scream into the inner passage of his ear. De Sang shrank back in pain, but her grasp was firm. The scream became louder. Her mouth was distended to ugly, shocking dimension. The membrane-splitting shriek paralyzed him with a pain like hot needles drawn through the most tender, fleshy parts of his inner ear. The scream burned. It was a scream of hurt and fear and agony and hatred, an occult screech calling across the centuries. The scream set up an excruciating, dangerous vibration on the sensitive tympanic membrane. He thought his eardrum must burst.

Alex rushed into the room and the scream stopped. De Sang flung himself away, falling to his knees against the wall. He put his hand to his ear, and there was blood on his fingers. He looked at her, sitting on the chair, and she was grinning at him.

Grinning at both of them, with evil satisfaction.

FORTY-FOUR

"I have to fly," said Maggie.

"What?" hissed Ash. "Are you mad? Don't you think that would just be enough to tip you over the edge?"

Ash had a kind of contract with Alex to visit Maggie one afternoon a week while Alex was at work.

"You told me yourself what Liz said. If you've lost something, you have to go back and look for it where you lost it."

"It's madness!"

"De Sang can't help me any further. I need you to fly with me, Ash."

"But how is flying going to help you?" Ash protested. "You lost yourself in the shifting, not in the flying."

"Flying is to knowledge as shifting is to power. Knowledge and power. That's the difference between the two. You have to trust me over this, Ash. I have to see, to know. There are some things I need to find out. That's my only way back."

"I don't see the logic."

"Now you're beginning to sound like Alex."

"And anyway, Alex would never stand for it. He wouldn't allow it for a second."

Maggie clouded over. "Alex will have to accept it. That's exactly what this whole thing was about in the first place."

Ash recognized the determination in her eyes. He'd seen that look before. How Maggie had changed over the time he'd known her. And yes, it was true, that was exactly what this whole thing was about in the beginning. He could see how she would tell Alex, and how Alex wouldn't be able to stop her.

"Remember the time we flew together, Ash? It was wonderful. Our love protected us. You can be there for me, protect me again. I gave you something that day, Ash. Something no one else could have given you. You owe me."

How could he argue? "It'll never work, Maggie. Alex would never forgive me. Haven't I encouraged you enough? Made you ill with it?"

"You can persuade Alex for me."

"Me? He's not going to listen to me!"

"You owe me."

Alex, as predicted, hit the roof. Maggie had persuaded Ash to wait with her until he returned from work. She sat her husband down and told him.

"Is this your fucking idea?" he snarled at Ash.

"No, it's mine. Ash was firmly against it. But he's agreed to help me if I'm determined to go ahead. Which I am."

"It's not going to happen."

"You can't stop it."

"I'll stop it. Whatever it is you do, I'll be there. I'll stop it. It's lunacy! Sheer lunacy!"

"Then we'll simply go somewhere else to do it."

"Does De Sang know about this?"

"What do you care about De Sang? You don't value his opinion."

"He won't allow it! He simply won't tolerate it!"

Maggie took hold of Alex's hand and spoke to him, calmly and gravely. "Alex, the days when you have the last word are over. You have to understand that, or all of this will have been for nothing. I'm still here because I love the children and I think that there is still a possibility for us. But the way we were before is over. It has to be. There will be times when I have to decide what's best for me, and you'll have to accept that. We're moving forward or not at all."

Ash had been sitting quietly listening to this exchange. "Can I say something?"

Alex looked at him. "No, you fucking can't! You've done your piece to get Maggie in this state! Maggie is my wife, not yours, and while we're talking you'll just keep your fucking mouth shut."

"Can you leave us, Maggie?" said Ash.

Maggie let go of Alex's hand and went out. Alex scrambled to his feet.

"WHERE ARE YOU GOING? GET BACK HERE!"

The door clicked softly behind her. Alex was left red-faced and impotent.

"Are you going to sit down?" said Ash.

"No, I'm not."

"Fine. Then I'm going to stand up." Ash did so, and took two steps toward Alex. He had a height advantage of at least four inches. Alex tensed.

"She's decided she must do this thing," said Ash.

"I don't have to listen to any of this."

"You're going to listen to it all. And if you don't, I'm going to walk in there after Maggie and I'm going to take her away from you. Which I could do."

"Don't flatter yourself."

Ash took a step closer. "Want to put it to the test?"

Alex looked away.

"I could go in there now and she would come with me. And nothing would make me happier than to have an excuse to take her away from you. A lot of this is down to you. Now you have a choice. You let her do what she's going to do anyway, or you lose her for ever. Simple. Now, are you going to make that choice?" Ash could see that he already had. "And don't think about bleating to De Sang about this. He doesn't need to know."

Ash called Maggie back into the room. "I've managed to persuade Alex to accept this course of action. He won't stand in your way."

Alex had tears in his eyes. "What if you die, Maggie? What if you die?"

"*I'm* not going to die."

FORTY-FIVE

The final ritual was to be conducted at Ash's house, in his study. This was not merely to spare Alex's feelings. There it was that they'd conducted the early, successful flying experiments and the room was charged with positive associations. Maggie persuaded Ash that flying would be enough. Flying was to knowledge, she said again, as shifting was to power. In any event, Maggie couldn't face the depredations of the shifting again, and Ash would have nothing to do with it; the flying was itself terrifying enough, and Maggie knew it would take them where they wanted to go.

They were fastidious in their preparations, trying to recreate exactly the conditions which had blessed their early experience. The process was begun at dusk: incense was set to smoulder in brass bowls, red and white candles were lit. Separately they took a purifying, aromatic bath. The only thing absent was the aphrodisiac tea and the love scent. Maggie certainly didn't want to complicate what was already a confusion. As before, she wore an engraved copper talisman round her neck. Ash also wore one.

Ash was a knot of anxiety, but in Maggie he found a focus of resolution. Even so, she was sensitive to his anxiety. "You don't have to join me, Ash."

"It's all right."

"You could simply watch over me."

"It'll be all right."

The hour came. They slipped off their dressing gowns and stepped into the rope circle. Maggie closed it behind her. They were naked but for their talismans. They dipped their fingers in the bowl of water and made the banishments: *I have purified myself and my heart is filled with joy. I bring gifts of incense and perfume. I anoint myself with unguents to make myself strong...* They watched each other apply the flying ointment. Ash had an erection which wasn't there the first time round. Maggie had the bloom of perspiration on her; Ash was sweating heavily. She leaned across to him and kissed him full on the lips. *Grant me the secret longings of my heart.*

Ash sat cross-legged, his erection bobbing angrily, stimulated by the tingling heat of the flying ointment. They'd pretended to each other, tacitly, that it wasn't going to happen; but in a moment she was lowering herself onto him. The moment eclipsed all external considerations. Both could feel the heat of the flying ointment inside and out. Ash made love to her as though it might be his last time on earth, and she writhed in his arms like a bitten serpent. They were already hallucinating in each other's arms before orgasm catapulted them almost into loss of consciousness. Ash saw their bodies replicate, locked in an endless procession of loving and birthing, a girdle of light spinning from their glowing, corporeal and coupled form, spreading round the planet; Maggie saw it as an unbroken scallop of light, an eternal caravan of reincarnation fanning from the circle and sourcing from this act of love. His hot seed was inside her, running like the mercurial thoughts firing in her brain, each seed a ball of energy she could ride to take them anywhere she wanted to go.

Maggie passed out of consciousness and came to in that familiar, timeless gray corridor. Ash was there. Gray and black geometric shapes drifted by, fracturing, reforming. The helping face appeared. Maggie promised a gift, and the face changed to become the parting in the gray corridor. This time the parting revealed nothing but an ethereal light. She moved toward the light and Ash wanted to follow her. She made him understand he couldn't come with her; that he must wait behind, stay and safeguard a way back for her. They were beyond speech. She was unable to explain. She waved him back, turned and stepped . . .

Into the turquoise light! Swimming, flying in the turquoise light! The light of far memory. Far memory. And she sits in a chair, in the middle of a room she should know. She is waiting. They are coming for her, but she no longer has any fear. She has placed herself beyond terror, with her secrets, which are also safe. Only she knows where they are, hidden behind a fireplace boarded with wood, where they will never look. She sits, patiently waiting, knowing of their approach, sensing that they are close. It is summer and the smell is high. Odor of decomposition and sadness, from within the house. Her dog and two cats lie decomposing in the kitchen. Flies are thick in number. She herself is starving, but she cannot eat. She has placed herself beyond hunger.

There comes the hammering on the door. Again. Then a splintering of wood as they force their way in. Oh, Bella. The splintering noise becomes a ripping sound, like a tearing not of cloth but of the ethereal light as she is flung again—into the turquoise light!

And she is no longer Bella, and they have her at the gibbet and the rope sore round her neck. The gibbet, and the gibbering crowd. Faces. She recognizes faces in the crowd. The light goes out as the hood falls over her head, her legs kicked away and she swings, oh swings, and the small crowd gasps and is silenced, for her neck has not snapped, only burned on the hemp rope, and she swings, choking, and there is a rumor and consternation from the crowd, and they cut her down.

The Scottish way, they say, they will the Scottish way, and they parade her bare-breasted and carrying the brands of the irons on her breasts, as they taunt and spit. She is carried to the place in the square where she sees them, bundling faggots high in the place of burning.

And again faces she should know. The women bundling the faggots high, she knows them! Two red-headed women, and another old woman with loose skin at her throat like a turkey's wattles.

The old woman spits at her as she draws near, curses her, pushes her toward the pile of faggots. Confusion. Betrayal. The men leave off her and let the women take up the cry, spitting, cursing, and this old woman is among the most vicious, though drawing close and taking her roughly, and under cover of this action presses something into her hand. Here, little sister, *she says in a whisper, an under-breath that betrays her own fear,* here, little sister. *And it is a pressing of the herb dwale, belladonna, which will be her only relief from the flame. She is comforted in her torment, knowing her sisters have not abandoned her; she bends double in disguise of swallowing the dwale and the old woman pretends to cuff her and heap curses upon her head.*

Yes, she is beyond all help, and her only fear now is for the Chain. How shall she pass the Chain when they will not let her little sisters draw near? How shall she chant the song of dying to a one? Two thousand years and the Chain broken? And how shall she, Annis, truly die if not by the Death Lullaby? Oh, little sisters! Oh, little sisters! My heart is a little bird! Tear it from my breast!

And they are surely other sisters heaping high the faggots of wood to burn her! And there are others she should know. Here the white-haired priest whose name she should know, damning her, book and bell; and here another man whose bed she should know full well, bearing the torch to ignite the wood. Who are these men?

The dwale takes effect, clouds sense, closes her eye, glory to the little sisters who did not forget her in her hour. And though the fire licks lazily at the wood under her, trailing thick gray plumes of smoke, she sees the sisters watching, watching in stillness while others bray, names she should know, names which confuse her, Liz the elder, Bella the redhead, and this other flame-haired one turning her face is Maggie.

Confusion! The dwale has befuddled her senses. How can this be if she is Maggie? I am Maggie; no, I am Annis. The dwale. And there comes the pungent smell of burning chestnut in her nostrils. Chestnut! The sisters! They know!

The flame gutters out. She comes to, still alive, unburned. Rumor and fear in the crowd. They light the faggots of chestnut brush again. A second time it smokes and it'll not catch. The sisters! Oh, the sisters!

Three times they light the wood. It smolders, thick, acrid coiling serpents of smoke, but it will not catch. Three times. The sisters know, piling the wood high with sweet chestnut of the season and it will not burn! Chestnut scarce at all: who has the knowledge of the wood? Sisters, you have saved me from the noose! You have saved me from the flame! Come to me now and take the Chain! The dwale has made me weary of this world and it is for you and no other I am ready. Come, those of you who are maiden, and let me print on your lips the lullaby of death and departing! In the midst of smoke and death I am in song!

Annis! Maggie!

But they cannot draw near lest they betray their natures, those sisters. And worse is to come. She passes from consciousness and they take her down, many even afraid now to handle her. For what work is this? What trickery? What truck with demons?

The white-haired priest. He approaches, bell and book. His voice quavers. So be it. If she shall so defy death, then grant her a living death. They say she can curse. Then sever her hand and foot that she may not point her curse at any man! They say she speaks magic words to her like. Then brank her that she be denied all faculty of speech. They say she can fly. Then bury her, so that if she sprout wings they be no help for her! And keep her alive that she endure her living death. Do this in God's name!

And they sever her hands and her feet, and cauterize the bloody limbs with burning brands. And they brank her head, and the spike bleeds her tongue. And they squeeze her into a tiny casket and bury her, leaving a breather pipe with which to water her and make hers the torment of many days and nights.

And in the night the brave sisters come, whispering words to her though she cannot answer them, and trickling potions to her lips to assuage her agonies. And they bury moon plates and knives and ask for the intervention of Hecate, to keep her heart from hatred. But the potions and her agonies derange and confuse her, and one night there comes a one, a sister. The sister whispers to her, whispering strange words in the blackest hour, rare words in the darkest night of her suffering.

I have come to you, *says the voice.* I am Maggie, and I will take away the brank of time.

Maggie woke inside the rope circle, cradled by Ash. She was shivering and weeping. Ash had draped one of his white shirts round her shoulders.

"I was there, Ash," she wept. "I saw it all."

"You're back; you're safe. It's all right."

Ash had come to some time before Maggie. On recovering he realized Maggie was still out cold, but weeping. Maybe she was dreaming, but in her unconscious state she was racked by a profound, distressing sobbing. He'd tried to make her come to. Then he'd found something to drape over her shoulders, returning to cradle her in his arms until she recovered consciousness. He got her to sip a little water.

"I was watching. I saw everything. Yet I was Annis at the same time. I was both Maggie and Annis."

"Drink this."

"She was one of the innocents, Ash. They twisted her. I know what she wants. They hurt her; oh, how they hurt her." Maggie sobbed in his arms. The things he was unable to see were tearing her heart. "Did you see it? Did you see it?"

But Ash hadn't seen it. He'd been left waiting in that gray place, that mysterious corridor between seeing and understanding, the memory of which was already fading for him. Whatever she'd witnessed was not for his eyes. Now there was nothing he could do but believe what Maggie told him.

"I understood, Ash. All of us. We're all branked by what life does to us. You. Me. Alex. Amy and little Sam. All of us, Ash. We're all waiting to take the brank away. And it hurts. It hurts."

Ash held her, until her sobbing had exhausted itself.

FORTY-SIX

Maggie told everyone what she wanted and whom she wanted. De Sang was recalled and Ash dispatched on an errand. Maggie asked Alex to stay close by. She wanted him to be there, to know.

Maggie's feverish sense of authority betrayed to De Sang that something had occurred, but in performing what was required he kept his suspicions to himself. He was skeptical about what else he could offer; he was also deeply apprehensive after the experience of Annis' occult scream.

"On the count of three I will touch you lightly and you will come to us as before, calm, and rested. One, two, three. There. Hello, Annis. You've been away."

The session was conducted in the lounge, as before. She blinked and looked at De Sang. Then she looked at her hands.

"How do you feel, Annis?"

A sneer came across her face. "Priest."

"No, I'm not the priest. Not anymore, Annis. I'm a friend of Maggie. You know who Maggie is, don't you?"

She looked blank.

"You don't have to play with us, Annis. Maggie is the one who will help you."

She licked her lips, and spoke with difficulty. "Water."

De Sang handed her a glass and she drank painfully.

"Maggie wants you to tell me the Death Lullaby. The song of death and departing. She wants you to tell me."

Silence.

"You know you want to, Annis. Then you can be free."

Silence.

It was broken by a ringing on the doorbell. Alex went to answer it. De Sang heard muffled voices in the hallway. He resumed the interrogation.

"Let me ask you something else. Who taught you the Death Lullaby?"

"A one."

"And you have to give it to another one? But it can't be a man? What happens if a man sings the Death Lullaby?"

"No man can know it."

"But if he did?"

"No power. Only women can know. Deeper in the cycle of life. Spring from womb, grow a womb, spring from a womb."

"I understand. So I don't want you to tell it to me. I want you to tell it to Maggie."

Silence again. Then: "No need. I have it for her."

"But if you don't, then two thousand years of craft will be broken, Annis. A hundred generations of witches, and the Singing Chain broken. Forever. Give it to Maggie. Let her take it."

"No need. We are one."

"No, no, Annis. You are separate. You must separate. She doesn't have the Chain. You have it."

No answer.

De Sang was already at the end of his rope. He didn't even believe in the existence of the Singing Chain, whatever it might be, and therefore wasn't surprised when he was unable to find it. He belonged to a school trading only in the cantrips of logic. But Maggie had given him a key she claimed would unlock the secret. He sighed. "I have a message for you from Maggie. She wanted you to have this special message."

"Tell."

"She asked me to say to you the following words. Are you listening. Annis? She asked me to say: *I am Maggie. I will take away the brank of time.*"

Her eyes flared open. She rotated her head slowly to look at De Sang. There was lambent fire in her eyes, but for the first time there was also loss, confusion, doubt, hurt. She started to tremble. It was the onset of a fit, the profitless finale of many of these sessions.

"Don't run away, Annis! Don't run away!" He was terrified she would simply hide from the conflict he'd set up for her, hide behind her fit. Already her breathing was deepening and she was closing her eyes. "Keep your eyes open, Annis. Look at me. If you won't tell us, we're going to have to kill Maggie."

She came to again. "You won't." Her demeanor had switched. She'd become protective.

"You said it, Annis! I'm the priest. I'll have her taken!"

"DON'T TOUCH HER!"

"I'll burn her. I'll have her buried alive, Annis!"

"DON'T YOU TOUCH HER!"

"It's why you're still here! If we kill her, we can kill you!"

"DON'T BRANK SISTER! DON'T BRANK SISTER!"

"Then tell Maggie! For heaven's sake, tell Maggie the Death Lullaby! Tell her!"

"I can't! Don't you see I can't!" She was screaming. Crying and screaming.

"You can, Annis! You want to! She can take away the brank!"

"She can't! She can't!"

"Why can't she? Why?"

"Because because because MAGGIE IS NOT MAIDEN!"

De Sang was astonished. Maggie had persuaded him Annis was ready to pass on the secret. She'd been certain. Plausible even. He'd believed it really might happen, if only because of her own conviction. Suddenly he felt crushed, defeated. Not maiden. He understood for the first time it was not that Annis didn't want to pass on the Chain to Maggie; she was unable. In Annis' mind, the

Death Lullaby could only be passed on to a virgin. The play had been made, and it had failed. De Sang didn't even know if there was such a thing as a Death Lullaby, or a Singing Chain. The convolutions of Maggie's unhinged mind had simply turned another flip, rendering the solution inaccessible. She had placed herself beyond reach. He had failed.

Behind him the door opened silently. De Sang turned and saw, advancing into the room, an old woman. He thought she must have been eighty years old. Her face was wreathed with care lines and her hair was iron-gray; loose flesh, like wattles, hung from her chin. She walked with a stick, yet moved forward with a light, fluid step. He guessed her name.

It was Liz. Before her was Amy, blinking shyly. Liz had one clawlike hand clasped on her shoulder. Ignoring De Sang, she propelled Amy toward the chair. The two women locked eyes. The sky outside was beginning to darken.

"I'll give you a one," said Liz.

"No," said Alex, hovering uncertainly by the door.

"And all things will be well," said Liz.

There was silence.

Liz leaned across the chair, and spoke gently. "This is the gift. She will take away the brank. Come on, old gel. You in your turn. Me in mine. And her in hers."

Maggie shuddered at Liz's words. Then she looked at Amy, her eyes blue glass. "The brank of time," she murmured. She beckoned to Amy with a tiny gesture. "Come here."

Amy looked at Liz. She was afraid.

"Go to her," said Liz. "Remember what I've told you."

She gave Amy a gentle push and backed off. "Well?" she said, turning to Alex and De Sang. "Get you out! This is not for you."

Neither Alex nor De Sang showed any inclination to move. Ash was also hovering in the hallway, having delivered Liz to the house at Maggie's request. Alex started to protest.

"*Out!*" shouted Liz, rushing at them. "*Out!*"

Startled, they went, and she slammed the door after them. She took up position against it, like a sentry. "Now," she said, "you have your gift. And the way is clear."

Amy looked at her mother. She was still afraid of her.

She didn't seem like her mother. Behind those features she saw an older face, the face of an enemy. But it had softened. Amy saw pain and sadness and suffering in that face, and a hunger for revenge that had only tormented herself. Amy understood nothing of this, she only felt it. She looked into her mother's eyes and saw again that impenetrable blue glass, and behind that rivers of ice, running, congealing, thawing, refreezing, running free again. The rivers of ice were hundreds and hundreds of years old. Her mother took her left hand and gripped her third finger tightly. She was silent for a while before she intoned in a kind of chant:

"My dark sister was Stella. And hers was Celinda. Hers Isabel. Hers Lizabeth. Hers Jean. Margaret. Ciss. Annie. Hers Peg. MyraRuthRowena. HazelBessElla. Melusine and Mag. Greta-ClaraAlwyn. CorrinnaFredaMalekinUlrica. JeanneAmeliaMicol-MaugElfredaMina. EricaIsolda. EilianMurielGwynethMorgan. RhonwenEnaBridged SheelinganMoiraCatti. Una. Hers Tryam. MolleeGlastie BoodKirreeCaithBrythMaeveSheena. Ethna. Etain-RoanneeLhiannon. CarridwenFuamach and An an Fionn. Nuala. Sadbh and Lorreeak. And Alethea from across the great sea.

"That is the line. Now it is yours, and you must remember. Many names. But you will remember them all. Because this is the Singing Chain. This is the far memory."

Amy felt her mother's hand tighten round her finger. The ice rivers were running free.

"Now give her the song," urged Liz. "The Death Lullaby. And you will be free."

Maggie sighed and ran her tongue along her lips, and sighed again.

"Come on, gel," Liz urged, "push it out." But patient, like some shadowy, unknowable midwife at the foot of the bed.

Maggie beckoned Amy forward and kissed her hard on the mouth. She fell back and stared at the ceiling. Then she began

singing, so softly Amy had to strain to hear the words, words
which meant nothing, but which she would never forget.

> *Baby born is born to die*
> *Even Mother's tears will dry*
> *By 'n' by*
>
> *All is none and none all*
> *Baby die 'fore baby crawl*
> *By 'n' by*
>
> *Dead men lie still*
> *But truth they will*
> *By 'n' by*
>
> *When baby live*
> *Then all's to give*
> *By 'n' by*
>
> *When baby live again*
> *No more a witch's pain*
> *By 'n' by*

Maggie closed her eyes and went to sleep. Amy stared at the
rhythmic rise of her breast and knew that Annis had gone forever, and that her mother would soon be well. Liz came up slowly
behind her. She put her gnarled old hand on Maggie's brow and
nodded with satisfaction. Then she ran her hand gently through
Amy's hair.

"No telling. Ever." Amy nodded. She knew. "When I'm finished, when my time comes, I shall call you, and you shall have
my line too. Two lines joined in one. And what a one you shall
be!"

Amy looked up at Liz. And her eyes were pure and clear.

FORTY-SEVEN

Maggie was mending. She was well enough two weeks later to make an expedition to see Liz, along with Alex and the children. When they got there Ash was nursing a glass of elderberry wine. He kissed Maggie and told her how much better she looked; he was relieved not to have to pretend it was true. A rose flush was back in her cheeks and she'd regained her lost weight.

Liz pronounced that spring was painting the hedgerows, and that they should all go out for a "blow," but Ash wanted to leave. He made his excuses. Alex tried to persuade him to come along, but he couldn't be tempted.

"That's right," said Liz. "You bugger off."

Ash kissed Maggie again, shook hands with Alex, and got into his car.

"And don't come back till the next time!" Liz growled after him. She opened the gate and they went walking across the field. Her collie stared after Ash as if it couldn't understand why he wouldn't come with them.

Liz was no stranger to Alex anymore. After the evening at his house, Liz had left Maggie to sleep and had taken charge, mobilizing people, giving instructions, heaping abuse where necessary. She'd emerged from the room with Amy to tell them Maggie was "mending" and needed putting to bed. When De Sang said he wanted to give Maggie a sedative after the punishment she'd been through, Liz gave him a tongue-lashing. De Sang looked round nervously for someone to grin at, and concluded he had no option but to accept this colorful new authority in the household. Liz snapped at him that he should make himself useful by getting the kettle going, and no one seemed more amazed than himself when he jumped to it.

Hadn't Alex got work? she demanded before scolding him for getting under everyone's feet. She busied herself with cooking up a weak broth, which she stipulated was for Maggie and no one else. Meanwhile Ash, seeing that Maggie was in the safest hands possible, slipped off quietly without telling anyone.

He hadn't the heart to stick around.

Amy had stolen the show by sitting regally in a chair with her hands folded in her lap. Occasionally she would approach Liz and whisper something in her ear, some question or other, to which the old woman would nod and answer simply yes or no; a little conspiracy which vexed De Sang and dismayed Alex. Most of the time Amy sat apart from the others, with her head slightly cocked, as if listening to some internal music, or as if she was counting. Or reciting in time to a rhythm only she could hear.

Sam just seemed baffled by it all. Liz, with whom he never felt entirely secure, had turned the premises upside down. Her presence was like a spice wind blowing through the house. Amy, after receiving permission from Liz, told him he had nothing more to worry about from "the lady," that he wouldn't be troubled again. He sensed that something had happened to Amy, but was no more party to it than were either his father or his erstwhile psychologist. They were all three adrift in the same excluded boat of ignorance, and he sat staring stupidly at his sister.

For the next few days Alex was subdued. A renegotiation of rights had taken place at a mysterious level almost beyond words. He was coming to terms with it. He knew he'd have to yield up his taste for control if things were going to work, and when that actually started to happen, he began to relax; soon he learned that he'd lost nothing but an angry pride.

"You had some idea of what you wanted from our life together," Maggie told him. "And the pictures in your head were more important than the people in your home. You're going to have to fix that."

"What can I do to make you stay?"

"You can't do anything. If I stay now it's because I choose to."

"So if you want to whistle up the wind every time there's a full moon, I have to put up with that?"

She laughed. "I actually don't feel the impulse for all of that anymore. Not today, at least. But I won't go back to the way things were before. I feel like I'm starting over. It's up to you if you want to start over with me."

Meanwhile Alex was fêted over his archaeological discovery in the castle grounds. His reports on the excavations appeared in academic and popular journals, and in all his writings he freely acknowledged the mysterious assistance of his wife in the "dig here" episode. He offered the information up to his readers exactly as it had happened, without senseless speculation.

Sam at least wasn't at all unhappy about the idea of going for a walk across the fields. Inside Liz's cottage, he gave the pantry a wide berth.

It was indeed a beautiful spring day. They climbed a stile and walked beside hedgerows cloudy with May blossom. Lapwings had returned to the field in number. Amy had her arm linked with Liz's. Occasionally the old woman would stop and point her stick at something in the hedge or growing in the grass. "Shepherd's purse. Can stop a bleeding wi' that one. You mark it," she said. Or, "Groundsel. Lady's friend. Tell you when you're older about that one."

Sam noticed how closely his mother and father, walking behind Liz and Amy, were marking this blossoming relationship. Amy seemed to glow in the attention. The sun lit up her golden hair and there seemed something changed about her. Tagging along behind, he could only gaze in awe and admiration at his sister.

His shining, dark sister.